# Wendy

# Vella

# Duchess By Chance

A Regency Rakes Novel

Duchess By Chance published by Amazon
Copyright © 2013 Wendy Vella
ISBN: 978-0-473-25423-0

# Dedication

When everything goes to hell, the people who stand by you without flinching - they are your family. *Quote by Jim Butcher.* For John, Rob and Kim, love you xx

And to my writing sisters, Cheryl, Shar, Trudi and Kate, who are sharing my journey every step of the way. Couldn't have done it without your support and knowledge and I can't wait until it's your turn. You girls' rock!!

# Also by Wendy Vella

**Historical Romances**
*Regency Rakes Series*
Duchess By Chance
Rescued By A Viscount
Tempting Miss Allender

*The Langley Sisters Series*
Lady In Disguise
Lady In Demand
Lady In Distress
The Lady Plays Her Ace
The Lady Seals Her Fate

*The Raven and Sinclair Series*
Sensing Danger
Seeing Danger

**Novellas**
*The Lords Of Night Street Series*
Lord Gallant
Lord Valiant

Christmas Wishes

**Stand Alone Titles**
The Reluctant Countess

**Contemporary Romances**

# PROLOGUE

Bedfordshire, England, 1794

*S*pencer Winchcomb watched the Duke of Stratton slowly place his hand on the table before him.

"Dear God!" The peer slumped back into his chair as Spencer laid the last card.

A fierce gust of wind rattled the windows, yet neither player flinched, keeping their eyes trained on the cards. The small parlor reeked of spilt ale and tobacco. The candles had burnt low, their wicks flickering with whorls of smoke as they struggled to stay alight. Chairs were thrown back from the table, indicating recent departures, and glasses and bottles lay discarded on the floor. The game had started two days ago and now only two men remained. One sat with a pile of coins and scraps of paper before him; the other, with nothing.

Their bloodshot eyes held. Exhaustion had been and gone; the duke was now motivated by desperation and Spencer by greed.

"I have a proposition for you, your Grace." Spencer eased back in his chair and rubbed stiff fingers over his bristly face.

"Anything," the duke rasped.

Silence filled the small room for several heartbeats and then he spoke.

"I will let you leave here this night with your estates and wealth intact if you betroth your son to my daughter."

"Impossible!"

Spencer leaned on the table, his eyes intent as he studied the duke. He knew what he asked was outrageous, yet he also knew that if the duke did not take the offer he was a ruined man. A feral smile flickered across his face; for the first time in many years it would be he who came out the victor.

"I want your signature on a piece of paper stating that your son will wed my daughter upon her eighteenth birthday. Only then will I return your markers."

Lowering his head, the duke closed his eyes and Spencer knew the rush of excitement that had flowed through the old man's blood while he gambled had ebbed away, leaving him aware of what this night had cost him. He knew he was beaten and his son would pay for his weakness.

"Do you agree, your Grace?"

The duke said nothing as he rose on unsteady legs and walked from the room. Spencer heard the murmur of voices and minutes later the duke returned, followed by the innkeeper who held paper, quill and ink in his hands.

After taking a deep breath, the duke then began to speak as he wrote. "I, Charles Daniel Loftus Irving, sixth Duke of Stratton, vow to wed my only child, Lord Daniel Charles Loftus Irvine to…?"

"Miss Berengaria Evangeline Augusta Winchcomb," Winchcomb said as the duke looked at him.

"In the year of her eighteenth birthday. Declared this day January 5th, 1794."

Placing one hand on the paper as the duke began to sign, Spencer Winchcomb said, "I want it written that the marriage must be consummated."

The old man did not raise his head although his fingers tightened around the quill as he added the necessary words.

"I'll be glad to be of service to you any time, your Grace," Winchcomb said once the second copy was signed and tucked into his shirt pocket.

The duke did not speak again. Pulling on his coat, he walked from the room.

# CHAPTER ONE

Bedfordshire, England - 1812

*H*ad the seventh Duke of Stratton the ability to choose the weather, he could not have matched his mood better than with the relentless fall of rain and grey gloomy skies that met his eye as he stared out the carriage window.

"Will we arrive soon, your Grace?"

Daniel was surprised to hear his wife's voice, as they had not spoken since the journey began hours ago. Unclenching his fists, he drew in a deep, bracing breath, then looked at the carriage's only other occupant.

"Under two hours." His tone was cold and clipped.

She, too, looked out the window, her ugly black bonnet obscuring most of her pale face. Daniel actually had only a vague idea what she looked like as she had kept her head lowered ever since their first meeting at their wedding ceremony four hours ago. Her eyes were possibly blue…or green. He had only spared her a fleeting glance during the service. Her hair was stuffed inside the bonnet so it could be white as snow or flaming red for all he knew. And her dress, although he was not an expert in ladies' fashion, was a drab brown with no shape, worn underneath a coat that had elbow patches on sleeves that began five inches above her skinny wrists. At least he could never forget her name, although God knew he wanted to. Berengaria Evangeline Augusta Winchcomb. It was a cruel twist of fate that he, the Duke of Stratton - one of the most eligible peers of the realm - was now married to a timid mouse who jumped every time he made a sound.

"Is there a problem?" he queried as she sighed, her breath forming a small white circle on the glass pane before her.

"No, your Grace."

Wife, he thought in disgust. Lord, how he hated her bloody heathen family. But most of all, he reserved a special seething rage for his own father and prayed daily the man was now residing in the hottest part of hell with Lucifer himself as a roommate.

"I...I, um..."

"Yes?" Daniel kept his eyes on the window as she stuttered. If she didn't have the decency to look at him when she spoke, then neither did he.

"Tis nothing, your Grace."

"It obviously is something, madam."

He watched her reflection in the glass as her grey, gloved hands curled into tight fists in her lap, but still she kept her eyes averted.

"I have need of a rest break, your Grace."

Looking at the landscape, Daniel searched for a

landmark. "There is a small inn ten minutes from here. We will stop there."

"Thank you."

Daniel fought the cold knot of fury in his chest and the sudden urge to roar something foul at her. He was not his father and never would be; he kept his temper firmly leashed.

Spencer Winchcomb had tied him neatly to his only daughter, binding the contract so tight; Daniel would never have been able to escape even if he'd known of his impending doom before his father's death. Well, now they had a title in their family but that was all they would get; he refused to have anything further to do with any of them, including his wife.

His friends had laughed when he'd told them he was leaving London during the height of the season to get married. No one had believed him - and indeed why would they have? Daniel had had trouble believing it himself.

"I have arranged for you to marry Miss Winchcomb."

Daniel could still hear his father's words echoing in his head. He had loathed his sire since he was old enough to realize the man who conceived him was a monster. The old duke had been a tyrant who had never bothered much with his only child unless it was to mete out punishment. Theirs had not been a relationship based on the bonds of love; they had basically ignored each other until the Duke of Stratton had summoned his son to his bedside to say his final farewell before he departed these fair if slightly chilly lands for the glories of heaven. Or, as Daniel now liked to believe, the eternal fires of hell.

"It was a promise made at her birth, a promise you must now honor."

And with those fateful words, the duke had finally succumbed to an inflammation of the chest. There was no wife to mourn him or daughters to weep and rather than the relief Daniel had believed he would feel, he had instead been filled with burning rage. Even in death, it seemed, the old bastard would play a hand in his life.

Realizing the carriage had stopped, Daniel opened the door and stepped down. He then turned to hold one hand out toward his duchess.

"Hurry!" he snapped when she did not move quickly enough. Grabbing her waist, he lifted her down. "I have no wish for my day to deteriorate any further. Run!" he added loudly as the heavens opened in earnest, although after what they had endured already today, a few seconds in the rain could do them little harm.

The proprietor met them at the door and ushered them inside.

"'Tis my belief it's setting in," he said, to which Daniel grunted something in reply. After handing his wife over to a woman who came to assist her, he followed the proprietor to a small parlor where he slumped into a chair before the fire.

"'Tis mulled to my own special recipe, my lord."

Daniel nodded to the man as he took the proffered mug. Pushing his nose into the vessel, he inhaled the spicy scent. Taking a large mouthful, he held it briefly in his mouth, enjoying the taste of cloves and cinnamon before he swallowed and the warmth slowly filled his body.

Dear God, I'm married. His mind kept repeating the words over and over again.

"I-I am ready to leave, your Grace."

Daniel looked to the doorway where his wife stood with her head lowered.

"Would you care for a drink, Duchess?" Squinting, Daniel tried to get a look at her eyes as her head shot up. Damn, still too far away. Why had he not looked closer when he helped her from the carriage?

"No, thank you," she said, unmoving.

"However, I wish to finish mine," Daniel added in a steady voice that took a great deal of effort. Just looking at the woman made him furious. How the hell he was supposed to dredge up some degree of passion to consummate their marriage before he left for London, he could not fathom. He had told Winchcomb he would not bed her, yet his father had given his word the marriage would be consummated, and so Daniel would oblige. The old duke had never kept his word on anything; this was one more thing he would do to ensure he was nothing like the man who had sired him.

"Of course. I will wait in the carriage for you, your Grace. Please take your time."

"Come and sit d -" Daniel heard the front door close before he finished his sentence. Growling at no one in particular, he gulped the last of his tankard, then slammed it on top of the table, enjoying the satisfying clunk. After handing several coins to the proprietor, he stomped out into the night.

Eva shot her husband a quick look. Husband! Dear Lord, he was so big. Large hands were clenched on muscled thighs, and polished booted feet twice the size of her own were propped on the seat beside her. She'd first set eyes on him striding down the aisle toward her and she had never seen a man so handsome. Even with his dark brows lowered and anger etched in every line of his face, he had made the breath catch in her throat.

His huge shoulders were encased in black super-fine cloth over a crisp white shirt. His black breeches were equally fine-looking. Across from her, his large hat rested on the seat. He was, to her untutored eye, everything a gentleman should appear to be.

He had been chillingly polite to her since their journey began, yet his anger filled the small confines of the carriage. In his eyes, she had crossed him, or more importantly, her family had, and he was not going to differentiate between the two. She was here and he was angry; therefore Eva would bear the brunt of that anger.

She watched as he pushed one large hand through his thick sable-brown curls as he once again looked at her through the glass. Black lashes and brows formed a frame for eyes that were the color of an overcast day, and the one time he had looked at her during the service they had been smoldering with rage. On any other face, his nose would have been oversized, but on his, it was perfect, complementing wide, high cheekbones and a jutting jaw.

Eva had not known what to think when her father told her she was to be married today. Stunned, she had sat in silence as the carriage carried them to the church. Her father had talked of how a hand of cards was about to change her life and how she should always be grateful to him and never forget that it was he who had given her this opportunity. She did not question him further. Spencer Winchcomb was too handy with his fists and it would have been just a waste of breath anyway as he had never listened when his daughter spoke.

Was she trading one tyrant for another? This was her biggest fear since meeting the duke. She had no idea how a duchess should behave, but this she could learn. However she had no wish to learn how to evade another man who insisted on controlling her by force.

"It is stated in the contract that you must consummate this marriage!"

She had overheard her father roaring those words at the duke before the wedding service, and Eva had wanted to curl into a ball and hide from the humiliation when she heard her future husband's response.

"Never! I may have to marry her, Mr Winchcomb, but I will never produce the heir you and my father wanted."

His words had been laced with loathing and when her father had continued to roar at him saying things like, 'honor bound' and 'gentleman', the duke had not uttered another word. Eva had felt a fierce pain in her chest when she realized she would never have a child of her own - someone who belonged to her alone, relied on her for its love and survival.

The wedding service had been cold and informal, with the duke arriving just minutes before the allotted time. He had not looked at Eva when he placed the ring on her finger. It was an ugly gold band studded with different colored stones and seemed more suited for a man, as it was clearly too big for her finger. It now hung on a chain around her neck.

There had been no wedding breakfast and no celebration. All her silly, girlish dreams of tears, flowers and happy friends flew away with the other dreams she'd once had of a handsome, joyful husband who would declare his eternal love for her. The duke had merely taken her arm as the reverend uttered the last words and escorted her from the church. Outside, Eva had hastily hugged Reggie, her youngest brother, begging him to come and see her soon, and then, ignoring the rest of her family, she had climbed into the carriage.

Eva was relieved when the carriage finally drew to a halt at Stratton Hall. The atmosphere inside had left her tense and nervous. The duke had not spoken again, and the silence had been deafening. She could feel the sting of tears behind her eyes as she gathered her things. Yes, she no longer had to put up with her family and their demanding ways, but she now had to deal with servants and running a household. Admittedly, she had done so since she was a child, but this was a huge estate with a multitude of rooms and staff. Her father had been miserly and had relied on two servants and Eva to run his house. Surely Stratton Lodge would house many more. How was she ever going to fulfill her duties?

"Are you ready, madam?"

"I am, your Grace," she said again, placing her hand in his and stepping from the carriage.

He released her at once and started toward the house, his feet making a crunching sound on the stones as he walked. She could not see the great stone building clearly in the dark, but she could feel its sheer size looming above her. Was she really to be mistress of this?

"Luton!" the duke bellowed as he walked into the house.

"Your Grace, we had not expected you until tomorrow."

Eva stood inside the doorway looking at the dirty water her husband's large, booted feet had left on the polished tile floor. The butler was tall with black hair that was liberally streaked with silver and his mouth was bracketed with lines, which hopefully meant he knew how to smile.

"We made good time," the duke grunted, motioning Eva forward. "Duchess, this is Luton. He is the butler here at Stratton Lodge and he will be the one who will help you settle in."

"Your Grace." Luton bowed.

"Luton," Eva said managing a small smile. "It is a pleasure to meet with you."

"Luton will show you to your room, Duchess. Tomorrow will be soon enough to meet the rest of the staff," the duke said with a stiff bow before stalking away.

"This way, your Grace."

Eva pulled her eyes away from the retreating back of her husband and quickly followed Luton toward the stairs. Lamps lit their way, yet Eva saw very little of her new home. Nervous, she kept her eyes on Luton's very straight back. They climbed a long set of stairs and then walked down a narrow hall that had windows along the right side, though the curtains were drawn to keep out the cold night air. Her rooms were at the end and Eva held her breath as Luton opened the door and she walked inside.

"Dear heaven!" Eva whispered, moving slowly over the plush carpets.

Turning a full circle, she tried to take it all in. Surely this was not her room? Painted in the palest shade of peppermint, the walls blended beautifully with carpets of apricot and cream. There was delicate-legged furniture which looked too precious to sit on, and at the windows hung matching swathes of striped satin. The room seemed to reach out and welcome her while the bed was fit for a princess. How could she have ended up here? The daughter of a worthless gambler, a man who earned his living by stealing from others - surely she was not worthy of such a room. She trailed her fingers down one of the four turned posts that held up a gossamer canopy of soft white fabric before walking toward a window seat scattered with pillows.

"This is Molly, your Grace," Luton said.

Eva turned to greet the young maid who was bobbing a curtsy.

"Shall I have a bath drawn for you, your Grace?"

"Yes, please, and some tea if it is not too inconvenient." Eva couldn't believe she was to have a bath she had not prepared herself.

"At once, your Grace."

With the click of her bedroom door Eva felt the last of her strength flee. Burying her face in her hands, she slumped onto the seat. In one day, she had left the only home she had known, and married a duke and was now going to live out her days in a mansion.

Eva's thoughts went to her brother. How would Reggie survive without her? He worked for the local farmer, but at seventeen he was not a big man and too young to deal with the bullying ways of his elder brothers singlehandedly. She must find a way to bring him here to safety.

The maid returned with two footmen carrying a large bath. Eva had never seen one so big; surely she could lie flat in it.

"I will help you undress, your Grace," the maid offered once the bath was filled and the footmen had left.

Eva had never had assistance to undress but she felt too tired to argue. Wearily she climbed to her feet and allowed the maid to pull off her damp coat.

"Thank you, Molly." She felt color flood her cheeks as her dress was removed. Her undergarments were a dismal shade of grey and repaired several times over.

"I will return in a while with your tea, your Grace."

Biting her lip as she stepped into the bath Eva felt the heat start to thaw her toes. Slowly she sank down, then lay back until only her head was out of the water.

So this is to be my life, Eva thought as her eyes did a survey of the room. She could find some peace here alone. Eva had no doubt her husband would not stay at Stratton for long. She knew he hated looking at her, being reminded of the fact that he had a wife he did not want. He would leave at the earliest opportunity and until then she would stay out of his way. Maybe in time her husband might wish for an heir, but for now she would be content with her life. There would be no more fear, just her and the servants. And they would rub along together nicely; she would make sure of it.

Molly returned with her tray as the water began to cool. She helped Eva climb out of the bath and slip into her nightdress. After she had drunk her tea and dried her hair, she climbed into the huge soft bed and fell into a deep sleep.

For one heart-stopping moment when she opened her eyes, Eva felt the same sinking feeling she'd experienced every morning when she woke in her small bedroom, located in the drafty attic of her father's house. But then she realized where she was.

"No more," she whispered, looking around the beautiful room. "They can hurt me no more."

Climbing out of bed, Eva then walked to the windows and opened the curtains. It was still early. The rising sun cast a soft shadow over the land, and she had a feeling her new home was going to be a wonderful place to explore. She could see gardens with hedge-lined paths as well as beds filled with flowers and different varieties of plants. In the distance she caught a glimmer of water. A lake? She hoped so. Perhaps she could go swimming when no one was looking. Though who would be there to look, she asked herself, remembering the anger in her husband's eyes and knowing he'd be leaving as soon as he could. Thinking of the duke made her heart plunge to her toes so she pushed all thoughts of him aside and hurried to answer the maid's knock on her bedroom door.

After dressing, she left her room. Following Molly's directions, she headed down the long hallway, stopping to look out the floor-length windows along the way. Her new home was beautiful but a little tired, Eva thought as she looked at the worn carpets that ran the length of the hall. Perhaps she could restore Stratton Lodge to its former glory.

"If you will follow me, your Grace, I will take you to the breakfast parlor."

"Luton!" Eva squeaked, startled by the butler's sudden appearance. "Good morning."

"Good Morning, your Grace." Luton offered her a smile before turning and making his stately way toward the stairs without further comment.

"Mrs. Stimpel, the cook, and Miss Sullivan, the housekeeper, will meet with you at your convenience, your Grace. Please let me know and I will take you to them when you are ready."

"Thank you, Luton." Eva suddenly felt queasy at the prospect of meeting the women.

The breakfast room had a faded red-and-gold patterned carpet and pale gold walls. She could imagine that in its day the room had been very grand. The table, thankfully, was not overly large and was draped in a soft white linen cloth. She sat in the chair Luton pulled out for her and noticed that only one place was laid.

"The...the...uh, the Duke has eaten already?"

"He had a tray in his room, your Grace."

"Oh, well then, I'll just have tea and toast, if you please, Luton." Eva wasn't sure, but she thought Luton tsked as he left the room.

"Your breakfast, your Grace," Luton said a while later.

"Tea and toast, Luton?" Eva queried, looking at the plate piled high with ham and eggs. A small basket held toast and muffins and the pot of tea would have served at least ten people.

"Mrs. Stimpel does not often have someone to cook for, your Grace," was all Luton said before he left the room.

Eva, who had never been a fast eater, took nearly forty minutes to finish the meal. Staggering out of her chair and feeling stuffed to her toes, she then asked Luton to take her to the kitchen where she would tackle Mrs. Stimpel first.

"If you will wait in the lemon parlor, your Grace, I will have Mrs. Stimpel brought to you."

"That is not necessary, Luton - I am more than happy to go to her," Eva skirted around the butler to head off in what she hoped was the correct direction.

She smelt the kitchen before it came into view. The sweet scent of spices tickled her nostrils as she walked into the heated room. She found the cook - a small, stout woman - scrubbing vegetables in a tub of water. Beside her, drinking tea and eating a large wedge of fruitcake, was an older lady, her grey hair scraped into a neat bun.

"Mrs. Stimpel?"

"Yes, I'm Hepitatia Stimpel," the cook said. "And who are you?"

"The Duchess of Stratton," Eva said, holding herself very still as the cook looked up.

Silence filled the kitchen as color came and went from Mrs. Stimpel's cheeks. She lifted her hands out of the water and hastily wiped them on her apron. "Please, your Grace, accept my apologies. I...I was not aware... I mean, you should have sent for me, your Grace. Tis not right for you to be down here."

Eva smiled as the woman hastened toward her. "Please, Mrs. Stimpel, do not concern yourself. We have not yet been introduced, therefore you did not know my identity." And I do not look like a Duchess, Eva thought, looking down at her worn grey dress and faded leather boots. Her toes had made small, white marks in the black leather as she had grown. "I merely wished to discuss menus and meal sizes."

"Your Grace," the other lady said as she, too, came forward to meet Eva, "I am the housekeeper, Miss Sullivan."

"I hope you were not displeased with the breakfast, your Grace?" Mrs. Stimpel rushed in.

"Oh, no," Eva quickly said, looking at the horrified expression on the cook's face. "The breakfast was wonderful and the eggs lighter than any I have tasted. However I do not have extravagant tastes and although my appetite is healthy, I would be happy with smaller meals."

"Smaller meals, your Grace?"

"Yes, Mrs. Stimpel, smaller meals. And once the Duke has left, I would be happy with simple fare," she added.

"Simple fare, your Grace?" The cook appeared confused at the concept.

How did one explain simple fare Eva wondered, having eaten it her entire life. Waving her hand vaguely, she said. "We will discuss my needs once the duke has left, Mrs. Stimpel. For now I would just like you to know that I do not eat a large amount of food. Therefore I have no wish to sit down to a meal the size of the wonderful but large breakfast you served me today."

"Of course, your Grace," the cook said, lowering her eyes and bobbing into a curtsy.

Next, Eva talked briefly to the housekeeper, assuring her

that until she found her feet she was happy to leave things as they were.

Feeling a flush of elation as she left the kitchens over her success with the cook and housekeeper, Eva thought maybe she could establish a civilized relationship with her husband. Surely he would not get angry with her for approaching him? Throwing back her shoulders, she asked directions to his study and before long was knocking on the solid wooden door.

"Enter!"

Eva nearly ran as he roared out that single word, but instead, she gripped the handle and opened the door.

He rose slowly as she entered and, dear Lord, if possible his scowl had grown more menacing since yesterday.

"Good morning, your Grace."

"You require something, Duchess?"

Eva forged on even though his tone did not suggest she should. "Would you care to take tea with me, your Grace?"

She stood very still while his slate-grey eyes ran over her. He looked like an angry beast that had been disturbed in his lair. His hair stood off his head, a shadow marked his jaw, which suggested he was in dire need of a shave, and his clothes appeared so rumpled, Eva wondered if he had, in fact, slept in them.

"Please accept my apologies, Duchess, but I have no time for tea this morning."

Eva bit her lip as he held her gaze for several long-drawn-out seconds. His grey eyes were piercing in their intensity and she wanted to shuffle from one foot to the other like a child. Yet she was made of sterner stuff; she held herself still and waited.

"I will be leaving for London as soon as my work here is complete and I would like to reach there by the end of the week. Therefore I have little time for...tea."

She winced at his precise pronunciation of the word; there was little doubt in her mind he found her request ridiculous.

"Is everything to your satisfaction, Duchess?"

"Pardon, your Grace?"

"Is everything here at Stratton to your satisfaction?" Eva watched as he unclenched his fists and braced them on the desk before him, his eyes steady and unwavering as they studied her.

"Yes thank you, your Grace."

"Excellent. Well, if that is all, Duchess, I really must return to my work."

Eva dropped into a curtsy and quickly turned to leave the room.

"Do you ride?"

Gripping the door handle, she nodded but did not face him after he asked the quesiton.

"I have a grey mare that will suit your needs and will instruct my staff to show you the best paths to ride when you are ready."

"Thank you but I do not want to put you to any trouble, your Grace."

Eva wasn't sure but thought he sighed.

"This will be your home, Duchess, I think in time you will wish to explore it."

Eve heard the impatience in his voice and reluctantly turned back to face him. "Of course, thank you again. She waited to see if he said anything further and when he did not she bobbed her head and quickly left the room, closing the door softly behind her.

# CHAPTER TWO

*S*inking into the chair, Daniel stared at the door. The anger in him was so close to the surface, he feared one wrong word or action from someone would see it unleashed. He would be just like his father then.

The old duke had raised his son using discipline. No matter the situation, if he felt Daniel needed whipping, he undertook the punishment with relish. Daniel had learnt to keep out of his father's way, yet he'd never learnt to be submissive when the punishment was being meted out. He had taunted his father, smiling through his pain, enraging him further until one day his mother had tried to intervene.

Closing his eyes he let the memories come; perhaps the pain would keep his anger in check.

The late Duchess of Stratton had meant everything to her son. Daniel had loved her from his first breath. She was beautiful, kind and loving - everything her husband was not. He remembered the day his father had dragged him into his study after he had broken a vase, demanding an apology that at twelve years of age, Daniel had already been strong enough to refuse. His father had flown into a rage, and then, bending Daniel over, he had begun to whip him. Only this time he didn't stop.

Hearing his cries, the Duchess had burst into the room, demanding he stop whipping her son. The duke had stopped, but only long enough to turn the birch on his wife. Daniel had screamed and tried to stop the punishment but he had been pushed aside and by the time he regained his feet his mother had fallen and hit her head. She had never regained consciousness.

He never spoke to his father again and after the funeral, Daniel was sent away to school, where he learned to tuck his grief and anger deep inside him. It had stayed there until now.

He needed to leave Stratton soon before he took his anger out on the woman who was now his wife. Only then would she be safe.

. . .

Eva explored her new home thoroughly over the next week, making sure that in doing so she kept away from the duke's study. She found many a parlor and room filled with sheet-covered furniture. Most were lovely old pieces that simply needed a good polish. Many of the drab, faded curtains and carpets, however, needed replacing. Eva decided she would talk to the housekeeper and together they would take an inventory of everything and then decide how best to tackle the problem of restoring her new home to its original beauty.

The only glimpse she had of the duke was from her window seat one morning. He had walked beneath on his way toward the stables. She could tell he was still angry because he had swiped his riding crop at a poor, hapless rose bush, sending a flurry of petals and leaves in all directions. Eva observed his long strides and tall muscular form. He was a man who drew a woman's eye, a man many would long to wed. Something inside her believed he was not like her father and ready with his fists, yet Eva was not about to place herself in his path to test that theory.

For once in her life she was left to do exactly as she wanted, exactly when she wanted to do it. She was sure in time that would get lonely, but for now Eva reveled in her newfound freedom and when she stumbled across the music room high up on the third floor she thought her happiness, for now, was complete. Eva wondered who had played. The old Duke, perhaps, or maybe his wife?

Daniel tensed when he heard the first strains of music. Opening the door, he listened as the sweet melody filled the empty halls of his home. The last person to touch those keys had been his mother. It had to be his wife; no one else but he played and he had not sat at a piano for many years. He was amazed at how good she was; it seemed her horrible father had at least allowed her some joy. Leaving the door open, he walked back to his desk. Re-seating himself, Daniel picked up another piece of paper from the pile his steward had left him and began to make notes.

He would finish his duties this evening and then go the Duchess's room to consummate the marriage. Dear God, when had he approached a women's bed with such trepidation? Had it not been a stipulation of the contract, he wouldn't have contemplated the act, but it was, and therefore he'd fulfill his side of the obligation no matter how much he disliked the idea.

A knock sounded on his door minutes later and Daniel scowled at Luton as he moved to stand before his desk, his face set in its usual pleasant mask.

"Will you and the duchess be dining in the main dining hall this evening or shall I have the small parlor prepared?"

What the hell was the old reprobate up to? Luton surely knew by now Daniel had no wish to dine with his wife. "I will have a tray in here again, please."

The butler's expression remained unchanged and the two men silently stared at each other.

"What, damn you?" Daniel thundered after several long seconds, and to his credit, Luton never so much as twitched.

"It will take but a moment to prepare the small parlor and Mrs. Stimpel has baked your favorite apple dumplings."

Not many men took Daniel on head to head, yet Luton had challenged him for as long as could remember.

"I have no wish to eat with my wife, Luton, and I would ask you to remember who is now master of this household."

"I believe Mrs. Stimpel has also prepared the beef exactly as you like it with a rich burgundy sauce," Luton continued, undaunted.

"And yet I have no wish to dine with my wife," Daniel reiterated.

"Your grandmother would be saddened, your Grace." Luton bowed deeply. "Your wife will be dining in the small dining room if you should have a change of mind."

Luton always dragged Daniel's grandmother into any

argument he wasn't winning. "I will not change my mind." He dismissed his butler with another hard look.

As the day progressed, visions of his wife having her evening meal on her own filtered through Daniel's head, until by nightfall they were a permanent fixture. Why he should feel guilt over his wife eating a solitary meal, he had no idea. Many married people did not eat together. In fact, they often lived separate lives and surely other marriages had not started with such tumultuous beginnings as his.

Sighing, he climbed to his feet. I will give her one night, and one night only, he thought as he left the room to change.

"Good evening, your Grace." Daniel entered the dining room thirty minutes later and moved to take the seat opposite his wife. She stumbled to her feet and sank into an awkward curtsy, listing slightly to the right in her haste, then re-seated herself.

Placing what he hoped was pleasant expression on his face he instructed Luton to bring the first course.

Daniel was pleased that a flower arrangement partially obscured his wife from his line of vision, although he was still afforded a partial view of one side of her face. This consisted of half a matronly white cap into which every lock of her hair had been stuffed, and one eye with a delicately curved eyebrow. Blue, he thought. Her eyes are blue...or were they? It was hard to say in the candlelight. The curve of one cheek was flushed with pink and below there was half a pair of surprisingly full lips and a small chin. Her skin was smooth and he noted a small smattering of freckles on the bridge of her nose. Once again she was wearing a hideous dress, this one in dull grey.

"Wine, your Grace?"

"Thank you," Daniel said absently as he viewed the ill-shaped bodice. Who the hell was her dressmaker? Or had she been forced to make it herself? He wondered what size - if any - breasts she had. He supposed he would find out soon, or possibly not if they just got down to the business of consummation.

"May I fill your glass also, your Grace?"

"Oh yes. Thank you very much, Luton."

She had a voice which did not grate on the senses, unlike some he could name.

"I heard you playing the piano, Duchess."

His words took her by surprise and Daniel watched her fork slip through her fingers to immerse itself in the burgundy sauce nestled between Mrs. Stimpel's tasty beef and fluffy potatoes.

She muttered what he thought was, "Oh dear." As Luton deftly passed her a new fork and removed the other with a pair of tongs, she said, "Would your rather I did not play the piano, your Grace?"

"No this is your home now. Make use of whatever you wish."

"There is a great deal of music in the room. May I also use that?"

"You may."

He knew she wanted to ask who played the piano in his family and he was intrigued to see if she had the courage to do so.

"Do you play, your Grace?"

"I do not." Daniel did not give her the answer she sought to see if she would ask a more direct question.

"Potatoes, your Grace?" Luton asked.

Daniel waved his hand to indicate that he would pass on the potatoes, then looked across the table once more. He watched her long, slender fingers pick up a napkin. He now understood how she was able to play the piano so well. They were unadorned and he felt a tug of shame that in his fury he had given her his grandfather's ugly ring instead of his grandmother's beautiful ruby. She lifted a mouthful of beef and then licked her lips as a drop of sauce touched them. He was surprised to find the small gesture strangely appealing; perhaps if he kissed her before bedding her Daniel would be able to rake up some enthusiasm for consummating their marriage.

"Did your mother play, your Grace?"

"Yes." Daniel did not elaborate, as he had no wish to discuss the matter further and especially not with the woman he had been forced to wed.

"I'm sorry." She said the words in a rush, almost as if they tasted foul

"For what?"

"That you were forced by your father to marry me."

What the hell was he supposed to say to that?

"'Tis done, therefore we must make the best of it." He made his words dismissive, wanting to put an end to the conversation before his simmering anger had a chance to boil.

"Will you take tea in the lemon parlor, your Grace?"

"Thank you, no, Luton," Daniel said, climbing to his

feet. The tension in the room was becoming unbearable and he had done his duty so now he could leave. "Duchess, I bid you good evening," he said to the floral arrangement, behind which she sat. He then turned and left the room.

Daniel had never been a coward, yet here he was still at Stratton and his wife remained a virgin. He should have visited her room last night after their meal; instead, he had chosen his own bed where he had slept a deep, dreamless sleep until dawn. Disgusted with himself, he walked into the stables, hoping a hard ride would clear his head. The sound of his stableboy's laughter made his lips twitch and he wondered who had evoked such a reaction in the lad who was usually so serious.

Daniel stopped in his tracks as he heard a voice say, "I hid behind a bush once and lobbed a rotten apple at my eldest brother as he cantered past."

"And what happened then, your Grace?" he heard Holby ask.

"My brother fell sideways into a conveniently located puddle. And I don't mind telling you it was one of my finer moments."

Could this really be his timid wife speaking so freely to one of his stable hands?

"Do you not like your brother?"

The duchess was silent for several seconds and Daniel wondered if she would answer the boy's question.

"It is wrong of me to say so, Holby, but I do not care over much for my elder brothers. However my youngest, Reggie, is wonderful and I miss and worry about him very much."

He could hear the longing in her words.

"How come you and your youngest brother are nice and the others aren't?"

"Well, Holby, the thing is we have different mothers so Reggie and I are thankfully different inside and out."

Daniel's mind flicked back to his wedding and seeing the youngest Winchcomb looking pale and drawn as he stood beside the carriage as they prepared to leave.

"Posy's ready for you now, your Grace. But I'm not sure as you should be riding out alone."

"It is sweet of you to worry, Holby, but I have been riding alone my entire life. I see no reason to stop now."

She said the words so easily as if riding unaccompanied was something every young lady did. Daniel knew that, in fact, this wasn't the case and put another black mark against the Winchcomb men.

"I will accompany her, Holby, if you will saddle Dickens," Daniel said as the boy led Posy from her stable.

"Your Grace!" the duchess gasped.

Daniel frowned as both his stableboy and wife turned to face him with identical expressions of horror.

Green. Her eyes were green, or were they? Damn, she'd lowered them again before he could be sure. Her hair was once again covered in a silly cap but he had noted that her eyebrows were dark so possibly her hair was, as well? Looking around the edges of the cap, he searched for a stray lock but could find none.

"I - I have no need of an escort, your Grace."

When Daniel took a step closer, his wife grabbed the mare's reins as if she was preparing to flee.

"Yet I will accompany you, Duchess, as you have no idea of the lay of the land around Stratton."

"I would not want to inconvenience you and as this is to be my home, I am sure riding alone will be something I do often."

Daniel lifted a hand, intent only on running it through his hair in frustration, yet his wife caught the movement and quickly ducked under the mare's neck, placing the horse between them. Daniel was stunned as she then vaulted onto Posy's back, the movement effortless and surprisingly graceful, and then she was gone, simply waving a gloved hand above her head. The little mare was suddenly galloping out of the stables as if the hounds of hell were on its heels.

"Bloody hell! Hurry, Holby - the little fool will kill herself if she keeps up that pace."

Daniel urged his black stallion out of the stables minutes later, then gave him his head. He could see his wife in the distance. Pulling alongside her minutes later, he reached for her reins and eased the mare into a walk.

"That was foolish,"

She didn't look at him, instead keeping her eyes between the horse's ears. "I had no wish to inconvenience you, your Grace."

She was terrified of him; Daniel could see it in the set of her shoulders and rigid line of her jaw. What the hell had her family done to her? "You have nothing to fear from me."

"I do not fear you, your Grace. However I say again that I had no wish to inconvenience you any further."

"Yet I will reassure you that I present no danger to you

and it is not an inconvenience to show you around the land."

Daniel realized that she was as much a victim, if not more so, than he in this mess they called a marriage. He'd never had a woman fear him and was at a loss to know what to do to reassure her that he meant her no harm.

"If you will follow me, please." He nudged his mount forward and hoped she would follow.

They rode in silence for over an hour, rarely speaking, just the occasional word from him about the land or buildings and a responding murmur from her. Strangely, it was not an uncomfortable ride, perhaps because Daniel always enjoyed viewing the lands around his home. He knew every dip and rise and lush, rolling inch of pasture, and took pleasure in showing it to others. She followed where he led, the thud of Posy's hooves the only indication of her presence.

"Stratton is a beautiful place, your Grace, and one I am honored to now call home," she said as they neared the stables again, and Daniel heard the honesty in her words.

"I hope you will be happy here, Duchess."

She didn't reply, instead urging Posy past his mount into the stables. He watched her dismount unaided and hand Holby the reins. She then talked to the boy for several minutes and Hobly was soon chuckling at something she said. Her eyes followed Posy as he led the little mare away and Daniel wondered what she was thinking. She turned then and caught him staring at her, offering him a small smile she then bobbed a curtsey and left the stables quickly. Shaking his head Daniel led his own mount into a stable and began unsaddling him. It would be best for both of them if he left, only then could they begin to build their lives once more, and perhaps then she would also believe she was safe here at Stratton, safe from the men she feared.

Later that day, Eva stood outside her husband's door once again. Taking a deep breath, she knocked twice. She had to do this one thing before he left for London. Thoughts of Reggie in her father's care were constantly in her head and she had promised him that she would send for him as soon as she could. Betsy, her father's housekeeper, was another she had vowed to rescue. If she could just get this interview over with, she would never bother him again. Wiping her sweaty palms on the skirts of her dress, she fought for calm.

"Enter!"

Dear Lord, he sounded angry again. Obviously his mood had darkened since this morning's ride. Eva felt her heart beat faster as she pushed open the door and slipped inside.

"Can I help you?" The duke rose as she approached.

Eva hesitated briefly, her eyes going to the hands he had braced on the desk before him. They were very nice hands - big strong hands, with blunt-filed nails. They were hands you could place your heart in and know it was safe. Hands that would hold a child secure.

However, not her heart and definitely not her child.

"Well!"

Eva felt a spark of anger as he barked the word at her; she had done nothing to deserve it. When they'd last met, at least he'd been civil. Taking a deep breath, she then recited the words she had practiced long into the night. "I have need of your assistance, your Grace."

"Of course. Speak freely."

Eva was relieved when he sank back into his chair. She felt safer with him sitting.

"I wish to have my brother and a servant brought over from my father's house, your Grace."

"And you want my help?"

Eva nodded. "My father will not release either of them into my care if the request comes from me."

She desperately wanted to lower her eyes - anything to avoid his intent stare - but she needed this one thing and then she would never ask him for anything more for as long as she lived.

"I would not ask if it were not important, your Grace." Eva wanted to yell at him to speak but he just kept looking at her almost as if he was searching for something. When the silence became unbearable, Eva turned to leave. "I will intrude on you no further." She would have to find another way to get her brother and Betsy here.

"Give me the name of the servant and I will see it done."

"And my brother?" Eva faced him again.

"I know his name and will try to have him brought here to you. However, it may not be as easy because he is still under your father's care."

She pulled a piece of paper from her pocket and handed it to him. He flipped it open and scanned the contents.

"Betsy Mullholland is the name of the servant and this is your father's address?"

"Yes."

"And it is important to have both her and your brother here with you?" he asked softly.

"Yes, your Grace."

"I will make sure the request is made before I leave tomorrow."

"Thank you, your Grace. I fear my father will not care for them now I am gone." Eva felt an explanation was needed.

"I am to leave soon, however my steward will call upon you in two days' time, Duchess. He will always be at your service, should you require anything, and will explain the accounts I have set up for you that will look after all your needs."

"Thank you, your Grace," Eva quickly sank into a curtsy, then turned and walked toward the door. It was as she opened it that something inside her urged her to speak. "I wish you good health and happiness."

Sleep did not come easy that night for Eva and it was just as she was drifting off that she heard the sound of her bedroom door closing.

"Who is there?"

"It is your husband, Duchess."

"Is something wrong?" Eva pulled the covers aside and swung her feet out of bed. Surely something must be terribly wrong if he was forced to come into her room.

"Nothing is wrong. I have come to consummate our marriage."

Eva was shocked at the cold, hard words and could not believe what she had heard. "You said to my father you would not c-consummate the marriage, your Grace - that you do not want an heir." Eva clutched her chest where her heart was thumping with painful ferocity.

"I may have said that to your father, yet because it is stipulated in the vow I always intended to do this as my honor is at stake."

Eva felt panic claw at her as he moved closer to where she sat on the edge of the bed.

"I will make it as painless as I can, Duchess."

"I do not want you to…not like this!" Eva said, realizing she meant every word. Yes, she wanted a child, but not one conceived in anger. Jumping to her feet, she ran for the door but did not get far as the duke merely stretched out one arm as she raced past him, his fingers caught her and hauled her to his side.

"This must be done," he then muttered, wrapping his arms around her as she began to struggle.

"Why! Who will know?"

"I will know." He pulled her into his chest and held her tight. "I must do this!" he rasped, "I must honor the vow my father made."

"P-please don't," she sobbed, struggling to break free from his hold. "Yes, I long for a child but not like this, not one conceived through pain and rage."

"Many children are conceived in such a way." His grip tightened as she renewed her struggles. Her efforts proved hopeless, however, against a man whose strength was twice hers. "You will harm only yourself if you do not stop this foolish struggling."

"Please let me go."

"I cannot."

"Wh-why are you loyal to a man who cared so little for you?" she cried, still trying to push herself away from him.

She knew he was naked beneath his robe; she felt the heat from his body pressed against her own. She took a deep breath, and her senses were instantly filled with his scent. Fear gripped her as Eva realized that once again she was at a man's mercy. "I-I thought you were different."

"I am," he said softly. Eva stiffened as he ran a hand down her spine. His fingers felt warm through the material of her nightdress. "But it is a matter of honor."

She knew further resistance was futile; the strength seeped from her body and Eva slumped into her husband. His hand continued to stroke her, as if soothing a skittish mare, and she could never remember being touched this way - not in kindness. "Honor is a word men use so they may commit a multitude of sins."

"I will not hurt you." Eva felt his breath in her hair.

"Men always s-say that but they do not mean it."

"I mean it," the duke vowed. "I know you have little reason to trust me, Duchess, yet I would ask that you try."

"Please, your Grace, don't do this now, not when we both harbor such a distrust of each other."

Daniel fell silent and just held her close. Her heartbeat had eased; one of her hands held his robe, the other lay flat against his chest. He could feel the dampness of her tears as they trickled down his neck and something inside him moved. Something clenched in the region of his heart, and he was discomfited to realize he felt at peace holding her, almost as if they were comforting each other. His fingers absently loosened the silken length of her plait as his mind worked through the emotions that raged inside him. Her words kept repeating themselves inside his head: Why are you loyal to a man who cared so little for you?

"Honor is the one thing my father has not taken from me." He heard the pain behind his words. The anger and sense of betrayal still ran deep within him.

"I...I have known you such a short time, your Grace, yet I had believed that unlike the other men in my life you were a man of honor, a man who would not force a woman to do his bidding."

Daniel listened as his wife spoke, her soft words tickling his skin and seeming to soothe the ache in his chest. Lifting a handful of her hair, he buried his face in the sweet-smelling curls. "I will never be like my father."

"As I will never be like mine," she vowed.

Her fingers were stroking his chest, the movements light as a child's touch, but Daniel felt the sensation through his whole body. "I lived my life believing I knew the future I had mapped out for myself," he said, "yet in the end, as he did in my youth, my father betrayed me." Daniel felt the small puff of his wife's breath on his skin as he finished speaking. "My words amuse you, Duchess?"

She lifted her head to look up at him but in the darkness, her expression eluded him. "At least you had the choice of how to live your life, your Grace. Traveling here with you is the first time I have left my father's home."

Slowly, Daniel trailed his fingers over her face, tracing the jut of one cheekbone, the rounded tip of her nose, then the full softness of her lower lip. Everything was different here in the darkness. Inside this room, they were two people who spoke only the truth. He could not do it, could not take her against her will knowing she had been mistreated her entire life.

"No one will hurt you again," Daniel vowed, swinging her up into his arms.

"No!" She struggled as he carried her toward the bed.

"Ssssh," Daniel whispered, lowering her onto the mattress. Pulling the covers back, he slid her inside. Bracing his hands on either side of her head, he looked down at her.

"You are right, Duchess. I have no right to take you with so much rage inside me. I apologize for causing you more pain when the reality is that you have had more than your share for one so young." Lifting a handful of her hair, he smoothed it on the pillow. "I must leave here now before the anger that burns deep inside forces me to do something I would regret. I will return someday under different circumstances, and then we will consummate this marriage and you will have your child, but until then, know that here at Stratton you are your own mistress, safe from the hands of your father."

She touched the side of his face briefly, her fingers soft as they ran down his cheek.

"Goodbye, Duchess."

"Goodbye, Duke."

Taking her fingers in his he gave them a final squeeze and then walked from the room, closing the door quietly behind him.

# CHAPTER THREE

"*I* have written to Reggie but have still received no reply, Betsy. I'm so worried for him."

Eva raised her face to the sun as she handed Betsy Mulholland a sheet to hang on the line. The heat was soothing on her skin.

Betsy had arrived one week after her husband had left with an armed outrider and Eva knew the Duke had guessed correctly that her father would not give up the woman without a fight. However, of Reggie there had been no sign. Her father had refused to let him come and she knew this was because he had taken Eva's place in the Winchcomb household.

"We will find a way to get him here, your Grace," Betsy said, "and in the meantime he is used to your father's ways."

Yes, Eva had to believe that and if she could not find a solution soon, she would ask the duke for help again.

She had thought about him a lot since that morning two months ago when he had left Stratton for London. Eva had watched him walk to his carriage, his eagerness at leaving obvious in his long strides. She'd leant on the window ledge to get a final glimpse of him, and as if he sensed her presence, he had looked up and their eyes met briefly. She had raised a hand in farewell but he simply climbed inside and closed the door behind him.

"Your Grace!"

Eva watched Luton hurry toward her. Tomorrow, she decided, they would hire a young boy to serve as his helper. Surely it was not good for a man of his age to be running about collecting his mistress? And two new gardeners, she thought with a spurt of independence. Stratton deserved to be restored to its former glory and since her husband was not here, that task now fell to her.

"Your Grace, Miss Belmont and Mrs. Potter have called to see you." Luton clutched his side as he drew in a deep breath.

"Oh dear." Horrified, Eva looked down at her drab grey dress. "Who are they, Luton?"

"I believe Mrs. Potter is the reverend's wife, your Grace, and Miss Belmont's father owns property which borders Stratton".

"Oh dear," she said again, feeling her newfound confidence wane.

Eva patted and tucked and fiddled with her hair on the way back to the house, took out her handkerchief and scrubbed her face, then tried to brush the grass stains from her skirts.

"It is you who are the duchess, your Grace," Luton said as they entered the house. "Therefore perhaps they are at this very minute doing the same to themselves."

Eva's hands stopped in mid-pat and she looked into his wise old eyes and smiled. "You, Luton, are a prince amongst men."

"Thank you, your Grace." Luton opened the parlor door for Eva to enter.

"I'm so pleased to meet you, your Grace."

Eva watched the beautiful woman walk toward her. She had hazel eyes and an open face and strawberry blonde curls peeking out from beneath her bonnet.

"I am Miss Belmont, your nearest neighbor."

"How do you do." Eva sank into a curtsy.

"And this is Mrs. Potter. She is the wife of Reverend Potter from the local parish," Miss Belmont added, squeezing Eva's hand hard, thus drawing her eyes upwards. Miss Belmont then winked at her.

Puzzled by the young lady's actions, Eva turned to face the other woman in the room. And I thought I had bad fashion sense, she thought, looking at Mrs. Potter.

The woman before her looked like a brightly colored Christmas parcel. She was as wide as she was tall, her body swathed in yards of bright red fabric that scooped low over her ample bosom and nipped in tight around her waist, which in turn was accentuated with a wide green sash. Then again, perhaps she resembled a gaily wrapped sausage, Eva thought, looking at the rolls of fat protruding over the sash. Even Mrs. Potter's hair was curled in tight sausage ringlets that framed a round face punctuated by two small eyes of indeterminate color.

"Please allow me to welcome you to the village, your Grace. Reverend Potter urged me to call upon you now you have settled in and ask if you will be attending services this Sunday." Mrs. Potter's smile was hopeful.

"Uh, I…"

"We are delighted to at last have another duchess living here at Stratton, and hope that soon you will honor our small village with a visit."

"O-of course," Eva said, feeling guilty that she had not already done so. "Please tell Reverend Potter I will attend church this Sunday, and forgive me for not doing so sooner. I am afraid it has taken me some time to settle in.'

"Oh no, your Grace." Mrs. Potter clasped her hands to her ample bosom. "Please do not apologize. We are aware of the pressures such a great lady must have upon her time and it will be such an honor to have you attend our service. I will have the Stratton pew cleaned in expectation."

"Please do not go to any trouble on my behalf, Mrs. Potter," Eva added. She had visions of the village all turning out to clean before she arrived and she did not warrant such attention.

"It will be our pleasure, your Grace." Mrs. Potter sank into a curtsy so low Eva wondered if she would need help rising.

"Would you ladies care for tea?" Eva looked longingly at the door. She had no experience with social chitchat and the prospect of sitting in a room with them was making her feel uneasy. She envisaged long, awkward silences.

"Tea would be delightful, would it not, Mrs. Potter?" Miss Belmont said, taking the lady's arm and leading her to a chair.

"Oh, indeed it would, Miss Belmont. Tea with the

Duchess." Mrs. Potter patted her sausage curls. "The ladies of the village will be most envious."

Eva did not say a great deal through the subsequent tea. She sat on the edge of her seat, very aware of her worn dress with its frayed hem, and listened to the other two ladies chat.

"I fear it is close to the reverend's lunchtime," Mrs. Potter said finally, struggling out of her chair, which took quite a bit of maneuvering, due to her bulk. "I like to be there when he takes his meals," she added, sinking into another curtsy, and then she was gone.

Miss Belmont chuckled at the startled expression on Eva's face as she looked at the closed door. "She is a kind-hearted lady who feels it's her duty to poke her nose into everyone's business. You are lucky she is in awe of you. The rest of us must suffer her moral sermons regularly."

Eva returned her gaze to Miss Belmont. She looked so gracious in her lemon dress with satin trim. In fact, Miss Belmont appeared exactly as a duchess should and Eva felt a hot wave of shame at her own dowdy appearance. Catching sight of the worn toe of a slipper, she pushed her feet under the hem. What was she to say to this lady who had obviously been raised in society? Surely they had nothing in common.

"Do not feel guilty over not attending church, your Grace." Miss Belmont patted Eva's hand. "You needed time to settle into your new surroundings. Unfortunately, the villagers' curiosity has reached fever pitch and now they have made up all sorts of convoluted tales about you."

"Oh dear, that was never my intention. I merely needed

time to adjust and did not feel comfortable…" Eva's words trailed off as she lowered her eyes.

"Can I help you with becoming more comfortable?" Miss Belton said gently.

Eva spread the skirts of her dress wide. "I fear there are so many things, Miss Belton, I would not know where to start."

"Perhaps your dress is not quite the thing, but we could -"

Eva could do nothing to stop her splutter of laughter. "Not quite the thing!" She lifted her head. "That is a polite way of saying my dress is a rag."

"Yes, well…" Miss Belton studied Eva. "If you will allow me to assist you, we shall soon fix that. If you are free, perhaps you could come to tea tomorrow afternoon and meet the local seamstress. Her dresses are adequate and will surpass what you are wearing." She waved her long, elegant fingers toward the skirts of Eva's dress.

Eva found herself laughing again. "I could not impose on you like that."

"Nonsense. I would love to help you," Miss Belton said. "In truth, we would be doing each other a favor. I can help you feel comfortable and you can stop me from incurring my mother's wrath, as in her eyes, all I do is read, sleep and ride my horse."

"And this is bad?" Eva questioned.

Claire rolled her eyes. "Very. I should be hosting tea parties and visiting local ladies with whom I should stitch quilts and make myself useful."

Eva felt sick at the thought. "Oh dear, should I be doing that, too?"

"Yes, and now we shall do it together and my mother will be happy."

"I'm not sure I'll be much help." Eva felt she had to point this out.

"Nonsense, you're a duchess, and therefore all you need do is turn up and it will be enough."

A rush of excitement had Eva nodding. Although the idea of taking tea and visiting people sounded terrifying, she had always longed for a new dress and perhaps now she was worthy of such a treat. The duke had left instructions that he would pay for any new clothes she acquired, so perhaps she would even order two!

"Once you reach London, you can have a new wardrobe made, but for now the local seamstress will do."

"I have no plans to go to London, Miss Belmont," Eva said quietly.

Miss Belmont smiled and patted Eva's hand. "You will one day. Now tell me what changes you have made here at Stratton besides Luton's clothing."

Happy to change the subject, Eva launched into a detailed inventory of what she had changed and hoped to change.

"Well I am pleased to see you taking an interest in the place, your Grace. No one has for many years."

"It is so lovely here," Eva said meaning every word. "And I hope, given time, that I can restore some of its beauty."

"There are plenty of skilled local tradesmen, should you need them, and they would be happy for the work."

"Of course." Eva knew that often villages survived off the trade from big manor houses in the surrounding area.

"I do not yet know any of the local people but I will endeavor to change that soon." She was the Duchess of Stratton now and would live out her life here. It was important she made herself known.

Miss Belmont then told Eva about the local community and some of the more colorful characters that lived in it and before Eva realized it, they had been talking for another hour.

"And now I must return home to accompany my mother on her afternoon visits, however before I do I would ask that you now call me Claire, as we are sure to be firm friends."

Were they? Eva had never had a friend, firm or otherwise.

"And you must call me Eva, Claire," she said, hoping this was the right thing to say.

Apparently it was, as Claire smiled at her and then rose to leave.

"I will see you tomorrow, Eva."

"I look forward to it," she replied, surprised that she meant every word.

"A gentleman has called, your Grace."

With a final wave to Claire, Eva turned to face her butler. "A gentleman, Luton?"

"He did not furnish me with his name, your Grace, but said you would be pleased to see him."

"Where have you put him?"

"In the small blue parlor, your Grace."

Dear Lord, could it be her father? That thought wiped the smile from her face. However she was a duchess now and would have to see whomever it was. Throwing back her shoulders, she walked through the door Luton directed her toward and came to a halt as she saw who sat inside.

"Berengaria, it is lovely to see you again."

"Dear God!"

"I hope you are as pleased to see me as I am you?"

Eva stiffened as Lord Gilbert Huxley walked toward her. She hated this man. He was evil and lecherous and took liberties with those weaker than himself. Always dressed impeccably, no hair out of place, he looked at a person only to calculate his or her weaknesses and then determine how best to exploit them. He had touched and taunted her for years, telling her what he would like to do to her, and she had always run and locked herself in her room when he was in the house.

"I would ask you to leave my property at once, Lord Huxley." Eva tried to sound calm. This man could hurt her no longer.

"It seems you have forgotten you manners, Berengaria." He kept walking, stopping only inches from where Eva stood. "It would be remiss of me not to reacquaint you with them in your father's absence."

"Do not touch me!" Eva pushed his hand aside as he reached for her. "I loathe and detest you and I will ask you again to leave my property."

Gilbert Huxley was a nobleman and she had never really understood why he spent so much time in her father's company, until the day she'd overheard them talking.

"I have travelled all day to see you, my darling little Berengaria." Huxley moved closer, backing her into the side table.

She had heard her father and Huxley discuss how best to cheat the men they were meeting out of their money. It seemed they had done this often, the commoner and the nobleman making money though lies and deceit, and if there was a slur cast upon Huxley at any stage, he simply challenged the accuser to a duel and won. Eva knew many men had been maimed or lost their lives at his hand. Her father had told her he was one of the most skilled swordsmen in England.

"I have no idea how you found me, Lord Huxley, but your journey has been wasted as I have no wish to see you, now or ever."

"Your father told me where to find you, my sweet, as he thought you would grow bored, now your husband has returned to London."

Her father's betrayal shouldn't have had the power to still hurt her but it did.

"Leave my property at once, Lord Huxley, or I shall -"

Eva did not see him move but suddenly his hand was fisted in her hair, pulling her closer. She shuddered as he put his mouth on hers, his teeth biting into her lower lip.

"No!" She tried to scream and fight her way free but he was too strong and within seconds he had her beneath him, lying on the table. She heard the vase crash to the floor and several books follow as he lifted her onto the surface.

"I have wanted you for a long time, Berengaria, and now that your husband has taken your innocence, I will teach you the art of how to really please a man."

Eva bit him.

"Bitch!" He slapped her cheek and then reached for the bodice of her dress.

"Unhand her at once!"

Eva nearly wept at Luton's voice.

"You evil beast! This time I should do the world a favor and shoot you right between the legs. Get off her now!" Betsy Mulholland yelled.

Suddenly Eva was free. A firm hand hauled her upright and pulled her toward the doorway. She was then thrust behind a wall of her servants. Mrs. Stimpel slipped an arm around her and pulled her close. "Tis alright, your Grace," she said softly. "You are safe now."

Eva took several deep breaths to stop herself from collapsing onto Mrs. Stimpel's ample chest. Betsy Mullholland held a shotgun pointed at Gilbert Huxley's private regions. Luton held a kitchen knife; Mrs. Stimpel, a rolling pin. Geoffrey, the footman, had an axe.

Panting with fury, Gilbert Huxley glared at her. "How dare you allow your servants to speak to a nobleman in such a manner, Berengaria!"

"How dare I?" Eva swallowed the hysteria and then moved to stand in front of Betsy, whom she thought just might shoot him if the moment presented itself. "You dare to preach to me of your noble birthright when you have just demonstrated you do not carry a noble bone in your body!"

"You dare to question me? You, a worthless little slut whose father gambled her into marriage?"

So that was how Spencer Winchcomb had forced the old duke into marrying his son to her. Eva would think about that later; for now she had to deal with Huxley.

"Worthless I may be but I am also a duchess and my duke is one of the most powerful men in this country.

Therefore, it should not be me who treads carefully, sir."

She'd surprised him with her words. His eyes widened briefly and his hands fisted at his sides.

"You, Gilbert Huxley, make my skin crawl," she continued, "and if I did not believe it would go unpunished, I would shoot you myself." Inside, Eva might be a quivering mess but she would never show him that. Never again would she be that frightened young girl in his presence.

"Hear me well, Gilbert Huxley, for I mean every word I speak," Eva said slowly. "You will leave my property and never return, and if you disobey these orders, I will have you shot."

He laughed in her face. "You could not get away with killing a nobleman, Berengaria, and it is my belief that you are too timid to do so."

"I am a duchess, my Lord. I am sure my misdeeds would be overlooked, should my husband wish it to be so." Eva braced her shaking knees together as he glared at her. She shivered at the murderous rage in his eyes.

"This will not end here, Berengaria, and you will be sorry you ever crossed me."

"Have him removed from Stratton, Luton, and see he leaves the area completely," Eva ordered holding his eyes. Taking the shotgun from Betsy, she then left the room.

. . .

Daniel had hoped returning to London would prove to be a diversion. His anger would abate and he would forget what he had left behind at Stratton. Eight weeks he had been back and instead of easing, his anger and frustrations were growing. He was heartily sick of everyone asking after his wife. Instead of waning, the interest in his nuptials appeared to be gaining momentum. He had attended balls, routs and card evenings. When questioned as to the whereabouts of his wife, he gave a polite but curt reply, saying she had chosen to remain in the country. Some had given up asking, especially as his explanation was always followed with a dark scowl, but the more determined had kept probing.

"So soon, Duke. We wondered at the rush to wed…"

"Is her condition too delicate for travel, perchance?"

"Miss Winchcomb, Duke. Most unexpected. We had thought you would set your sights higher…"

He had ground his teeth so many times at each innuendo and question, he was sure they would shatter. And then there were the eligible young ladies, the ones who'd all thought to catch him in their snares. They now sent him teary, reproachful glances. Their mothers and some of the more promiscuous widows, however, were sending him covetous glances, and he was besieged by invitations to share beds. It seemed now he was to be hunted by another sort of female - the bored, attached kind whose husbands turned a blind eye to their wives' little affairs. Of course he was usually more than happy to oblige, but somehow it all seemed a bit tawdry that due to his marital status, he was now fair game - which just showed what a hypocrite he was, as he had spent many long pleasant interludes in the beds of wives, widows and any number of society ladies.

Last night at the Simpkin ball, Lady Louisa Hall suggested she and Daniel have an encounter at the

Trengally house party that was to take place in a month's time in Essex. Daniel had smiled politely and said he was honored but would have to decline. Rather than be put off by his refusal, Lady Louisa had merely fallen on his chest – accidentally, of course – before blowing in his ear.

Shuddering, Daniel remembered her thick, cloying scent. He had left the ball to visit his mistress, but Amelia had pouted and cried over his long absence from her bed and then asked after his wife, indicating her displeasure that he had not informed her of his nuptials. He had simply pulled his breeches back up his legs and stalked from her room, aroused, frustrated and bloody furious with the world.

At present, he was drowning his sorrows at his club - or he had been until his friend Simon, Lord Kelkirk arrived. Having just returned to London, he'd heard of Daniel's marriage and demanded to know why he had not been invited to the celebrations.

"I told you I was leaving London to get married," Daniel said.

"Yes, but I did not believe you!" Lord Kelkirk scowled at his friend. "Good Lord, man, you are always saying one thing and doing another. How was I to know this time you were telling the truth?"

Daniel didn't respond, just stared into the depths of his glass.

"And that, Stratton, is the fourth sigh in as many minutes." Lord Kelkirk added.

Daniel had left his estate with the intention of pushing all thoughts of his wife from his head. However since his arrival in London, she seemed to have taken up permanent residency there. He remembered that night in her room, when the darkness had allowed them to speak honestly. Daniel had been surprised how good it had felt to share some of his feelings with her. He could still feel her soft weight in his arms, the swell of her breasts against his chest, the feel of her tears on his skin. She had smelt of roses and every cloying scented woman since had seemed distasteful to his senses.

His guilt had steadily risen at leaving her behind, her words replaying themselves over and over inside his head. "At least you had the choice to live your life, your Grace. Traveling here with you is the first time I have left my father's home." He imagined her walking aimlessly from room to room at Stratton with only her thoughts for company.

"Five sighs."

"Shut up, Kelkirk!" Daniel scowled.

Viscount Kelkirk and Daniel had been friends since they'd studied together at Eton. Both Simon and Daniel's fathers had cared more for appearances than their sons' happiness and so the two of them had formed a bond as close as brothers. Like Daniel, Simon was big, but where Daniel's hair was brown Simon's was grey, and had been since he turned nineteen. Women loved his silver tresses threaded with black strands, believing they gave him a distinguished air.

"You should just return home and apologize to her," Simon told him.

"How do you know I have anything to apologize for?"

"Because you are preoccupied and withdrawn, two traits

I have never before attributed to you," Simon stated. "And as the last person you saw before coming back to London was your new wife, I surmised she was the source of your ill humor. So either you owe your duchess an apology or she owes you one."

Daniel had not told him the whole story of his marriage, only that his father had been behind it and that his wife now resided at Stratton Lodge. "Haven't you business somewhere? I'm sure there is someone else you could pester."

"Why should I wish for another's company when you are such a delightful companion?" Simon enquired with a smile that made Daniel's scowl deepen. "So what is she like, your new duchess?"

"Timid."

"Warts, moles, bent back or other inflictions?" probed Simon, his eyes fixed on his friend's face.

"None of the above. Skinny wrists and a terrible fashion sense." Daniel took a long swallow of brandy, which burned down his throat in a most satisfactory manner. And she fitted perfectly into his arms. He still had no idea what color eyes his wife had and for some reason, this made him feel guiltier.

"Have I met her family?"

"No."

"No, they are not part of society or no, we have yet to be introduced?"

"Kelkirk, my mood can at best be termed mean. Therefore, it would be in your interest to stop this line of questioning."

"Did she have a season?" Simon asked, seemingly unworried by his friend's threats.

"No."

"Because her family is not part of society or because -"

"Because she was already betrothed to me." Daniel's words sounded weary, as if dredged from his soul. Lord, it seemed he was either seething with rage these days or so tired he felt like he could sleep where he stood.

Simon studied Daniel. "And you had no idea that you were betrothed?"

Daniel's laugh held no humor. "No. I found out as I stood dutifully beside my father's deathbed. He did not ask after me or my future plans. He merely said I was to marry her. It was a touching paternal moment I will carry with me until my own death. I have arranged for you are to marry Miss Winchcomb." Daniel mimicked his sire's voice. It was a promise made at her birth, a promise you must now honor."

"But why?"

"Now that -" Daniel took another deep slug of his drink "- is something I do not know, since my father, with excellent timing, passed away before I could press him further."

"Did your lawyers look over the document?"

Daniel sent his friend a foul look

"Of course. Forgive me." Simon waved a hand. "It is just such a shock."

"Try standing in my shoes."

"And I presume the duchess was as shocked as you?" Simon said.

More guilt landed on his shoulders. "Yes, I now believe she was."

"Now?" Simon questioned.

"Now that I have distanced myself from her and my anger has eased, I can see things more clearly."

"Stratton!" came a voice beyond Simon.

"Have mercy!" Daniel hissed as he looked up into the faces of two of his new brother-in-laws. Thankfully, it seemed he was to be spared their father.

"Lord, Monty! If it isn't our brother-in-law," Bartholomew Winchcomb said. He then brayed loudly, sounding like a farmyard animal.

The elder Winchomb siblings were like two peas in a pod with their short and stocky frames, thinning red hair and wide, bulbous eyes. They looked nothing like the duchess, even though they shared a father.

"Have to thank you, old man. Your name has given us entry into places we had only ever dreamed of before," Bartholomew added. "See you've left the wife at home. Good move. Eva's an ugly little thing and would put you in a very bad light."

"Eva?" Daniel asked.

"Course, you only know her as Berengaria. The bloody Mulholland started calling her Eva ten years ago and it just sort of stuck."

Eva. Daniel didn't like to think of his little wife as Eva. Somehow that made her seem more vulnerable. The name Berengaria had always reminded him of a maiden aunt, but Eva...

"Won't have to worry too much about keeping her busy now the wedding night's over, as Lord Huxley will soon pay her a call," Bartholomew Winchcomb said with another bray of laughter before punching Daniel in the shoulder.

Daniel thought briefly about punching Winchcomb back. Just one well placed jab and he would fall easily with minimum fuss. He could then have them both thrown out of his club.

"And why would Gilbert Huxley pay my Duchess a visit?" Daniel said as he climbed to his feet.

"He's partial to Eva, always has been. Spent a lot of time in our house, you know." Bartholomew Winchcomb puffed out his chest. "Our father is in business with him."

"I'd hardly call cheating men out of their money 'business', Winchcomb," Daniel said. What had Eva's life been like at the hands of these idiots?

"It's business is what it is, Duke! And about now Huxley will be seeing to unfinished business with your duchess, too!"

Montgomery Winchcomb was not as slow as his older brother and had picked up on the change in the large duke's demeanor. Eyes as cold as sleet were at present fastened on Bartholomew. "Uh, Barty," Montgomery said desperately, trying to get his brother's attention. Bartholomew, however, was not listening.

"Really?" Daniel raised a brow.

Happy for once to be the centre of attention, and most especially in front of his very powerful brother-in-law, Barty was not about to relinquish the reins to his younger brother.

"Indeed. Father, you know, let Huxley play with Eva a little, but said he wasn't to touch her -"

"Barty!" Montgomery said with more urgency.

Two very large hands were now clenched at the duke's sides.

"At least until she had wed you, then after the wedding night you would dump her somewhere. Well who wouldn't want to, ugly little thing like that? It makes one shudder thinking of her amongst us."

"Are you saying Huxley will make inappropriate advances to the Duchess of Stratton?"

Bartholomew Winchcomb stilled. Suddenly, all the air squeezed from his lungs as he looked up at the Duke. His brother-in-law's eyes were like looking into the pits of hell. "Uh, well, um…as to that, I'm just, uh…"

"Of course Lord Huxley was just rambling. Harmless fellow, loves Eva like a sister," Montgomery added with a high-pitched laugh. "He wouldn't dream of touching our sweet Eva, would he, Barty?"

"Nooo," Bartholomew shook his head. He then allowed Montgomery to grab him and together, the brothers made a hasty retreat.

Daniel watched the Winchcomb brothers flee, their coattails flicking as they ran through the quiet, exclusive club.

"Do you know if Huxley is in town?" Daniel asked Simon as they both headed for the door through which the Winchcomb brothers had recently fled. The Duke had a very bad feeling in the pit of his stomach all of a sudden. Was his duchess in danger?

"I returned this morning, Daniel, and have not had a chance to catch up on the gossip." Simon fell in beside him as they collected their horses and started through the busy streets of London. "Do you think there was some truth to their claims, then?"

"I cannot afford to discount it. I have only elderly retainers at Stratton Lodge except for Tibbs, my stable master, and he goes to the village most nights. There would not be a lot of protection, should she require it."

Simon digested this for several seconds.

"They are fools, both of them, Daniel. I find it hard to believe that Huxley would pursue your wife, a duchess, to Stratton Lodge and attempt to take her against her will."

"I may not have wanted a wife, Simon, but I have one and can not discount any possible threat to her. She is under my protection now and I have left her vulnerable in my haste to leave Stratton."

"We need to find someone who knows about both the Winchcombs and the threat from Huxley," Simon added, looking around him as if that someone was milling on the streets before them.

Several curses filled the air as Daniel's shoulders slumped. "Grandmother will know."

"Well this, my friend, is where we part ways," Simon said, patting his friend's shoulder in sympathy.

"Coward."

"Sad but true," said Simon, waving farewell and setting off in the opposite direction before Daniel had time to draw another breath. The duke's grandmother had that effect on people.

# CHAPTER FOUR

*T*he Dowager Duchess was Daniel's father's mother. She'd always been a formidable woman, terrifying every new season's debutantes with her vicious tongue. She went through a new household of staff every few weeks and was perhaps the only constant in Daniel's life, though that constant was like a barb being repeatedly jabbed into one's side. She challenged her grandson on every front, just as she had challenged her son. It was she who had visited him regularly at Stratton Lodge, checking his tutors were schooling him correctly to be the next duke, and later she was the one who'd pushed him through Eton.

There were plenty of carriages filling the streets at two o'clock on a sunny afternoon, yet it took Daniel only minutes to direct his horse to his grandmother's doorstep. After handing the reins to a groom, he knocked on the large, white front door.

"Your Grace," the immaculately clad butler said with a deep bow.

"Thompson." Daniel responded with a nod and handed

over his outer clothing. Thompson was the only long-term member of the duchess's household, and had remained in his position for as long as Daniel could remember. "Is my grandmother at home?" he asked, not sure what answer he hoped for.

"If you will come this way, I will take you to her at once."

Damn, she must have heard about his wedding, Daniel thought. Otherwise he would have been left to cool his heels in one of her elegant parlors for at least an hour before she condescended to see him.

"His Grace, the Duke of Stratton, your Grace," Thompson said, ushering Daniel forward.

The Dowager Duchess of Stratton was a big woman who had lost little of her indomitable presence with age. Daniel had no idea of his grandmother's exact age and she was not likely to ever disclose it to him, but she had to be over seventy, he thought, though her black hair was only lightly sprinkled with grey. Her big shoulders, large hands and long, hawk-like nose all added up to a formidable matron who was not to be messed with. They shared the bond of blood but little else. They rarely hugged or touched, she never offered words of kindness of sympathy and in truth, he would not have known how to take them from her. She had a sharp tongue and little wit and Daniel had never really worked out how he felt about her.

"Grandmother." Daniel bowed over her hand.

"So you have been back eight weeks and now you finally visit me?" the duchess barked.

"Yes, I am well, and you also seem to be the picture of health." Daniel moved to take the chair opposite her.

"Do not bandy words with me, Grandson. I was at your father's funeral and you did not say one word, so I had to hear of your marriage like everyone else, through the newspapers." To let him know how angry she truly was, she picked up a book from the table beside her and whacked it soundly on his knee.

"Did you know of this marriage contract?" Daniel rubbed his knee, noting he'd been taken to task by The Marauding Adventures of Captain Veesley on the High Seas.

"Of course. Bloody fool. Your father was an idiot in his youth and he gambled nearly everything away. Had that Winchcomb not offered a marriage contract instead of demanding the money your father owed him, we would all have been out on the streets."

Stunned, Daniel sat back in his chair and stared at his grandmother. Winchcomb had saved his father and the Stratton name?

"You could have warned me," Daniel said quietly, still reeling from what she'd told him.

"How? By telling you that your future was decided? That would have changed who you have become, changed the path you trod. And more importantly, the chit could have died - both your father and I had hoped for her death. Alas, she did not oblige."

That was twice in one day his wife had been insulted - first by her brothers and now by his grandmother. Daniel was beginning to feel angry, which was ridiculous, as he had no feelings for the woman other than pity. Needing to look anywhere but at his grandmother, he studied the room around him, seeing but not really seeing. Not much had changed since his last visit. It was still dark and austere, just like its owner. The only pleasing thing to Daniel was that all the furniture was solid and well-built, unlike the current trend of spindly legs and narrow seats, grossly unsuited to his large frame.

"I met her brothers before I came here and they mentioned that Gilbert Huxley has an interest in my Duchess." Daniel watched his grandmother closely. Her reaction surprised even him. Her hands clenched and her cheeks puffed. These displays did little to alleviate the feeling of unease in his stomach.

"That pathetic excuse for a nobleman - makes my blood boil just to hear his name."

"Is my wife in danger, Grandmother? Her brothers alluded to the fact that Huxley had unfinished business where she was concerned."

The older woman nodded her head. "Huxley was there when I visited the Winchcombs for the last time a few years ago."

"You visited my wife's family? Why?" Daniel shook his head, confused.

"I visited the Winchcombs to see what sort of family they were and look over the girl. She was only a baby the first time but I wanted to make sure the future Duchess of Stratton did not have a squint or clubbed feet."

Daniel remained silent; interrupting would get him nothing but a lecture.

"The little girl was pretty. She gurgled and smiled and I was most pleased. Her father was an idiot and tried to kiss me."

"I beg your pardon!" Surely Daniel hadn't heard that right.

"I, of course, unmanned him instantly, by, well, you understand."

Daniel couldn't help smiling as his grandmother glared at him. He could well imagine what she had done to Winchcomb.

"I am pleased you were able to protect yourself, Grandmother," he said solemnly.

Thompson arrived then with tea, and Daniel knew better than to ask his grandmother to continue while a servant was in the room so he ground his teeth and waited. The elderly woman nodded for the butler to leave, then proceeded with the long drawn-out ritual that was needed to prepare a good cup of tea. He watched as she turned the teapot four times to the left, then four times to the right, counted for twenty seconds, then repeated the procedure. Usually Daniel found this quaint little ritual quite endearing. Today, however, he would cheerfully have reached across the table, grabbed the bloody teapot and hurled it across the room, but again, he knew better than to hurry her along. One did not hurry his grandmother, so outwardly calm he sat and waited.

"My second visit was, as I said, only a few years ago," she continued after she had taken a small sip of tea. "I had wanted to check on the girl again, make sure that the tutor I had sent to school her was doing his job and that she was up to the mark. We could not have the new Duchess of Stratton appearing to countrified."

"And you did not think at this stage that I should have been informed of my impending doom." Daniel's tone was terse.

Snorting, she reached for her tea and took a long swallow.

"You would have run for the hills or gone into the army, had I informed you."

She had a point there but he was too angry to acknowledge it.

"Your wife was a small, mousy thing, but for all that she seemed to have pleasing manners and as she had no idea of your contract either, I did not enlighten her. Her father told her that I was a long-lost relative who had come to see the family and that I was the one responsible for the tutor. The girl didn't question me, yet I could see confusion in her eyes."

"You hardly look like a benevolent benefactress, Grandmother."

"It was the only thing that seemed plausible without alerting the girl to the contract between our families, and I will ask you to mind your tone, Grandson."

"Huxley, Grandmother," Daniel said, steering the conversation back to what he needed to know.

"Huxley was at the house when I arrived. He appeared familiar with the family and most especially the girl. I, of course, knew who he was as I was unfortunate enough to know his father."

Daniel watched his grandmother take another mouthful of tea before continuing with her story. Why did he have this feeling of unease inside him?

"At least the youngest two Winchcomb children do not share the elder brothers' looks. Different mother, from what I gather," the Dowager Duchess added.

"What happened to her, their mother?"

"Died in childbirth, so Winchcomb told me."

"Tell me of Huxley, Grandmother."

"I was invited to dine that night. I was staying at the nearest inn and knowing what Winchcomb was capable of, I had two servants accompany me at all times." Seeing her nephew's raised eyebrow, she snapped at him. "I may appear old to you, my boy, but to some, I am still a very attractive woman."

"I have no doubts as to that, but still you digress," Daniel said, barely restraining the urge to yell at her.

"The girl," she said glaring at him, "appeared to be the servant for the night. Her brothers and father ordered her hither and yon, and Huxley touched her intimately on several occasions. She was red-faced with rage by the time dessert arrived and she dumped an entire bowl of very bland apple pudding on Huxley's head. I, of course, applauded and held out great hope that she would indeed one day be able to fulfill the role as Duchess of Stratton."

"Are you saying her family just sat there and allowed this man to touch and abuse her in your presence and did little to assist her?"

"Indeed, I was quite disgusted and when I took my leave later that night and found Huxley in the hall trying to kiss the girl. I instantly set my footman upon him, then told Winchcomb senior that if I found out this reprobate had touched the future Duchess of Stratton again, there would be hell to pay."

"And he kept his word…until now," Daniel said, leaping to his feet and heading for the door.

"Bring her to London!" his grandmother called as he shut the door.

Something was urging Daniel to return to Stratton

Lodge immediately. Running down his grandmother's stairs, he then mounted his horse and headed for his townhouse. Fifteen minutes later, he was once again dismounting, this time to hand the reins to his butler.

"A note has arrived for you from Luton, your Grace."

Stripping off his gloves, Daniel took the note and broke the seal, his eyes scanning the neat writing.

A Lord Huxley visited Stratton, your Grace. His actions were not that of a gentleman and the staff was forced to take measures to ensure the duchess's safety. She was distressed by the incident but expressed a wish that you not be informed. However, after careful consideration, I believed the best course was to do so with some expediency, as when Lord Huxley left Stratton, he threatened to return and harm the duchess. We, the staff, are, of course, ever vigilant and should he return, we will alert you instantly.

Luton

"Please have a fresh horse brought round, Werhnam." Daniel folded the note and slipped it into his pocket. "I have decided to return to Stratton right away. I will be bringing the duchess back to London with me so prepare her rooms," he added before heading to his own to change clothes. When he had made the decision to bring her back with him he had no idea, but he knew he wouldn't leave her behind again.

"So you are going back to Stratton?" a voice greeted him

as he walked back out the front door twenty minutes later.

"I thought you'd run for cover, Kelkirk." Daniel shrugged into his greatcoat and pulled on his gloves. Simon was dressed similarly and stood waiting at the bottom of his stairs.

"Me?" Simon said, placing a hand on his chest. "I'm wounded. I merely went to retrieve my horse, and leave a message that I was accompanying you to Stratton for a few days."

"And why did you think I would be returning to Stratton?" Daniel looked down at his friend, who was now slapping his hat against his thigh and looking vaguely interested in a large barouche that was trundling past.

"A hunch."

Daniel snorted, then rolled his eyes for good measure, yet remained silent.

"And I yearn for the wide open spaces and lush green hills of Stratton," Simon said, adding with a wide smile, "It has been an age since I visited there and I feel that Luton has been denied the pleasure of my company for far too long."

"You attended my father's funeral." Daniel's voice was dry as he walked down the stairs to take the reins of his horse from his groom.

"Is it wrong to want to meet the wife of my dearest friend?"

"Dearest?" Daniel responded. "I'm flattered."

"Don't let it go to your head," Simon muttered, urging his horse forward to fall in beside Daniel's.

"I just received a missive from Luton indicating that

Huxley called at Stratton and that his intentions were not honorable. The servants saw him off, yet Luton was sufficiently concerned to write to me."

"Good Lord, so the threat was real. Is the duchess all right?"

Nodding, Daniel added, "Yes, but she asked Luton not to inform me of Huxley's visit, however that combined with what Grandmother told me was enough to alert my fears."

"You can't be surprised by your wife's request, surely, Daniel." Simon looked at him. "She was raised by those heathens and then forced into marriage with a man she does not know. Even taking into account the threat from Huxley, she's hardly likely to want you to return now, when she has probably found a measure of peace for the first time in her life."

Daniel knew his friend's words were true, yet that did not make him happy about the fact that she had not notified him. He was her husband, and she was his responsibility whether he liked it or not. He should not have had to rely on his butler to alert him of Gilbert Huxley's visit.

"In truth, I may need your help," Daniel said.

"How so?"

Daniel looked at his horse's ears and then viewed the streets before him. Lord, this was hard. "I don't know if trouble awaits me but if it does, I would be pleased to have you at hand."

Simon nodded but remained silent, sensing Daniel had not finished.

"And in truth, my wife may be more comfortable with you around."

Simon stared at him. "What?"

"You can converse like a woman," Daniel growled.

"I don't believe that was a compliment."

"It wasn't."

Simon mulled on that for a minute. "So you're having trouble communicating with your wife? You, the silver tongued duke who woos woman as easily as the rest of us breathe?"

"It's different with a wife, Kelkirk, especially one wed under duress. The words don't seem to come as easily as they would in a ballroom."

"Or bedroom."

Giving his friend a foul look, Daniel continued. "I want her to return with me to London and hope that having you there will put her at ease and give us a chance to grow comfortable with each other." Daniel pushed aside the memory of how he had held her in a darkened room and how they had both spoken without reserve then. He knew that in the light of day things would be different between them.

"I shall, of course, be at your service, your Grace. My silken conversational skills and ready wit will be on hand, should you require them."

Daniel growled something rude and ended the conversation by nudging his boots in the side of his mount so that it sprang forward into a gallop.

They stopped for the night and were up again at dawn the following day to continue the journey, arriving at Stratton as the sun was sinking behind the hills.

"It is a vision to gladden the most hardened heart,"

Simon said as they rode up the long driveway. Stratton was at its most picturesque bathed in golden light.

It was a beautiful sight and one Daniel liked more now his father was not waiting for him inside.

After stabling their mounts, Daniel, followed by Simon, walked to the house. It loomed before him as it always had, large and austere, but this time it would be his duchess greeting him.

"Your Grace, we were not expecting you," Luton said, hurrying forward as Daniel and Simon entered the house.

"It was a last minute decision, Luton."

"For my part, I have missed you, Luton," Simon said, shrugging out of his overcoat and handing it to the butler.

"Where can I find the duchess?" Daniel said, ignoring his friend.

"The duchess is from home, your Grace."

Daniel stopped in the act of removing his gloves and stared at his butler.

"What? Where is she?"

"Visiting with Miss Belmont, your Grace."

Stunned that she wasn't here where he had left her, Daniel simply stood there for several seconds, gaping at his butler.

"And when do you believe she will return?" Simon asked when Daniel remained silent.

"We are expecting her soon, my lord."

"Excellent. We shall take a tray in the study, Luton, and if Mrs. Stimpel has baked any of that excellent plum cake, I shall not be offended if you place a slice or two upon it," Simon added.

"I shall see to it at once, my Lord."

"What the hell is she thinking?" Daniel snapped. "To leave the protection of Stratton on her own!"

"Doesn't the Belmont estate border yours?"

"That is not the point."

Following Daniel as he stalked to the stairs, Simon said, "For my part, I have only met Miss Belmont briefly. However, I did not think her a woman with nefarious intentions."

Opening the door to his study, Daniel stomped inside and headed straight toward the fireplace, where he dropped to his haunches and lit it. "Claire does not have a nefarious bone in her body, you idiot, but with the threat of Huxley still looming, I hardly think it a wise move to leave Stratton alone."

Simon found the brandy and poured two measures.

"How do you know she has gone alone? She could have taken an army of servants with her."

Rising, Daniel took the glass Simon handed him and then fell into the nearest chair.

"She should be here, not cavorting around the bloody countryside."

"What are you annoyed about, Daniel? Should your wife have spent her days at Stratton seeing or visiting no one? That hardly seems fair or indeed, worthy of you."

"She is an innocent who knows nothing of the world but what she learned in her father's home! She dresses like a servant and is timid and skinny. The woman should not leave here until she has gained experience."

Daniel could hear himself and how stupid he sounded

yet did not seem to be able to stop. Arriving at Stratton to find his wife was not where he had left her had rocked him. He was angry and worried and and frustrated by both emotions, especially the first, as he had sworn he would not show her his anger again when next they met.

"Your reaction seems a bit dramatic, my friend. However, as the food has arrived, I shall not continue this conversation, as it may lead to you roaring again, and I intend savor this plum cake and give it the respect it deserves."

"She's a lovely lady, that Miss Belmont."

"Yes, she is, Molly." Eva smiled across the carriage at her maid.

She had spent the afternoon and evening with Claire. They had discussed fashions and the latest hairstyles and Claire had told her about society and some of its more colorful people. Never having mastered the art of womanly conversation due to the lack of friends, it had come as a shock that she actually enjoyed it. She'd caught herself giggling a few times and marveled at the feeling. She was changing. Her life was so different now that she lived without the abuse from her family. Eva had enough food and rest, and more importantly, she had a friend. And although she was consumed with worry for Reggie, she was content for the first time in her life. A child would complete her - a child and a husband - but Eva knew that neither of these was likely to happen anytime soon, if ever. Therefore, she would content herself with this life. She could ride when she chose to, play her piano for hours at a time and read under a tree if the mood struck.

"Thank you for accompanying me, Geoffrey," Eva told the footman as he opened the door and helped her and Molly down.

"It was a nice night for a drive, your Grace," the young man said, looking at Molly.

Eva watched her maid return the look and swallowed her smile.

"I will not need you until later, Molly." She waved a hand over her head as she headed toward the house. She liked both Molly and Geoffrey and would not stand in the way of any blossoming relationship.

"Good evening, Luton. I hope you've had a pleasant night," Eva said, taking off her bonnet and gloves.

"The duke and Viscount Kelkirk have arrived, your Grace, and are at present awaiting you in the study."

Much like the duke earlier, Eva stood still for several heartbeats as she took in this news.

"He's here at Stratton?"

"Yes, your Grace."

Why? She had not thought to see him for a very long time. Why had he returned now and with company? Panic made her chest tighten as she clutched her gloves. She wasn't ready to see him. Would she ever be ready to see him? What did he want?

"I, uh...should go up then," she finally managed to say.

"That is the duke's wish, your Grace." Luton smiled.

"All right then, I will," Eva said this time with more force.

Pausing in the mirror, she checked her appearance and was pleased she still looked presentable. Squaring her shoulders, she then made her way upstairs. Pausing briefly outside the door, Eva drew a deep, steadying breath and then tapped lightly on the wood.

"Enter."

Pushing it open, she walked inside.

Daniel looked up as his duchess walked through the door and his first thought was that she'd played him for a fool.

"Good evening, your Grace. I had not expected your return or I would have been here to greet you."

She was beautiful. Her hair was the color of midnight and piled on top of her head, leaving the length of her pale elegant neck exposed. A delicate blush filled her cheeks and her eyes were the deep blue color of the Stratton sapphires and surround by thick, dark lashes. Her white outfit with peppermint trim did little to hide the gentle sway of her hips or the full curves of her breasts. Daniel's eyes travelled the length of his wife's body and wondered how he had failed to notice what had obviously been beneath those ugly dresses she had worn. Elegantly arched brows rose as he remained mute.

"You should have told me Huxley had visited you," he finally said because he couldn't think of anything else.

Color leeched from her face at the words. He saw the fear in her eyes and if Daniel had needed confirmation of the threat Huxley presented, she had just given it.

"There was no need, your Grace - "

"There was every need," Daniel said, moving closer until that subtle rose scent reached his nostrils. "What if he returns?"

"I would have taken measures to have him removed again."

She was trying to stay calm as he crowded her but her breathing was rapid and her hands were clenched together. She'd gained weight, he noticed. Her cheeks had filled out, as had her wrists, and she was now a woman who would draw any man's eye.

"I was told that he threatened you, Duchess. Is this true?"

Rather than dropping her eyes as she had when first they'd wed, she kept them on his, and again he wondered if she'd played him for a fool.

"Daniel, must you interrogate your duchess when we have yet to be introduced?" Simon came to stand beside him. "Good evening, your Grace," he added, holding out one hand. "My name is Viscount Kelkirk and it is an honor to meet you."

"Good evening, Lord Kelkirk."

She offered Simon an elegant curtsy, unlike the lopsided affair she'd been prone to when he'd first met her.

"If you will excuse me, your Grace, I am bound for my bed now, but shall look forward to becoming better acquainted with you in the morning."

"Of course. Good evening, Lord Kelkirk."

Daniel grunted something to Simon as his friend left the room.

"Did Gilbert Huxley threaten you, Duchess?"

"It matters not, your Grace, only that he left," she said in a quiet voice.

He ran his eyes over her again, lingering on the curves

of her breast. Damn, Daniel had never wanted a wife he could lust after.

"It appears much has changed in my absence, Duchess. Had my carriage reached the end of the drive before you threw away your dowdy clothes?"

"Wh-what are you accusing me off, your Grace?" She wasn't precisely glaring at him but to Daniel's mind it was pretty close. "I was informed by Mr Neil, your steward, that I was allowed to spend some money on my clothes. Would you rather I had not?"

It seemed the timid mouse had found a backbone.

"I have no problem with you spending money on clothes, Eva, as long as the change in you is an honest one."

Color washed her face, and she took a step backwards. Daniel wondered if she was protecting herself or him.

"I will ask again, what are you accusing me of, your Grace?"

What was he accusing her of? It was true he was an untrusting devil but had she really duped him? Now he had got over the shock of seeing her, he thought not, especially considering where she had come from. Daniel did not often speak without thought but in this case he believed he had.

"Forgive me. Your appearance surprised me." He was like any man in that an apology never came easily and his words sounded gruff.

She nodded.

"Why are you here, your Grace? Surely you did not come just for the purpose of censuring me about Huxley and questioning my clothing?"

"Need I have a reason to visit my home and my duchess?"

"I had thought when you left that it would be for some time."

His eyes roamed her features before he spoke.

"My reason for returning to Stratton is twofold, Duchess." She looked up at him, silently waiting for him to continue. "Firstly, I wish you to return to London with me."

"But I had thought my life would be here."

Daniel saw that the idea of going to London did not sit well with her. In fact, it terrified her.

"You are my duchess and under my protection and it is time for you to take your rightful place in society."

"But I was not born into society, your Grace, and have no idea how to behave amongst them."

Her words were calm, yet her eyes told another story. The deep blue depths were anxious.

"My grandmother told me you were tutored in what was required, Duchess, and I shall be with you to help ease your path."

"Wh-what was the second reason?"

Daniel decided to leave the subject for now, there would be plenty of time to discuss it further over the coming days.

"I want us to have a child."

He knew it was what she wanted and knew it had been wrong of him to deny her simply because he wanted to thwart both his father and hers by not having an heir.

"You want to have a child?

Daniel saw the flare of hope that accompanied her words.

"Do you wish to have a child?" he countered.

She bit into the soft flesh of her lower lip and he had the

urge to lean forward and kiss her. "I do wish it, your Grace, with all my heart." It was a solemn vow. "And are you no longer angry, your Grace?"

Daniel briefly closed his eyes at her question, remembering how she had begged him not to take her in anger. "I have promised to never touch you in anger, Duchess."

For some reason, the intensity in her eyes made Daniel hold his breath. He released it when she nodded.

"Will you want to…I mean will you come to my room tonight?"

He wanted to, Lord how he wanted to, yet Daniel knew she needed time to grow comfortable around him.

"Not tonight, Duchess, go to your bed and I shall see you in the morning."

He watched her go, following the sway of her hips and then she was gone. Shaking his head, Daniel poured himself another drink and went to stare into the fire. He thought to find his timid, dowdy duchess threatened and scared by Huxley, yet he had found a woman whose beauty rivaled many, a woman who still feared yet had grown strong enough to face those fears. A woman he now wanted.

# CHAPTER FIVE

*E*va usually woke early and this morning was no different. After a night spent tossing and turning over her husband's unexpected return and his reasons why, she was eager to leave her bed.

Pulling on a pair of Reggie's breeches, she then stomped her feet into boots. Eva only wore the breeches in the morning when she was sure no one would see her. Riding astride was wonderful, yet she was not foolish enough to do so at any other time of day. Buttoning up the jacket from her riding habit, she quickly plaited her hair and tied a ribbon around the ends. She didn't think her husband or Lord Kelkirk would rise until late morning, so there would be plenty of time to change before she saw them again.

She tiptoed down the stairs, walked to the front door and picked up the small basket sitting beside it, then opened and closed it softly behind her. The sun was beginning to rise and the ground smelt fresh and crisp as Eva made her way to the stables. She had tried to persuade Holby that she was more than capable of saddling Posy and that he could stay in bed but he would not hear of it. Therefore it was a blurry-eyed boy that greeted her as she walked into the stables.

"Good morning, Holby."

He mumbled something which Eva knew from experience was his greeting. She did not engage him in further conversation, but once he had finished tightening Posy's girth, she handed him the piece of jam and bread she had Mrs. Stimpel place beside the front door every morning.

"Thank you, Holby. Now go back to bed." Eva gave the boy's arm a gentle pat as she nudged him toward the loft he had crawled out off. Minutes later, she was leaving the stables.

Little puffs of white formed in the air as Posy snorted her pleasure at the exercise she knew she was about to have. Eva had ridden many of the vast acres that made up Stratton and she never tired of her morning rides. Sometimes she rode up hills, other times she followed the stream. There were tracks she galloped down, too, and this morning, she chose one of those. Gathering the reins, she gave the mare a gentle nudge with her heels and she sprang forward. Eva loved the freedom of galloping - the wind in her face, just her and Posy as they raced over the ground. She laughed as Posy stuck out her neck, eager to run and stretch her long legs.

Sleep had not come easy to Eva last night; visions of her husband had filled her head. How long would he stay at Stratton? Would he stay until she had conceived? Did he really want a child?

Her brothers had told her in detail exactly how a man

got a woman with child. They had used foul language and descriptions of the act, then told her all she would need to do was lie still until it was over. No husband wanted a wife for any other reason than breeding; anything else was left to his mistress.

What would it feel like to have the duke's big body lying on top of her? Eva knew it would be painful when he did what had to be done - her brothers had relished telling her that fact - but she also knew that to have a child, she had to do what was necessary.

Veering right, Eva directed Posy onto the path that ran between the trees and urged her over a fallen branch. Splashing through a puddle, they thundered along the shadowed route. Bending low over the mare's neck, she let her go. Posy knew exactly where they were going and Eva just held on, enjoying the ride. It was exhilarating and she felt the last of the sluggishness from lack of sleep leave her head. Minutes later, breaking free of the trees, Posy headed for the trail that led up the side of the hill. Reaching the top, Eva reined the horse in and walked to where she could see the village below

Smoke puffed from chimneys as slowly the little village roused. Eva imagined families waking and sharing their morning meal. Mothers would be dressing and caring for their children, a routine they took for granted. She would do that one day, care for her own child.

The church spire rose highest and she wondered if Miss Potter's night attire was as outrageous as her day wear.

Eva thought of Reggie and how he would love to ride over Stratton with her. He was never far from her thoughts and she vowed now the duke was back that she would discuss getting him here where he was safe. She would get him a tutor and then he would go to university as he had always wished to do. She just needed to pick the right moment, one when the duke was in an agreeable mood, preferably.

"If you have no care for yourself, Duchess, then at least care for your mount!"

Eva spun so quickly in the saddle, she tumbled straight off Posy and landed on her bottom. She heard curses as she struggled to draw in the breath that had been knocked from her body.

"Give me your hand."

Bracing them behind her, Eva ignored the duke and scrambled to her feet. Mortified that she was dressed in breeches and had fallen in front of him, she reached for the saddle, preparing to remount.

"Are you unhurt, Duchess?"

Shaking her head, Eva busied herself with collecting the reins

"Then perhaps you can address my earlier concerns."

Realizing that ignoring him would incite his anger, Eva reluctantly turned to face her husband. He, too, had dismounted, although she doubted it had been in such a spectacular fashion.

"I have been riding these paths for over two months now, your Grace. Posy was quite safe."

Dark brows lowered as he scowled down at her. Unlike her, he was once again impeccably dressed in grey breeches, black jacket with polished boots and a neatly tied neckcloth. The only thing not in order was the hair that stood off his head.

"You rode through those trees too fast, madam. There could have been more fallen branches in your path."

"I would never put Posy in danger, your Grace, and I apologize if you thought otherwise."

For weeks Eva had lived without the constant knot of anxiety in her stomach that had plagued her most of her life. The fear that at any moment someone would take her to task had been absent and she had reveled in that freedom...until now.

"It was folly for a woman to ride in such a manner."

She didn't want to be intimidated by the duke. He would not hurt her. Hadn't she believed that after the night he visited her room? The words they had spoken then had been open and honest.

"You think a woman is not as competent as a man in the saddle, your Grace?" Be quiet Eva. Don't antagonize him.

"A woman is not as strong as a man, Duchess, even if she is riding astride." His eyes ran over her legs as he spoke and her discomfit increased. What must he think of the way she was dressed?

"Strength does not necessarily determine skill, Duke."

"Are you suggesting you are a more skilled rider than me, Duchess?"

"I would be foolish to suggest such a thing." Eva reached for her saddle, eager to finish the conversation and head back to Stratton.

"Foolish because I am a man and you know I am more skilled or foolish because I am a man whom you feel threatened by?"

Eva gripped the leather so tightly, her knuckles went

white. He was trying to provoke a response from her but she did not want to answer such a loaded question. Putting her foot in the stirrups, she was about to pull herself up when two large hands grabbed her and tossed her onto Posy's back.

"Accepting defeat, Duchess?"

His taunt hit its mark. "I have no need to brag over my accomplishments, your Grace, nor do I willingly seek to incite your anger. However I will say that my skill in the saddle has never been tested, as I have never felt the need to do so." Turning Posy before he stopped her, she headed quickly back down the hill. Eva had all but called him an arrogant braggart and had no wish to wait about for his reply.

Tibbs waited for them as they entered the stables. Stopping before him, she then kicked her feet from the stirrups and prepared to dismount, but again, the duke was there and reached for her. Her heart thumped painfully as he lifted her off Posy and placed her gently on the ground before him.

"We will address the matter of your recklessness another time, Duchess."

That made her chin lift. "I was not reckless. Now please excuse me, your Grace."

He didn't release her immediately, but pulled her closer.

"Wh-what are you doing?"

He kissed her, just a soft brushing of his lips over hers, and then he pulled back, leaving her breathless.

"We will also address who is the better rider when time allows us to do so, Duchess, and I will add, once again, that you are under no threat from me and that I would never use force against you."

"I...I must go."

He released her and Eva tried to walk calmly from the stables when inside, her heart fluttered and her skin felt warm and all she wanted to do was run away from the large, disturbing male behind her.

She tried to push the memory of the kiss aside as she entered the house.

Why had he kissed her?

"Good morning, your Grace."

"Good morning, Molly," Eva greeted her maid as she walked into her room.

"Your bath is ready."

"Thank you," Eva said beginning to pull off her clothes. Why had he kissed her?

Thoughts tumbled through her head as Molly assisted her to bathe and dress and she was still consumed with the kiss minutes later as she made her way to the breakfast parlor.

Lord Kelkirk was already seated when she arrived.

"Good morning, your Grace."

"Good morning, my Lord." Eva waved for him to reseat himself as she took the chair opposite him. He, like her husband, was dressed immaculately.

Eva had never entertained guests at her breakfast table, especially a man she hardly knew. What should she say?

"I had a very sound sleep, I don't mind telling you, your Grace, and woke with a foggy head, however a cup of fortifying tea and one of Mrs. Stimpel's substantial breakfasts should rectify that," Lord Kelkirk said.

Eva looked at the many silver covered dishes on the sideboard and thought that Mrs Stimpel must be very happy with men to cook for again.

"May I recommend the grilled trout with white butter sauce, your Grace? Mrs. Stimpel does it better than anyone."

Eva couldn't quite hide the shudder at the thought of trout for breakfast.

"I tend to go for rolls and honey, my Lord."

"Good God, really? How do you keep body and soul together on that?"

She laughed at his horrified expression. Then, rising, she began to fill her plate. She still struggled to know that someone else had prepared all this for her when for years it had been she doing the preparing.

"I have the feeling nobility hold quite a lot of importance in food, Lord Kelkirk. In fact, my cook nearly took to her bed when I told her I liked simple food when first I arrived at Stratton."

When she reseated herself, he reached for the teapot. "Can I pour you a cup, your Grace?"

Flustered to have him serve her, Eva merely nodded.

"The thing is, your Grace, the nobility are traditionally a lazy bunch who spend a great deal of time indulging themselves," Lord Kelkirk said. "Food and drink being one of those indulgences, we like to do it well."

Eva's cup had been halfway to her lips when he spoke and it remained poised as she looked at him. She had never known a man to speak so easily to her and especially not a nobleman. "It is amazing that you are not all stout then, my lord, if indeed that is the case."

"Well, speaking for myself, I do a great deal of exercise to counteract the indulgences. Your husband, however…"

"Have you bored my wife to tears yet, Kelkirk?"

Eva drank deeply as the duke entered the room and ignored the tiny flutter in her stomach as he called her his wife. He had kissed her and she could still feel the imprint on her lips even though she had washed her face thoroughly.

"We were just discussing the nobleman's penchant for the overindulgence of food and drink, Daniel."

He stood beside her and looked down at the small roll on her plate. "Not a failing of yours, Duchess?"

"She nearly fainted when I mentioned the trout."

"Now that is not true, Lord Kelkirk. I merely shuddered." Eva felt moved to protest, besides which, it was easier to talk with Lord Kelkirk than her husband. He made her pulse do silly things.

"At least you have stopped wearing those ridiculous caps."

Eva watched her husband go to the sideboard and load his plate. "I beg your pardon, your Grace?"

"Perhaps you could call me Daniel, Eva."

Could she? It seemed to infer they were comfortable with each other when, in fact, they were anything but.

"And I am Simon, Eva."

"I said I'm glad you are no longer wearing those ugly caps that cover your hair."

Swallowing another mouthful of tea to soothe her suddenly dry throat, Eva stammered, "I…I…uh, I had no idea you noticed, your Grace."

"I was trying to work out what color hair you had, yet not one strand escaped those ridiculous things."

He sat to her right and Eva's eyes widened as she looked at his food-laden plate.

"I rest my case." Lord Kelkirk had a smug expression on his face as he noted her own expression.

"My caps were a sort of cover against my family, your Grace," she said after a moment.

"Daniel," he said around a mouthful of ham.

"Cover?" Simon pressed, intrigued.

"My family were not the easiest of men to live with, Lord Kelkirk, and sometimes I wanted to blend into the background and look…inconspicuous," Eva said.

Simon coughed and several drops of tea flew onto the cloth. Eva looked at the small splotches on the linen and hoped the stains would come out; this was one of their new cloths.

"Inconspicuous?" he finally gasped, begging her pardon.

"Yes, and perhaps a touch witless," Eva added.

"Witless?"

"Come now, Simon, you should be well versed in the word," the duke said with an evil glint in his grey eyes.

"Are you suggesting I'm witless, Stratton?"

"Well, there was that time at Eton when you set fire to Professor Maitland's front door only to find it was in fact Professor Hind's front door."

"That was not my fault!"

Eva had never heard her husband speak like this. He sounded as if he was enjoying teasing his friend. He even winked at her. She watched as the two grown men bickered, each giving as good as he got. When one drew breath, the other spoke. Her brothers had never teased each other and if they did, a fight usually ensued.

"Do you like it here at Stratton, your Grace?"

It took her a few seconds to realize the conversation had swung back to her. "Yes, thank you, Lord Kelkirk. I am quite content."

"You will like London even more. It is a wondrous place, especially on your first visit."

"I don't think I would, Lord Kelkirk. I am a country girl," Eva remembered the conversation she'd had with her husband last night. He wanted her to take her place in society and had said that he would protect her.

"And yet as we discussed, Eva, you are coming to London with me," the duke said calmly. She could feel his eyes on her as she played with the handle of her cup.

"And on that note, if you will both excuse me, I have an urgent letter to write."

Eva watched Lord Kelkirk hurry from the room. "It must be a very important letter."

The duke snorted. "Simon has never written a letter in his life. He merely wanted to give us privacy, Eva."

"I don't understand."

"He knew I wanted to talk to you about London."

Eva didn't want to discuss leaving Stratton so soon, so instead she tried to distract him. It had often worked with her brothers. "I would like to apologize for how I was dressed this morning, Daniel. I understand it is not acceptable for a woman to wear breeches."

Eva's words filled Daniel's head with visions of her shapely legs encased in the form- fitting breeches and the raven plait trailing to her waist. She had the sweetest curve to her buttocks and he'd had to fight the urge to caress it when he had helped her mount Posy.

"I have no issue with you wearing them in the privacy of your own home, Duchess. But considering how you looked in them, I would suggest you not wear them outside of Stratton."

"I understand."

He doubted she did but he wasn't getting into that now. "Besides, when I best you, I don't want you to have any excuses."

She smiled but chose not to reply, instead saying, "I wondered if I could ask another favor of you, Daniel, as I've still had no word from my brother Reggie and would like you to send another invitation to my father to see if he can visit."

"I will, of course, immediately write to your father informing him of our intentions, and ask that he let Reggie join us in London."

"Oh, but -"

"You will be protected there, Eva, and I will put you in no situation you are uncomfortable with. It need only be a temporary visit, until society is satisfied that you actually exist."

"My family - "

"Will not bother the Duchess of Stratton because she is far above them on the social scale," Daniel said firmly. "I have told you I will protect you, Eva and am sorry that my leaving Stratton led you to believe I would not do so. Can you not trust me in this?"

"I want to."

"Yet the circumstances of our marriage do not inspire trust," Daniel said softly.

Emotions flickered through her eyes, yet she did not voice them. "I just need more time to prepare, Daniel."

Daniel knew she was hoping to stall him but he would not change his mind. He truly believed this was the right decision for both of them. "I have no wish to prolong the journey to long, Eva."

He could see her trying to read what she believed he had not said. Mistrust from her past did not make acceptance easy and he knew it would be some time before that changed.

"I will, of course, be ready when the time comes to leave, your Grace."

He could hear how much those words had cost her, yet he would not back down in this. They would leave Stratton, and soon.

. . .

Eva lowered the book to her knees and stared out the window. She had slipped away to her room to curl up on the window seat and read, yet she couldn't concentrate. Her thoughts always seemed to return to her husband.

Neither of them had mentioned London again and she had spent the past few days getting to know both he and Lord Kelkirk and in doing so, had grown comfortable in their company. She had never spent time with men who simply wanted to be with her to talk or make her laugh. It was a revelation. They constantly bantered with each other and now included her in this. She was called on to referee and offer her opinion, and Eva could not believe this duke, with his easy manners and charm, was the one she had known in the early days of their marriage. He was a formidable man when required, yet with her he was polite and attentive and she slowly felt the barriers she had built to keep her safe begin to erode.

His touch unsettled her – his hand on her back or around her waist. The contact was always brief and Eva wasn't experienced enough to be certain, but she thought by the knowing gleam in his eyes that perhaps this contact was deliberate on his part.

A knock on the door disturbed her thoughts. "Enter."

"Miss Belton has called, your Grace, and wishes to see you with some expediency," Luton said, coming into the room.

"Of course. Please have tea brought into….uh, where did you put her, Luton?" Eva questioned as she searched for her shoes.

"The lemon parlor, your Grace."

"Excellent. I will be with her shortly."

When Eva entered the lemon parlor - presumably named for the solitary lemon tree outside the window since the walls were painted peach - Eva noticed Claire was craning her neck to see the driveway.

"Claire, is something amiss?" she said, coming forward to take her friend's hands.

"Yes. Dear lord, Eva, I am afraid Mrs. Potter is on her

way here again. I was in the village and overheard her saying to that fish-faced Mrs. Plimpton it was her duty to call upon the duke now he has returned to Stratton."

"When?" Eva rushed to look out the window. She did not relish the prospect of Daniel meeting Mrs. Potter. What if the woman decided to push him into attending church?

"Now, as we speak. I had to warn you."

Both ladies stood still as statues as they listened to the wheels of a carriage drawing up outside the front door.

"Is your husband from home?" Claire whispered hopefully.

"No. He and Lord Kelkirk are in the stables," Eva whispered back.

"Perhaps they will stay there."

"Perhaps, but I don't believe so. Lord Kelkirk likes to take tea at this hour."

"Noblemen and their tea," Claire muttered.

"Mrs. Potter, your Grace," Luton said, showing the older woman into the room seconds later.

"Dear Lord!" Eva whispered, watching Mrs. Potter come bustling forward. She resembled a basket filled with fruit of every color and variety.

"Your Grace." Mrs. Potter curtsied, making her large hat tilt precariously to one side and nearly oversetting the small stuffed bird on its crown.

"M-Mrs. Potter," Eva said with only a slight quiver to her voice.

"Oh, Miss Belton, you are here also." Mrs. Potter deflated slightly. "I have come to see your husband, your Grace."

"Uh, I believe my husband is from Stratton at the present time," Eva said quickly.

"If it is not too much of an inconvenience, your Grace, I shall wait. It is the reverend's fondest wish that the duke attend his service this Sunday and I am here to issue the invitation."

Both Eva and Claire watched in fascination as she then lowered herself into the nearest chair, wriggled and twitched, patting the cushion at her back and finally settled, not unlike a small dog.

"He could be some time, Mrs. Potter."

"Mrs. Potter, I believe," said a deep voice from the doorway as Eva finished speaking.

Both Claire and Eva stiffened as the duke and Lord Kelkirk walked into the room.

"Mother of God!" Simon whispered, watching the small, round woman rock back and forth several times before gaining enough momentum to get out of the chair.

"Simon, this is Miss Belton." Eva waved a hand from Claire to Simon as she tried to hear exactly what Mrs. Potter was saying to her husband. "Allow me to introduce you to Lord Kelkirk."

"A pleasure," Simon bowed deeply over Claire's hand. "We met briefly in London, I think?"

"Yes, we did, my lord," Claire said, not sparing Simon a glance, Eva noticed, as she too, was attempting to follow the conversation between Mrs. Potter and Daniel.

"I am charged to convey an invitation to you, your Grace, to attend church this Sunday. My husband is to give a very fine sermon."

Eva held her breath. Surely Daniel would not tolerate Mrs. Potter making such a request?

"Of course, Mrs. Potter. All who reside at Stratton will be attendance."

"Oh, that is wonderful news, your Grace. Reverend Potter will be very happy indeed."

The duke turned to smile at Claire and Eva before continuing. "There are many here at Stratton, Mrs. Potter, who need spiritual guidance and it is my responsibility to ensure they receive it."

"He is a silver-tongued sod," Simon whispered to Eva from the side of his mouth.

"I have never once seen Minerva Potter at a loss for words," Claire added.

Eva wanted to giggle as she watched color flood the round face of Mrs. Potter after Daniel complimented her on the stylish arrangement upon her hat.

"Duchess, could you have Luton replenish the teapot?" Daniel asked, winking at the small group gathered by the door. "Mrs. Potter and I have much to discuss."

"Allow me." Simon made a dash for the door before Eva could even lift a foot.

"Come and join us, ladies," the duke added.

Grabbing Claire's arm before she, too, fled, Eva towed her to one of the couches. Sitting together, both ladies watched Daniel as he proceeded to ladle on the charm. Within minutes, Mrs. Potter was blushing and twittering like a debutante at her first ball.

"He should be on the stage," Claire whispered.

"I am coming to realize there are many sides to my husband."

"Oh, Daniel has a wicked wit when he unleashes it,"

Claire added. "And his smile has often got him what he wants."

"Is my smile not as distracting?" Simon said, returning. "Country manners are so charming," he added with a goodly dose of sarcasm, as both women ignored him and kept their eyes firmly trained on the now giggling Mrs. Potter.

"The male ego is such a fragile thing, Eva." Claire threw Simon a scathing look.

Eva swallowed another laugh as she peeked at Simon and noted his scowl.

"We are so honored that you are to attend dear Reverend Potter's service this Sunday, your Grace." Mrs. Potter clutched the duke's hand as she prepared to rise after drinking two cups of tea and eating two jam-laden scones.

"I shall look forward to it." Daniel bowed low over her hand.

The small group then walked outside and goodbyes were exchanged and finally Mrs. Potter left, casting longing looks at Eva's husband until her carriage was no longer in view.

"That was very well done of you, your Grace," Claire said, pulling on her own gloves. "Although I fail to see how you will rid yourself of her company now that she is halfway in love with you."

"Tsk, tsk, Claire, I was merely being friendly."

Claire snorted as they walked to the waiting carriage. "Be careful of this man, Eva - he can wrap any woman around his finger. Even my mother is infatuated with him. She used to make him play the piano and sing whenever he visited. If one is gifted with the voice of an angel, one must use it, she used to say."

"A woman with exquisite tastes, your mother," Daniel drawled.

"Or she's tone deaf with failing eyesight," Simon added.

"I assure you, Lord Kelkirk, my mother is in full control of her faculties," Claire snapped, the smile leaving her face as she faced Simon.

Simon's mouth tightened. Bowing slightly, he said, "Forgive my poor attempt at humor, Miss Belmont. I have little doubt after meeting you that your dear mother is both beautiful and in full control of her faculties."

Rolling her eyes, Claire ignored him. "I am for London next week and I am hoping to see you there also, Eva."

"Oh –"

"She will be there," Daniel interrupted Eva. Taking Claire's hand, he helped her into the carriage and once she was seated, he gently shut the carriage door.

"Excellent." Claire signaled to the driver that she was ready to leave.

Eva's eyes stayed on the carriage following Mrs. Potter's through the gates until it had left her sight and only then did she turn to face Daniel.

"We are to leave for London so soon?"

"Yes. We will return for the remainder of the season." Daniel had a feeling that if she hadn't thought it an unseemly display, his wife would have stamped her foot in frustration. "You cannot hide here at Stratton indefinitely, Duchess."

"I am not hiding. I am preparing myself for what is to come."

Color sat high on her cheekbones as she glared at him

and he wanted to take her in his arms and kiss her, taste her anger. "An excellent comeback, Duchess."

"I will not embarrass us both by appearing countrified, your Grace, therefore I would beg a bit more time to learn the role I must play."

"No."

He just used the one word but it was enough to have her expelling a breath loudly and then turning to stomp back inside without speaking another word.

"You handled that well, Stratton."

"I would not be one to criticize, were I you, Kelkirk. I have never seen Claire take such an instant dislike to someone as she did with you."

"She is thankfully not my wife. I have never known you to be so ham-fisted with a woman, Daniel. You weren't joking when you said you needed help conversing with your duchess."

"I am not ham-fisted, I am merely trying to get my wife to London and unfortunately I am going to need a firm hand to do so."

"She is a timid, wee thing, yet finding her backbone, I believe."

The two men headed toward the stables.

"I found her out riding, in breeches of all things, and she was careening recklessly over the countryside. My duchess definitely has a backbone."

"Lord, tell me you didn't take her to task over it?"

Daniel's silence was enough to have Simon tsking.

"Go to hell, Kelkirk!"

"Just reassure her, Daniel. Tell her she will be safe once there and she will come about."

Daniel pulled several leaves off trees as they walked. Crunching them in his hand, he released the fresh scent into the air. "I have done that and she has acknowledged that she will go, but her last words tell me she wants to prolong it as long as possible."

"Well, just don't bully her," Simon supplied.

"I don't bully women!"

"No, because they are usually only to willing to drop their drawers at your feet without a word of protest."

"Surely not all?" Daniel drawled.

Rolling his eyes, Simon said. "All I'm saying, Daniel, is give her time. Eva has lived with men who have mistreated her since birth. According to Betsy Mullholland, she has only survived because of her strength and humor."

"Who the hell is Betsy Mullholland?"

"The maid you had brought here from Winchcomb's household, you idiot."

Daniel vaguely remembered the name. "Why are you speaking to my maid?"

"She was in the kitchen when I went to see Mrs. Stimpel."

Shaking his head and muttering about Simon's appetite, Daniel entered the stables seconds later. He would talk again with Eva later, reassure her about London. He hoped Simon was right and that given time she would change her mind, but in all honesty he had his doubts.

# CHAPTER SIX

*D*aniel looked across the table to where Eva sat. She chatted with Simon, laughing as he said something amusing. She was comfortable at Stratton and he knew change would not be easy on her, yet he also knew she was stronger now – stronger, perhaps, than even she realized.

Candlelight played over her hair and face. The gentle curve of her nose and pout of her lower lip drew his eye. Tonight's dress was blue, simple in design, yet it caressed every sweet curve of her body and the need inside him that had been building would tonight be assuaged.

"I understand you play the piano, Eva?"

"Yes, Lord Kelkirk."

"Will you play for us tonight?"

Her instinct was to say no - Daniel saw it coming - but this time he thwarted her. "An excellent idea, Simon. Luton, please light the candles in the music room and we shall follow shortly."

"I am out of practice."

"Believe me when I tell you, Duchess, that Simon is tone

deaf and will not know the difference."

"Sad but true," Simon sighed.

"I shall just go up then and warm up my fingers." She stood so quickly, the chair rocked back on its legs, and she hurried from the room

"Promise me one thing, my friend."

Daniel looked across the table as Simon spoke. "What?"

"Be gentle with her. She would be easy to break."

"I am not now nor will I ever be my father, Kelkirk. I would never willingly hurt a woman and most especially not my duchess."

"So you finally believe that, do you?"

"Believe what?" Daniel snapped.

"That you will never be a brute like your sire."

"I am trying, Simon, but I fear it will take me some time to believe fully."

Standing, Simon refilled their glasses. "Having known both you and your father, I can say in all honesty, my friend, there were never two more different men. Unlike he, you have honor in your bones."

Like most men, Daniel did not feel comfortable with sentiment, but he thanked his friend for the words and felt lighter in his heart as they headed toward the music room. Maybe - just maybe - he was different.

Luton had lit two branches and they sat at Eva's back so she could read the music before her. She was playing a ballad as they walked in and took the two seats set out for them.

"Even my untrained ear can hear she's good."

Daniel nodded but remained silent, content to watch her.

Some people played music because it was expected of them but he could feel Eva played because it was a passion, as it had once been for Daniel and his mother. She was engrossed in the music as her fingers flowed over the keys. It was not a chore or something she did because it was expected of her. A small smile played around her lips and he wondered if she was even aware they had entered the room.

Had this been her escape? To play so well meant practice, and many hours of it. Had her family left her alone to do just that?

"You play well, Duchess." Daniel said when she stopped several songs later.

"Thank you. It is something I have always enjoyed."

"And on that note, I am ready for my bed. I shall say goodnight, Duchess, Daniel."

"Goodnight, Lord Kelkirk," the duchess said, rising. "I, too, shall retire, your Grace."

"Daniel," he said, watching as she headed for the door. "And thank you for playing for Simon and I, Eva."

She didn't turn, just nodded and left the room, leaving him alone with his thoughts, most of which consumed her.

Yes, she was beautiful, but there was more to her allure. She intrigued him. The woman she had been was still there, yet she was changing, growing stronger every day and he wanted to continue to see her grow. He wanted her to laugh freely and talk without restraint.

So you finally believe that, do you?

Daniel replayed Simon's words in his head. Had he also changed? Was he, too, starting to believe he was not now nor ever could be his father? Shaking his head, he made his way to bed, however it was not his he would seek tonight.

Too restless to sleep, Eva sat on the windowseat and pulled her knees to her chest. Her head was filled with so many thoughts. The life she always believed she would live was now so very different. She was a duchess with so much and with that came responsibility. She knew that she couldn't prolong going to London indefinitely no matter how much she wished to. Here at Stratton, she knew what awaited her at dawn each day. No surprises greeted her, no one wanted more than she could give and no one would force her to do their bidding. Surely in London all that would change.

The sound of her door opening drew Eva's gaze. Her husband walked through, dressed in his robe. He looked to the bed and then swung to where she sat. His legs were bare, which told Eva that he wore little beneath that robe, if anything. He had come to consummate the marriage and to start her quest for a baby. She now knew he would not hurt her, and that the man she had come to know over the past few days would not take her in anger either, of that she was certain.

Rising on unsteady legs, Eva walked toward the bed. "I...I know what I must do, your Grace."

His intercepted her in two long strides, one large hand wrapping around her wrist and stopping her before him. "And what is that, Eva?"

She felt a fiery blush heat her cheeks as she looked up at him. "I am to lie still on the bed until you are...um, finished, your Grace."

The hand that held her wrist moved up her arm to cup her cheek. "Did your brothers tell you that?"

Nodding, she watched his features soften into a gentle smile.

"I would ask you to forget anything they ever told you, Eva. Can you do that for me?"

His thumb traced her lower lip and Eva felt something stir inside her. "I can try."

His hand slipped around her waist and she was slowly pulled closer until her chest touched his.

"You are a very beautiful woman, Duchess, and this, what we are about to do, will not be a chore for either of us, I can promise you."

"Oh," was all Eva managed before he lowered his head and claimed her lips.

The stiffness in her body slowly eased as he teased them. Soft and coaxing, he drew a response from her until she reached for him, one hand clutching the material of his robe in a fist as she arched toward him. Where one kiss ended another started. The pressure that slowly built inside her as he took her mouth on a sensual exploration was beyond anything in Eva's experience.

"Do you like my kisses, Duchess?' His breath brushed her swollen lips.

"Yes." She couldn't lie, not when her body was pressed against his, need filling her eyes, she was sure.

His lips moved to her neck and then lower. She felt his fingers on the buttons of her nightdress and then cool air as he released the last one.

"You smell of roses. The scent has tormented me for days."

Eva felt his mouth move lower to touch the swell of one breast, and she felt it grow fuller as he placed a hot kiss on the sensitive flesh. How could anything so wicked feel so wonderful? Heat pooled in her belly and her nipple ached as he kissed the other breast. His hand moved to her back, stroking her heated flesh through the nightdress, caressing the swell of her buttocks.

Lifting the hem, he moved it up her body.

"Eva, will you let me remove your nightdress?"

"Yes."

"Then lift your arms," Daniel ordered softly.

In a daze, she complied and he pulled it over her head.

"Christ, you're beautiful," he rasped, and Eva saw in his eyes that he meant every word.

"No, don't hide from me."

He took her hands as she tried to cover herself, and held them at her side. She had always been slight, yet believed her breasts were almost too full for her body, his eyes told her a different story. She read the desire and need that she was sure was matched in her own. His hands moved to her hair releasing it from its restraints and then he tangled his fingers through the strands as they fell, the ends brushing her buttocks.

He kissed her again, took the lip she was worrying between her teeth and nibbled it slowly. Pulling her into his chest he ran his hands slowly over her body until Eva once again slumped against him. Only then did he lift her into his arms and carry her to the bed.

Eva lay where he left her, watching as he removed his robe. Light from the candle cast a golden glow over his muscled flesh. She should have been frightened, yet his touch had been the sweetest caress, his lips and hands creating a need that burned steadily inside her. No one had ever touched her in anything but anger, and now to have him, her husband, create such a wealth of feeling inside her, well, she wanted to weep with the joy of it.

"I won't hurt you, Eva."

"I know."

She saw the surprise in his grey eyes as he lowered his body down beside hers.

His fingers traced her jaw and wandered slowly, touching and teasing every piece of skin in their path and when he kissed her again, Eva felt herself melt. Her body was not her own but his to command. She moaned and pressed into his hand as he touched her breasts, his fingers stroking her nipples. He kissed her as his hands made her writhe and then he touched her there, the place only she had ever touched and she shattered as he stroked the sensitive bud and pushed a finger deep inside her.

"I promised not to hurt you, Eva, yet in truth this first time might."

She heard the anxiety in his words, laced heavily with need.

"Please don't stop, Daniel."

His lips brushed hers. "Nothing could make me."

She felt him at her entrance and then push slowly inside. Stretching the silken tissues, he eased into her until he reached her maidenhead and then he pushed through. There was pain, sharp and swift, and then he was buried deep inside her, almost as if they were one.

"Eva, are you all right?"

She heard the desperation in his words as he held himself tense above her. "The pain eases, Daniel." Arching off the bed, she placed a kiss on his lips. He followed her back down and deepened the kiss as he withdrew and reentered her. He did it again and Eva felt something build inside her, something that needed release.

"Wrap your legs around me, Eva."

She followed the rasped command and the change in position deepened his next thrust. The pain became pleasure as pressure built until it grew almost unbearable, and then Eva knew only ecstasy as she flew to sensual heights with Daniel following, seconds later.

Eva felt him lower himself onto the bed beside her, his breathing as rapid as hers.

"Are you all right?" he asked again.

"Yes, thank you."

She felt him look at her after her polite response.

"Should I leave you now, your Grace?"

He leaned on one elbow moving closer to look down at her. "Where would you go? This is your bed."

"Of course. It is just that I know you have no wish to share my bed, therefore I thought-"

"What?" His tone was curt and she sensed he was angry with her.

"I had believed...I was told you would want to leave after -"

"I thought I told you to forget everything those idiots you call brothers ever said to you, Duchess."

"It will take some time for me to do so, your Grace, they

were part of my life for many years."

"My name is Daniel, Eva, and I would ask you to try. They are fools and not worth a minute more of your time."

A yawn surprised her.

"Sleep now, Duchess. The morning is soon enough for you to don your worries once more."

Eva didn't fight him as he pulled up the blankets and then wrapped an arm around her easing her into his warm body and in minutes she felt the blissful tug of sleep.

Eva woke alone. Looking to the curtains, she noticed the sun had already risen. What time had he left her?

Stretching, she felt several unused muscles twinge. Remembering how she had incurred the aches made her feel warm inside. Last night had been one of the most wonderful of her life. Being held in Daniel's arms was something Eva was sure she could get used to. He had been so gentle and caring with her. Touching her lips, she felt them tingle. They were still sensitive from his kisses. Had he felt what she had last night?

"His lordship said you may need a bath, your Grace," Molly said, bustling into her room.

Realizing she was still naked, Eva pulled the covers to her chin as the maid opened the curtains.

"Tis a beautiful day, your Grace, and the duke said you would be leaving for church in an hour. I will bring your tray directly."

When Molly left, Eva found her discarded nightdress and slipped it on and was sitting up in bed when she returned.

"Molly, the sheets will need changing." Eva studied the teacup as she spoke. Evidence of her innocence was on the linen and she knew Molly would realize instantly what it was.

"I shall see to it once you are gone, your Grace."

"Thank you."

While she bathed, Eva reminded herself that for the duke, last night had probably been no different from many other nights. According to her brothers, he had shared his bed with plenty of women and would have a mistress in London. Eva needed to understand that even though to her the night had been special, to him it was not. Still, she loathed the idea of a mistress, the idea that Daniel would keep a woman just for his pleasure. Dressing with care, she made her way downstairs and outside to where the duke and Simon awaited her.

"Good morning, your Grace."

"Lord Kelkirk." Eva nodded as Daniel opened the carriage and held out his hand to help her inside. Once they were all settled, the carriage started down the driveway.

"Why must I go to church when it is you that Mrs. Potter wants to see, Daniel?"

Eva watched Simon scowl across the carriage at the duke who was seated opposite her, his long legs and large feet taking up most of the space. She couldn't look at him directly, as memories of last night filled her head, so instead she chose to study the scenery.

"Because if I must attend, then so must you," Daniel said.

"We are not children, Stratton. That rule no longer applies."

"Is this a new rule? Because correct me if I'm wrong, but a few months ago you had to visit your Uncle Horatio and you made me go with you because - and I quote - he terrifies me spitless," Daniel drawled.

Eva could feel his eyes on her but hers remained out the window. She had never had to deal with anything like this before. The man seated across from her had seen her naked, he had done things to her that Eva had never imagined and she was struggling to not blush fiery red at the thought. She could see his hands – fingers splayed - resting on his beige breeches, and remembered how they had felt upon her body.

"For some unfathomable reason, that mean-spirited old reprobate - excuse me, Eva -" Simon nodded to her "- likes you. Something to do with similar personality traits, I believe."

"I'm fairly certain that was a compliment, Kelkirk, and if not, I will take it as such."

Daniel watched the flush slowly bloom in Eva's cheeks as she caught his eye before once again looking out the window. She knew he was thinking about last night, and damn him for a randy fool, but he had thought about nothing else since leaving her at dawn.

She looked mouthwatering today, the darker blue pelisse caressing her beautiful breasts and fastened to the neck, the small buttons begging to be undone. Her bonnet was ruched velvet with a small brim, and several curls peeked from beneath. Daniel mentally shook his head, wondering how he had ever thought her plain. He had entered her room last night knowing she was an innocent and believing he would leave having done his duty. Instead, he had left shaken to his soul. His wife had responded to him like no other. Her innocence had caught him, her touch ensnared him, and when he had taken her, he had never wanted a woman more

Should a man lust after his wife?

He could never have imagined she would respond so eagerly to his touch. How could he, when each day she walked around carrying the burden of fear and pain that were the remnants of life with her family?

"I could simply wait in the carriage for you to return, Daniel, or there is a nice little pub -"

Daniel reached for the door as they stopped. "Think of it as cleansing your black soul, Kelkirk." He took Eva's hand while helping her down, then placed it on his arm.

"Yours is blacker than mine, Stratton, and in need of a thorough sluicing, if you ask me. Forgive me, Eva," Simon added.

"Lord Kelkirk, Simon."

"Yes, Eva?"

Daniel watched as Eva thought about her words. She rarely just rattled out whatever came into head, possibly because the consequences had not always been pleasant.

"I was brought up by three brothers and a father who spoke in whatever manner they chose, regardless of whether I was present or not. Therefore, I will not take offense if you and Daniel, in the course of your bickering, throw in a few insults or cusses."

"Bickering!" Daniel protested. "Men do not bicker, wife - we debate."

"I'm far too mature to bicker, Eva," Simon assured her. "Although I can't vouch for your husband."

Eva laughed but said nothing further as they headed toward the church. Daniel enjoyed the feel of her small hand on his arm and the occasional brush of her body as they walked. They passed small cottages with neat gardens, the crack of sheets flapping in the gentle breeze telling him that for many families it was wash day. Several children squealed as they ran past in their Sunday best.

People were gathered outside chatting as they arrived at the tall, cream-stone church. A large, round stained glass window gleamed in the morning light, casting shadows on the steps below.

Everyone stopped talking and cleared a path for them to walk through as they drew closer. Daniel noted that like he, Simon took it in his stride - smiling left and right, nodding and then entering the church. Eva was not quite so comfortable. Her fingers now gripped his sleeve.

"What?" Daniel questioned her as he helped her into the narrow front pew.

"Those people outside…"

"You're a duchess, Eva. That will happen if you are here or in London," he said, watching her fiddle with her gloves. "It comes with your title and in time you will get used to it. Is that not right, Kelkirk?" Daniel added, turning to his left to try and accommodate his long legs in the small space.

"I don't make a habit of agreeing with your husband, Eva, but in this case he is correct." Simon's jaw dropped as he glanced back down the aisle. "Dear Lord, don't look now but Mrs. Potter has something live draped around her head."

Of course, Eva and Daniel immediately turned to look behind them. Mrs. Potter was striding down the aisle dressed in a mustard wool dress which, while a little snug, was not overly outrageous. However on her head she wore a turban at least two feet high. At the top, Daniel thought he could see a small pair of beady eyes, though it was hard to tell in the church's dim interior. Eva, he noted, was biting her lip to stop laughing, however she still made a little snuffling sound.

"Did you just snort, Duchess?" Daniel whispered into her ear.

Keeping her mouth pursed, Eva shook her head; he knew she dared not risk talking, as she would surely burst into hysterical laughter.

"Is that a tail I see poking out of the bottom?" Daniel queried. He didn't think Eva had often had cause to laugh out loud and he wanted to provoke her into doing so. Inhaling, he breathed in her scent and was reminded of the taste of her skin last night. Not a wise move, thinking lustful thoughts when he was sitting in God's house

"And a foot by her right ear. I'm sure I see a claw." Simon craned his neck to get a better look

"P-please s-stop." Eva was now gripping her gloved fingers together.

"I wonder how it is secured? Could cause no end of damage were it to dislodge and land on someone," Simon whispered.

"Your Grace, Lord Kelkirk, your Grace!" Mrs. Potter stopped beside their pew.

"Mrs. Potter, how wonderful to see you again and in

such splendid health. May I compliment you on your headgear - it is really quite something." Daniel felt Eva shake beside him.

"Quite something, indeed," Simon agreed. "In fact, it is beyond quite something, your Grace - it is magnificent!"

They were incorrigible, Eva thought, dropping her eyes. Surely Mrs. Potter was not falling for their compliments? Sneaking a look, she noted the flush of pleasure on the woman's face. It appeared she was.

"You are both very bad men and today I will make sure to pray for your black souls," Eva said as Mrs. Potter went to her special pew, just a few feet below her beloved Reverend Potter's pulpit and elevated above the piano so she could oversee whomever was unfortunate enough to be playing.

Simon just laughed at her and Daniel winked, which made Eva's pulse flutter. Where was her serious-minded duke?

The service was thankfully not overly long and Eva was glad because her husband sat so close to her, she could feel him pressed to her right side. Surely it was wrong to feel this way in church...

Daniel had removed his gloves and laid his hand on the seat beside hers. His fingers brushed hers every few seconds, making it very hard for Eva to concentrate. Was he aware of what he was doing? Out the corner of her eye, she noted he was calmly looking forward. Perhaps it was a twitch?

"What?" He gave her an innocent look when she peeked at him.

"Tis nothing." Eva faced forward again. He confused her. She felt completely off balance around him today. Yesterday he was her husband the duke, the man who made her feel nervous, the man who was to give her a child. Today he was the man who had made sweet, passionate love to her last night and slept with her in his arms.

"Oh dear." Eva's eyes followed the squeal that suddenly rent the air at the completion of the service.

"I fear our pianist is about to be attacked by a rogue turban," Simon drawled, watching Mrs. Potter's headgear tilt sideways, then sail through the air and land on the pianist below.

"I believe now is the time to make a strategic retreat." Daniel nudged Simon out of the pew and tugged Eva behind him. "While our dear Mrs. Potter is preoccupied with retrieving her furban."

"Furban?" Simon questioned as they hastened out the doors and back to the carriage.

"Ferret-turban."

"I bet it took you the entire service to come up with that, Stratton."

"I like terret better - it sounds like it could be a hat," Eva volunteered, then felt foolish. They didn't want to know what she thought.

"Yes I can see you looking very elegant in a terret, Duchess, but Mrs. Potter is more likely to be a furban wearer, don't you think?"

Eva nodded and then took her husband's arm as they made there way back to the carriage.

"I wonder what delights Mrs. Stimpel has created for our

luncheon," Lord Kelkirk sighed.

"I heard her discussing chocolate cream yesterday, my lord." Eva realized she was hungry as her stomach rumbled at the prospect of such a treat.

"You'll have to have your coats extended soon, Kelkirk." Daniel gave his friend a steady look.

Eva enjoyed the rest of the journey to Stratton as Daniel and Simon bantered back and forth. She volunteered the occasional comment when called upon but for the most part, she was just happy to be in their company, or more specifically, her husband's company. Last night had changed much about the way she viewed him. No man could be that gentle and want to harm or dictate to her, surely? Did this mean he was happy to give her time to adjust to going to London also? Eva hoped that was the case.

When they arrived at Stratton, Eva hurried upstairs to wash up before lunch. Humming, she pushed open her bedroom door and nearly tripped over the trunk placed just inside. Looking around the room, she noted her clothes lying across the bed and several more trunks already filled with her things.

"Molly, what are you doing?"

Removing her bonnet, Eva searched for the maid and found her behind the screen.

"Packing for our trip tomorrow, your Grace."

Some of the warmth inside her began to chill as she struggled to understand what was happening.

"Trip?"

"London, your Grace. The duke has given orders that

we are to leave at dawn to make the journey in two days."

"We are to leave tomorrow, Molly?" Eva tried to stay calm as she waited for her maid's reply.

"Yes your Grace, and I can't tell you how excited I am. I've never been to London."

Eva replied but she had no idea what she said.

"You go on and have your lunch now, your Grace, and I shall see to the rest of the packing."

Stripping off her gloves, she placed them on the bed, followed by her pelisse and then she was walking back out the door.

"Do you know where my husband is, Luton?"

The butler was in the hallway when she arrived downstairs. "In his study, your Grace."

"Thank you."

Why had he not told her they would leave tomorrow? Of course she had known they would go, she just hadn't expected it to be so soon and after what they had shared last night Eva had hoped for another week, maybe two. Knocking on his door, she then opened it and walked inside.

He was seated behind his desk, but rose as she entered. Ignoring the flutter in her chest as he smiled, Eva stopped several feet away and said, "Why did you not tell me we were going to London, tomorrow, Daniel?"

She took a step backwards as he advanced. She couldn't think when he was near.

"I thought it best not to prolong it further, Eva. Your fears about London are not easing and in fact, I believe they are escalating."

It was all so simple to him. He had decided they were to go and he was the duke; therefore, they must.

"I had only wanted some time, Daniel - time to understand how to act and become comfortable in my new role as your duchess."

"I have business to attend to in London that cannot wait, Eva. You are my duchess and I am bound for London. Therefore, so are you."

He was being rational. His words were calm and concise and she hated him for his composure when inside she was terrified.

"You were born to live this life. Nothing you see can upset you, but I was raised in a small house with two servants, one of those being me. Can you not understand how daunting the prospect of London society is to me?" She could hear the tension in her voice; the uncertainty was making her hysterical. There had been many times in Eva's life when she had been scared, yet she couldn't remember one that filled her with the panic that consumed her now. "I will make mistakes and be laughed at." Lord, she sounded pathetic.

"Eva, there really is no need for this. Everything will go well, I promise you."

She heard the sympathy in his words, yet they did nothing to soothe her. "Do you think people will not laugh when I spill wine down my dress or step on my partner's toes because I am a duchess? That they will not laugh when I wear pearls at the wrong time of day or snub the king because I have no idea what he looks like?"

"I'm sure the king will be announced before he is upon

you, Eva, and if not, I shall make sure to alert you to his presence myself and as for the pearls, I'm sure Claire will know what is proper."

He was smiling now - a sweet gentle smile that urged her to respond – however, Eva was past the point of responding. "I'm glad you find my insecurities so amusing, your Grace. Perhaps in light of them, I should follow you to London at a later date." Please, Eva added silently.

He was closer now, his big, disturbing presence inches from where she stood.

"Firstly, your fears do not amuse me. They are real and justified but they will not ease until you go to London to see for yourself the place is not a city filled with heathens and evildoers intent on nefarious deeds. Secondly, you are coming with me because otherwise I will receive a letter once I get there stating that you need more time and then another after that."

"I could humiliate us both." Eva bit her lip after blurting out the words.

His big hands wrapped around her shoulders, sending little waves of heat through her body.

"I have vowed to protect you, Eva, and I don't believe eating with the wrong fork or missing a step in a dance will result in your being ostracized. You have more elegance in your fingers than half of society and I have no doubt you will captivate everyone you see. Now we shall speak no more on the matter, as the decision has been made and will not be reversed."

"If we are laughed from London, your Grace, you shall have only yourself to b-blame," Eva whispered.

His fingers cupped her chin. Lifting it, he then kissed her slowly and thoroughly and Eva remembered last night and all the delicious emotions he had created inside her. When he lifted his head, she was breathless and aching for more.

"Have a little faith in both of us, Duchess."

She didn't speak again. Instead she moved out of his arms and with a quick curtsy, left the room.

# CHAPTER SEVEN

They rolled out of Stratton early the next morning. Simon had decided to visit with family and would catch up with them in London so he bid farewell at the gate.

"I will call upon you the instant I arrive, Eva, and I know you will be settled, with your worries eased by then."

"I hope so," Eva said, and Daniel knew her smile was forced.

Daniel left his wife alone with her thoughts for the first few miles, hoping that with time, the rigid set of her shoulders would ease. She had not looked his way once, instead keeping her eyes fixed on the window, but he had read each change of emotion as it flashed across her face. She sat so straight, her back had to be aching, yet she seemed unaware of any pain - and unaware of him, too.

Eva had clearly struggled to walk away from Stratton and what she now viewed as her home, saying goodbye several times to the servants until he had simply taken her hand and urged her into the carriage. She had watched Stratton until it disappeared and he understood then that this was probably the first place she had really felt safe and now he was making her leave that safety behind.

"Unclench your fists, Eva."

"Pardon?"

"Your hands."

Surprised at his words she looked down at her fingers, almost as if they belonged to someone else.

Today she wore cream and lavender and her black hair was bundled into a matching bonnet and Lord, just looking at her made him want her.

"Do you trust me yet, Duchess?"

"Of course." Her response was instant and honest and he felt something ease inside him.

"I have already promised to protect you in London, Eva. So I would ask you to remember those words when you feel afraid."

"It is no longer you I fear, Daniel, just the unknown."

Daniel moved to the seat beside her. "By unknown, you mean society?"

Eva nodded.

Daniel took her hand in his and pulled off the glove placing a kiss in the middle of her palm.

"Daniel!"

"Eva!" Daniel mimicked, then captured her other hand and proceeded to peel off the glove and kiss each of her fingers slowly and thoroughly. He smiled into the soft skin of her palm as her breath hitched and her nervous giggle filled the carriage. It was a beautiful sound and one that made his body hum. Moving to her wrists, he placed kisses around each, then looked at her. Her eyelids were lowered as she watched his every move and her mouth was open slightly.

"W-we are in a carriage."

"And we have a long journey ahead of us, Duchess. Surely we must find something with which to occupy our time?"

Eva was yawning by the time they pulled into the small inn where they would stop for the night and Daniel was more than ready to stretch his legs. He had chosen to ride in the carriage with Eva to keep her company rather than ride his horse and even though the carriage was well sprung, he was a large man and sitting in the same position for many hours usually made him stiff.

"Come. It will be good to stretch our legs," he said, taking his wife's hand in his and leading her into the inn. He had sent a man on ahead to organize their lodgings so the proprietor was ready for them.

"If you will follow me, your Grace, I shall show you your room."

"Room?"

Daniel could have booked Eva in with her maid but he didn't like the prospect of her sleeping without his protection.

"Follow the proprietor, Duchess, or we shall not know where he goes."

Placing a hand on her stiff spine, he urged her forward and reluctantly, she moved her feet. They climbed a set of narrow stairs and then were ushered into a small room.

"Thank you, and if you could send a tray up for my wife, please," Daniel told the man as he prepared to leave.

The bed was not as big as the ones at Stratton but still big enough for the two of them. He watched as Eva walked to the window, which looked down on the courtyard below. She still wore her bonnet and her pale face was framed by a wide satin ribbon tied in a big floppy bow beneath her chin.

"We are to sleep here together?" She looked from him to the bed, then back again.

"We have already slept in a bed together, Duchess, however there is a chair if you'd prefer." Color flooded her face as he teased her. "Rest now, Eva, you are tired from the journey. Your meal will arrive soon and I would ask you not to leave the room at any time unless I am with you."

"You are leaving?"

"I need to organize a few things and then I shall return. But if you need me, send someone and I shall come. Lock the door behind me now. You are in no danger with me and my men close by, but I would still have you show caution, Duchess."

"Of course."

Daniel waited outside the door until he had heard the key turn in the lock and then he made for the stables.

Eva let the maid in with her meal a little while later and ate in solitude, wondering when she had grown to dislike her own company, seeing as she had endured so much of it in her lifetime. She had enjoyed spending time with Daniel in the carriage and was coming to realize she could easily become enamored with her husband. He was gentle and coaxing with her, happy to answer questions, but he was comfortable with silence, too. Eva had never been the chatty type and it seemed neither was her husband. She blushed remembering how he had kissed her fingers. Was it wrong to enjoy such things? Surely not if he enjoyed them too.

As the evening progressed, the mumble of male voices grew louder through the floorboards and she realized her room was directly above the taproom. Her brothers and father had always been loud when they drank - loud and violent.

She bathed in the water set out for her and changed into her nightdress when it grew dark and then, with little else to do, she climbed into the bed. Blowing out the candle, she settled beneath the covers and waited for Daniel to return.

The door to her room swung wide suddenly and slammed into the wall and she realized she had not locked it after the maid had left with her tray.

"I hear there be a lady in here!"

Pulling aside the covers, Eva quickly got out of bed. "Get out of my room at once!"

The man stumbled forward and she could smell ale on his breath as he drew nearer. "Hello, sweeting, come and give me a kiss."

Eva lunged for the pitcher she knew was on the dresser. "Leave this room now or I will hurt you."

"I like a tousle, lovely - the rougher, the better."

He moved closer and Eva realized she was cornered. She threw the pitcher as hard as she could. He stumbled backwards as it hit his chest, cursing as water covered his front. Seizing the moment, she ran for the door but he was quicker and grabbed her.

"Daniel!"

The man tried to kiss her but Eva swung her fist at his head.

"Bitch!"

He grabbed a handful of her hair and pulled it hard, the pain made her eyes water but it was not enough to stop her. She brought up her knee and rammed it into his groin. He groaned, falling backwards. Eva ran as he released her, out the door and down the hall straight into Daniel's arms as he arrived at the top of the stairs. He caught her, pulling her close.

"What's wrong? I heard you scream."

"A man - there is a man in my room."

He tensed, his arms tightening as he lifted her off her feet briefly before releasing her and pushing her behind him.

"I kicked him...there, so he may still be on the floor."

Eva tucked in behind Daniel's back as they walked back to their room.

"Stay here," he told her when they reached the open door. She watched him enter and then followed. She did not want the man to surprise Daniel and hurt him. If she could reach the nightstand, she could light the candle.

"Get up!" Daniel dragged the moaning man to his feet.

"That bitch - she kicked me in the pecker!"

"You just cursed at a duchess. What's more, she's my duchess."

Eva could hear the rage in Daniel's voice as she slipped into the room.

"I told you to wait outside!"

"I don't want to stand in the hallway, your Grace, awaiting the next man who comes along," Eva said.

"No woman deserves a man entering her room uninvited," Daniel said to the vile man through gritted teeth. "Chambermaid or duchess, you should respect her wishes."

"Eva, come and lock the door after me."

She watched as Daniel pulled the man's arm up behind his back and walked him toward the door.

"When will you return?"

"Soon, I promise."

Grabbing a blanket she quickly wrapped it around herself. If Daniel had not heard her scream, that man could have raped her.

"I'm sorry, your Grace, I didn't know she was your duchess, you have to believe me." The man was whining but Daniel was not listening, instead Eva watched as he forced him

from the room, she turned the key in the lock as soon as the door was closed. Sitting on the bed she then waited for her husband to return.

"Eva it's me."

Relieved when Daniel called to her a few minutes later, she hurried to open the door and after entering he closed and locked it again.

"Are you all right?"

Still clutching the blanket, she moved back to the bed. "Yes. Thank you for coming when I called, Daniel. I'm sorry but I forgot to lock the door after the maid took my tray and that was how the man got in."

"Did he hurt you in any way?" Daniel stood just inside the room watching her intently.

"I hurt him more," Eva answered.

He smiled at her words. "You certainly did."

"Get into bed now, Eva, and I will join you after I have washed."

Placing the blanket back on the bed Eva then climbed beneath the covers listening as her husband removed his clothes and washed. Sliding over to the far side she then turned her back to face the wall.

"Goodnight."

He didn't answer her, instead blowing out the candle and then climbing into bed beside her. Eva felt his arm around her waist and then she was being lifted back into his chest.

"Are you wanting to –"

"I'm sorry that man hurt you, Eva, sorry that I was not here to stop it happening sooner."

She turned in his arms then and burrowed into his chest seeking his strength.

"But you came when I called."

"As I always will," he vowed.

Eva felt his chin rest on her head and the last of her terror began to ease. She was safe here in his arms.

"Sleep now, Duchess."

Eva closed her eyes and went to sleep with the steady rhythm of her husband's heart beating beside her own.

They rose early and were soon back on the road for the final leg of their journey. Daniel had watched Eva grow more nervous with each mile until by the last few she was answering him with gestures and single, quietly spoken words. Her questions had long since ceased and now she sat stiff and pale. Entering the city of London, he feared she was about to relieve her stomach of its contents.

"If you don't breathe soon, you shall swoon, Duchess."

"It is very large and noisy," Eva whispered, her eyes, if possible, growing wider as she looked at a group of people gathered around a shop front.

"And smelly," Daniel added, picking up her slim fingers and twining them through his own. He had hoped to make her laugh, however, she remained silent.

"There is a lady wearing pattens on her shoes, Duchess. Remember I told you about those?" Daniel pointed out the window.

"I remember."

"We will go driving in my phaeton and I will show you all the sights tomorrow."

"Y-yes."

Daniel felt a tug of shame at the stammered word. He had forced this on her, compounded her fears by making her accompany him here. "Eva, I brought you here because I believed it would benefit us both, but I would not have done so if I did not believe I could protect you and keep you safe."

"And because society is curious about the new Duchess of Stratton."

"Yes," Daniel sighed." That too."

If possible, her body grew more rigid as the carriage slowed and stopped and Daniel decided to leave any further conversation until they were inside and she was more comfortable.

"Come and meet your new home, Duchess," Daniel urged, taking her hand in his and climbing from the carriage.

"Wernham -" Daniel led Eva forward to meet the butler who was coming down the stairs toward them "- this is your new duchess."

"Your Grace." The butler bowed deeply.

"W-wonderful to meet you, Wernham." Eva took his hand and squeezed it.

Startled, Wernham straightened, his cheeks flushing with color.

Daniel watched his usually stoic butler stammer a few words before smiling at his wife. She definitely had a way with servants; both Luton and Mrs. Stimpel had quickly joined the ranks of her devotees.

"Your maid has arrived, your Grace, and your luggage," Wernham said, his face now sporting a wide smile. Eva thanked him profusely for his efforts. Daniel refrained from rolling his eyes while watching his butler bow so low, his nose nearly touched the ground.

"I shall never bend him to my will again."

"Pardon?"

"In minutes, you have reduced my very correct butler to your devoted servant. How will I ever bend him to my will again?"

"It is important, I think, to get on with all the staff, but Claire told me the butler was the most important."

"Did she? Well, she's probably right and now that Wernham is your slave, I'm sure the rest of the staff will follow," Daniel said, taking her hand. "Come. We shall go inside."

Daniel knew his town house was a male domain, yet he

thought it a comfortable one. It was not stuffed full of furniture and the walls for the most were painted in dark colors or paneled with wood, but the pieces were well-crafted and comfortable. Eva trailed behind him as he walked her through some of the rooms, explaining that he rarely used them and that often they stayed locked up for months.

"I have purchased a piano for this room." He led her into a large, light-filled room. It was painted in daffodil yellow, with curtains of white and yellow satin stripes hanging at the windows. He watched as Eva studied each wall and piece of furniture, her eyes taking in everything.

"It will be a beautiful music room, Daniel, but are you sure?" She ran a finger over the backs of two large chairs he had placed around a fireplace, satin pillows heaped high on their seats.

"You like to play the piano and I like to listen so I have purchased one to go in this room. Yes, what is it, Wernham?"

Eva looked up as the butler appeared in the doorway.

"A young man has arrived, your Grace, and is requesting to see the duchess. He says his name is Mr. Reginald Winchcomb."

"Reggie!"

Eva was out the door and running down the stairs before Daniel had moved one foot. He followed at a more sedate pace, wondering how the youngest Winchcomb had made his way to London.

"Eva!" Her brother saw her coming and ran to meet her. They hugged and cried, both as eager as the other to talk.

"Will you introduce me, Eva?" Daniel said.

Giving Reggie a final squeeze, Eva placed an arm around his waist before turning to face her husband.

"This is my youngest brother Reggie, your Grace."

Daniel moved forward and shook her brother's hand. "Your sister has been eager to see you for some time, young man. Tell me, how did you make your way to London when your home is at least three days' ride away?"

As that was Eva's next question, she remained silent, content to look at her brother. His dark hair was too long and he looked as if he had lost weight. His eyes were big in his face and the clothes she'd altered for him many times hung off his body.

"I climbed into the back of wagons and onto carriages until I made it here."

"Dear Lord, Reggie, why?"

"It just got to hard, Eva, so I ran."

Pulling him back into her arms, she held him tight, rocking him as his tears began to fall. He let her hold him until he was finished, which showed how upset he was because Reggie, like she, was not one for demonstrations of affection.

"What has happened to him, Eva?"

She'd forgotten the duke stood nearby. Looking his way, she found grey eyes filled with concern. "My father and brothers have made his life hell since I left and he could take no more."

"I'm sorry. I should have tried harder to get him to Stratton."

Eva kissed the top of Reggie's head as he lay against her.

"Tis not your fault, your Grace. My father would not let him go, as he was earning money working for one of the local farmers."

"He will not return to them," the duke vowed, moving forward to place a hand on her brother's shoulder. "Wernham, have a room prepared for the Duchess's brother and food and a bath, please."

"At once, your Grace."

"Follow Wernham, Eva, as I'm sure your brother is in need of rest after his long journey. We will become better acquainted tomorrow."

"Come, Reggie." Eva took her brother's hand and led him upstairs.

She helped bathe and dress him in the nightshirt Wernham had produced. Fatigue was in every line of his body and he did not struggle as she put him to bed.

"I won't go back, sister." Eyes so tired looked up at her.

"No, brother, you will never return to them."

He nodded at the certainty in her words.

Looking down at Reggie, Eva saw how far she had come since arriving at Stratton. Was it only a few months? She, too, had been thin and broken, her will battered and her fears real when she had married the duke.

"It's over for you now, brother. I will never let them hurt you again and my husband will offer his protection also."

She had heard her husband saying those very words to her many times and had failed to believe them. She was determined her brother would.

"Is he a good man, Eva?"

"He is, Reggie. You can trust him."

Kissing his cheek, she pulled the covers to his chin and left the room. At least one of her fears was now allayed. Reggie was here with her and she would see he stayed.

Wernham was waiting for her as she closed the door.

"His Grace requested that I show you your rooms, your Grace."

"Thank you, Wernham, and thank you for your help with my brother."

"Think nothing of it, your Grace. You have only to ask if you require anything further."

There was something familiar about Wernham as he tilted his head at that angle.

"Do you know the duke's butler at Stratton, Wernham?" Eva followed him along the hallway as she spoke.

"Luton is my brother, your Grace."

"I thought I recognized the tilt of your head. He is a wonderful man, Wernham, and without him, these last few months would have been much more difficult, I can assure you."

"He is the elder, your Grace, and approached the duke about employing me. When the duke agreed, he then taught me everything I needed to know before I undertook this position.

"I'm sure the duke and I are very lucky to have you both."

The butler blushed.

"His Grace has told me to bring a tray to your room, your Grace, as he thought you would be tired and wish to stay near your brother."

"Yes, thank you that would be perfect," Eva said.

Her room was smaller than the one at Stratton, which suited Eva, but just as lovely. Molly, her maid, was waiting for her inside.

"Did you enjoy your trip here, Molly?" Eva sat on the bed, feeling suddenly tired. It had been a busy few days and having Reggie arrive had turned her emotions on their head.

"It was wonderful, your Grace, and London such an amazing site."

At least someone is happy to be here. "I'm glad you're happy, Molly."

Eva spent the remainder of the day in her room or checking on Reggie, who had not stirred since he fell asleep many hours ago. Daniel came to see her briefly telling her to call him if she needed anything and that he would be in his office working through the paper work that was awaiting his attention. When she was sure that Reggie would not wake until morning, Eva washed and retired early, exhausted she was asleep minutes.

# CHAPTER EIGHT

*D*aniel came upon Reggie Winchcomb the following morning as he walked past the library. It was early, but as was his usual routine, he intended to run through the day's correspondence before eating his morning meal. He found the boy on his way to the study.

"Good morning, Reginald."

"Reggie is my name. Thank you, your Grace."

Nodding, Daniel looked at the young man as he replaced the book he held. His eyes were like Eva's, filled with the same pain and fears, although he wanted to believe her fears were easing.

"Reggie, then. Did you sleep well?"

His nod was solemn. "It was the best sleep I have ever had."

"Excellent. Would you like to have breakfast?"

"I would. Thank you."

Also like Eva, each of her brother's words was spoken carefully and with thought. Daniel did not have much experience with young men - he had no siblings and he was not terribly close with his cousins – and therefore, he would have to go by instinct when dealing with Eva's brother.

"This way," he indicated, forgoing his study for the breakfast room. Once seated, he asked the boy what he would like to eat and drink. Reggie's response was to stare blankly back at him.

"No preferences? Ham, eggs and toast?

"Yes, please."

"Wernham, please bring us a meal worthy of two men and Reggie will have chocolate to drink and coffee for me, please."

The boy didn't move at all. His hands never reached for his knife or played with the tablecloth. Instead he sat very still and watched Daniel. Fidgeting was obviously not tolerated in the Winchcomb household.

"Reggie, have you given any thought to what you would like to do now you are here in London?"

"I don't want to go back to my father."

"That will never happen," Daniel vowed, holding the boy's eyes until Reggie nodded, acknowledging the words.

"I want to go to university."

"Away from London to university?" Daniel queried. Intrigued, he waited as Reggie formed his words before continuing.

"Eva taught me everything she learnt from her tutor. I know a great many things but I want to go to a school with other boys where I will learn more. I want to read books and study languages. But most of all…"

Daniel found himself leaning forward as a sparkle came into Reggie's sapphire blue eyes. "What, Reggie? What do you really want?" Daniel would find a way to give it to the boy, no matter the cost.

"I want to have friends."

Wernham brought their breakfast in and Daniel took the few minutes to think about what Eva's brother had said. He still had friends he'd formed at Eton - solid reliable friends who had made his time there something to remember.

"I will start enquiries today for Eton, Reggie."

"But I am not of noble birth, your Grace."

"Your brother-in-law is a duke, Reginald. Please remember that fact." Daniel winked at the boy and was rewarded with half a smile, which made him feel good. "And please call me Daniel."

"While I am honored that you would offer such a school for me, I would rather go to Edinburgh University."

Daniel sipped his coffee. "How old are you?"

"Seventeen, your Grace."

Lord, he'd thought the boy no older than fifteen. His height was no greater than Eva's and he would not weight much more.

"Why Edinburgh?"

Reggie lowered his fork, then wiped his mouth before speaking, both actions giving him time to think. "Edinburgh is open to anyone and I have no wish to attend a school where I will not fit, your Grace. Now I know Eva is safe in your hands, I have no need to stay near her and Edinburgh is far enough away from them."

"Why do you believe your sister is safe with me, Reggie?" Daniel was curious. This boy, like his sister, had suffered at the hands of their family, yet unlike Eva, he seemed willing to trust Daniel on short acquaintance.

"My sister said I could trust you, Daniel, and I can see in your eyes that it is true."

Clearing his throat, Daniel nodded. "If you want to stay here with your sister, Reggie, you can trust me to keep you safe also."

His smile was tired and should have been on the face of an older man. "I would rather you put all your efforts into protecting my sister, your Grace, as it is she who has suffered at their hands the most and it is she who deserves happiness."

Daniel kept his eyes level as Reggie stared at him. "Your family will never touch your sister again. You have my word on that."

Reggie looked at him a few seconds longer and then nodded, which made Daniel release the breath he hadn't known he was holding. "But I will have your word, Reggie, that if at any time you have concerns or are in trouble, you will come to me instantly."

"I promise."

"Good. Now finish your breakfast and I shall have my man look into Edinburgh. I'm guessing you wish to leave soon?"

"Yes. A fresh start and new city is what I crave, although Eva will not be happy at the prospect."

"Only because she worries for you, Reggie. I believe that is what sisters are meant to do," Daniel said. He'd always wanted a sibling and now it seemed he had one in the form of a brother in law.

When Eva walked in ten minutes later, Daniel and Reggie were still planning his trip.

"Good morning, Eva." Daniel rose to greet her. "Reggie, your sister is in the room. Please rise."

Surprise flashed across her pretty face as he spoke but she said nothing, instead moving to hug her brother. Then she found her chair. Daniel felt the foolish urge to request a hug, too.

"Eva, Daniel is going to help me go to Edinburgh University." The boy didn't say it loudly or sound overly excited but Daniel knew by the gleam in his eyes that he was. His sister, however, did not appear to be.

"Why do you want to go away to school when you have only just arrived?"

"You know it has always been my fondest wish, Eva."

"But I had thought you would stay here with me."

Me, not we, Daniel noticed. The ease with which they had shared each other's company on the journey seemed to have dissipated with their arrival in London and that of Eva's brother.

"I want this, Eva, and if Daniel is happy to help me achieve it, then it is something I must do."

"But we cannot ask it of the duke, Reggie, when he has already given me so much."

What had he given her? A marriage, shelter and food on her table, but had any of those things made her truly happy?

"I am happy to do this, Eva, if you agree." Daniel said nothing further as he continued with his meal, content to watch the siblings. They were not demonstrative, neither raising their voice to the other, both talking calmly as if they were discussing the weather.

Eva's hair was darker than her brother's was but their

eyes were identical. Her cheeks were fuller now and her skin had a healthy glow that Reggie's lacked. She wore a simple white dress this morning with a modest neckline and short sleeves, yet because of its simplicity, the lush body beneath was enhanced. He wanted her in his bed again - underneath him, on top of him. He wanted to explore and taste every inch of her.

"It would be selfish of me to stop you if it is your wish, brother. It is just that I will miss you so much." Eva felt as if her heart was being ripped in two. Reggie was here with her finally and now he wanted to leave.

"I cannot live with you forever, Eva. It is past time I did something useful."

"Suddenly you want to be useful? Is this a new development?"

Reggie's chuckle made her laugh. They had not done much of that over the past few years and it felt good to do so now.

"I will have my man look into Edinburgh," Daniel broke in, "but you will need new clothes and other items before you leave."

"Do not concern yourself further, your Grace. I shall look after my brother." Eva realized as soon as the words left her mouth how ungrateful they sounded.

"In that case, I shall leave you to your breakfast together."

The duke rose and bowed to her, then shook the hand Reggie held out to him.

"That was neither fair nor necessary, Eva." Reggie said

as the door closed. "The duke has been kind enough to assist me in finding a place at Edinburgh University. Without his support, sister, none of this would be possible. I would beg you to remember that fact."

A wave of shame washed over her. She had spoken without thought, something she rarely did, yet Reggie's welfare had always been her concern and everything seemed to be happening so fast. "I know. I'm sorry."

"'Tis not me you should apologize to, sister." His fingers clamped around hers where they lay clenched on the table. "Whatever is between you is your business, Eva, but remember that were it not for that man, you would still be living with our father and I would have had nowhere to run."

"Our destinies were determined over a hand of cards, Reggie. How can either of us hope to find a future together after such a beginning?" There were moments when Eva hoped they could overcome what their father had done, and then others when she would despair that their past would always dictate their future.

Reggie sighed, loud and long. "I should have known the reason would involve gambling. But the thing is, Eva, you trust him, and therefore, so do I. And now I want you to go and apologize to him in case he changes his mind and won't help me get to Edinburgh."

"He would never break his word to you, Reggie."

Her brother gave her a steady look. "You know this about him, yet still you doubt him?"

Pulling her hand free, Eva fiddled with her cup. "The doubts are mine, not his."

Reggie nodded but said nothing further on the matter. They finished their meal in silence; Reggie was the first to rise.

"I'm going into the library and you should find your husband and apologize, sister."

"Dear Lord, must I?" Eva did not look forward to the prospect.

"One thing neither of us has ever been, sister, is a coward."

She watched her brother leave and then followed. He was right. She did owe Daniel an apology and she needed to get it over with before she lost the courage to do so.

Tapping on her husband's study door minutes later, Eva entered. He was not seated as she had expected but standing before a shelf of books, his fingers skimming the spines.

"If I may have a few minutes of your time, your Grace."

"My name is Daniel, Eva. Your brother has no problem using it and neither did you until recently. Therefore I'm sure you can do so again."

She didn't have to like his rebuke but knew she deserved it. "I would like to apologize to you for my words at the breakfast table, Daniel. They were uncalled for, considering what you are doing for my brother. My only excuse is that he has been my sole responsibility for many years."

"And you resent accepting anything from me."

"No - "

"Yes, but I am a duke with a great deal of money, Eva. Your brother has a dream and it is within my power to see he achieves it."

He made her sound petty.

"I would ask you to try and accept both me and London, Eva, or our marriage will test both of us. I'm not asking for undying devotion, only that we rub along together."

"I shall try."

He nodded and turned back to the books before him, selecting one. "Do you think Reggie will want to read this? He told me he has an interest in old literature and this is very old."

Eva walked to where he stood and looked at the book. Ignoring the tingle as his fingers brushed hers, she opened the cover.

"They are letters written nearly two hundred years ago. He may not be able to read them, as most are written in French, but it will be interesting for him to look at."

Eva read the first few lines. "We both speak and read French."

"Excellente."

"Are you sure you wish him to touch it? These look very old."

"He is seventeen, Eva, not ten. I trust him not to damage them."

Handing him back the book, Eva offered Daniel a tentative smile. "It is sometimes hard to remember that fact and yes, he would very much love to look at this. Thank you again."

Eva watched him replace the book, his big hands sure and steady. "I will get a tailor to come to the house to have Reggie fitted for clothes, and if between you a list can be made for the rest of his needs, I will see it filled."

His face was inches from hers now, but she could read

nothing in his grey eyes. "I will say again that I'm sorry for the way I spoke and I realize now that if I had not come to London then I would not have been here when Reggie arrived. It will take time for me to adjust to this city, yet I promise to make every effort to do so."

"If that was your attempt at an apology, you will need to try harder, Duchess."

Eva flicked a glance at him, then away again. His eyes had changed. They were no longer cool and unemotional. "I think my apology is more than adequate, Daniel. I...I assure you it was delivered sincerely."

She watched him step to the right and Eva had to turn to face him and it was then she realized he had maneuvered her back against the bookshelf. Rather than feel fear, she instead felt anticipation.

He moved forward slowly, bracing his hands on the shelves on either side of her and kept coming until his breath brushed her lips. "I want you to promise me something, Duchess."

"What?" Eva shivered as his warm breath brushed her lips.

"That you endeavor to remain open-minded about London."

Eyes open, he held hers as he took her bottom lip between his teeth and bit softly into the flesh.

"I...I will try," Eva whispered when he released her.

He moved in again, this time to place a slow, sultry kiss on her mouth and Eva felt any resistance flee. She melted, her insides turning to liquid as he tormented her. Only his lips touched her, yet in seconds she was the puppet and he, the master. When one kiss ended, another started until she was arching toward him, wanting more.

"Daniel." She sighed as he moved to her neck, his breath warm on her skin. Running her fingers through his hair, Eva gripped the curls as he nipped her.

"I want you, sweet Duchess, very badly."

"Then take me." Eva could hardly believe she had said the words out loud.

He lifted his head to look down at her, his eyes burning with a need that mirrored her own.

"Soon, Eva, but for now we must satisfy ourselves with kisses. I would not want Reggie to walk in on us in a compromising position."

"Reggie!" Dear Lord, how could she have forgotten her brother was in the house? "I had not thought about him."

His smile was smug as he ran one hand up her arm and she shivered.

"I…I will go to him now."

"Not yet."

Eva tried to push him away, but he kissed her again and she did not put up much of a fight.

"I think that is everything, Eva."

Eva looked at her brother's excited face and swallowed her tears. The siblings were in his room finishing his packing before he left for Edinburgh. Daniel had secured a place for Reggie at the university and he could take it up as soon as he got there. This news for Eva was a double- edged sword, as on one hand, her brother would get what he wished for - heaven knew he deserved it after the life he had lived - and on the other, she would lose him again.

The past two weeks had been wonderful. Daniel had taken them to see many sights and they had shopped for Reggie, but more importantly, they had spent time together talking. Eva had seen another side to both her brother and her husband. She'd watched Reggie blossom without the threat of his father and brothers looming over him constantly. He laughed freely, talked constantly and asked Daniel endless questions, to which he had patiently answered. The duke had a wicked humor that often made them laugh and Eva felt comfortable around him now - comfortable and unsettled at once. Her skin tingled whenever he was near and she had a constant longing for him that was almost painful.

"I have everything packed in two trunks, Eva, and they are being loaded into the carriage as we speak."

"You have the books for the trip and the itinerary, plus Jacob, the duke's man, is accompanying you and will stay until you are settled." Eva ticked off the points on her fingers.

"Yes, and Daniel has secured a contact for me once I get there. He is Scottish and will be on hand, should I need anything at anytime."

Reggie was pulling on his new coat. He looked healthy after two weeks of good meals and plenty of sleep. She could feel his excitement and knew Daniel was the one to thank for that.

Daniel. Lord, she blushed just thinking of what they had shared last night in his bed. He had told her that in there, they were just Eva and Daniel. All the problems that awaited them outside the bedroom door were left there when they entered at night.

"Are you all right, Eva?"

"Of course." She forced herself to smile. "I'm so excited for you."

They made their way outside to where Daniel awaited them beside the carriage.

"Jaccob is inside and he has instructions on where you will stop and my letter to help smooth your way."

"Thank you, Daniel, for everything." Eva watched Reggie step forward and embrace the duke, which surprised him at first but he soon wrapped his big arms around the boy and squeezed him hard.

"Remember we are brothers now, Reggie. I will come if you need me."

"I will remember."

Eva bit her lip as Reggie turned to hug her. She would not cry; he did not want that. "Please write to me regularly, brother."

"I promise."

She cupped his cheeks and looked into his eyes. He was healing and this journey would finish that process. "You know I love you?"

Color stole into his cheeks as she held him still.

"I know it and you know your love is returned, sister."

She released him and smoothed his lapels. "Go now while I let you."

He kissed her forehead. "Thank you for being my sister. Without you, everything would have been so much harder."

Eva sniffed as he released her and climbed inside. Daniel

closed the door and then he was gone. She watched the carriage until she could see it no more and then the tears began to fall. Arms came around her and she fell on the warm, hard chest and sobbed.

. . .

"The Dowager Duchess of Stratton," Wernham said in his deep baritone.

Startled, Eva looked up from the letter she was writing as Daniel's grandmother walked in. The room instantly seemed smaller – just as it often did when her husband was near. Eva had met the Duchess once before; however, she had not known then that she was to become related to such a formidable woman. Rising to her feet, she knew her morning of letter writing had drawn to an abrupt halt. Shooting a quick look at the clock above the door, she was relieved to realize Daniel would be returning soon from his business appointment. He had not wanted to leave her, no matter how briefly, yet she had urged him to do so, she was safe here with their servants behind closed doors.

"Well, girl, it is long past time you showed your face in society," the duchess boomed as she took the seat opposite Eva's.

"Tea, please, Wernham." Eva smiled at the butler, who hovered in the doorway looking anxious. She then sat on the edge of her seat. Something told her that with Daniel's grandmother in the room, she needed to be ready for any eventuality.

"Although looking at that rag you have on, it is just as well you have not been seen in public."

"Good morning, your Grace, I am most pleased to meet with you again. This time it appears you are playing the part of your true self." Eva's cheeks were beginning to ache with the effort of smiling.

"Backbone. Excellent," the duchess said, her thin lips curling slightly at the corners.

Eva wondered if this constituted a snarl or a smile.

"We won't have time for tea now – there's much to be done!" she suddenly announced, regaining her feet.

She was very agile for an elderly woman, Eva thought, standing, too. It was all very strange. The woman had insulted her and then complimented her (she thought) and now she appeared to be leaving. Or did she have something else in mind?

"Come, girl, collect your things and I will wait in my carriage! Ten minutes, mind, and no more," the duchess added, giving Eva a gimlet-eyed stare which was disconcertingly like her grandson's. She then stomped toward the door she had only minutes ago entered.

"Uh, I seem to have missed something," Eva said. Dear Lord! Did Daniel's grandmother expect Eva to accompany her somewhere? Just the thought of the two of them spending time together sent chills down her spine.

"Shopping, girl! For pity's sake, have I not just explained it all to you? Not hard of hearing, are you?"

"I soon will be," Eva muttered, touching her ears as she watched the old woman leave the room.

"May I be of assistance?" Wernham appeared as if by magic before her.

"I appear to be going shopping." Eva knew she sounded dazed.

"I will inform the duke upon his return, your Grace." The butler looked grave.

"Thank you," Eva said, walking out of the room. She thought frantically of feigning a headache or having Wernham tell the Duchess she had fallen down the stairs and broken her ankle. But then she would have to stay inside for several weeks, which appealed to Eva but would hardly be fair to Daniel. She pulled on her pelisse and bonnet and prepared to leave the house.

"Hurry up, girl!"

Eva ran down the stairs as the loud voice reached her. Closing her eyes, she prayed silently for a safe return.

Two hours was all he'd been gone and in that time the old besom had swooped in and taken Eva away.

"Why did you let her go?"

Wernham did not flinch in the face of his master's anger.

"Of course you could not have stopped her. Bloody woman. A brace of beefy prize-fighters would struggle to subdue my grandmother," Daniel snarled.

"I will bring you some refreshments, your Grace," Wernham said. "Also, the Duchess's piano arrived today, and I had it placed exactly where you stated."

As if he could eat or drink! Just thinking of Eva in the hands of his grandmother and out on the streets of London without his protection made Daniel feel ill.

He had not taken Eva into society yet because he was giving her time to adjust to life in London. Then there had been Reggie and his needs, which had taken up more time. He had decided that this week they would attend their first engagement and now his grandmother had swooped in and taken her shopping. What must she be thinking?

"Lord Kelkirk has called, your Grace," Wernham said, re-entering the room minutes later.

Daniel nodded. At least Simon would take his mind off his wife. In truth, he knew his grandmother would never harm Eva, but he felt protective of her - too protective, he thought with a wry smile. The problem was, she occupied far too much of his thoughts. Over the past two weeks they seemed to have grown comfortable with each other and at night when he came to her bed, she was heaven in his arms. She was open and honest in what she felt, her responses to him were unguarded and she had him hotter than hell in seconds.

"That smile at best could be called licentious."

Daniel grunted, then climbed to his feet to shake the hand of his friend.

"How does Eva fair, Daniel?"

"If my grandmother does not force her to flee London then I am sure you will see her soon."

"You let your grandmother get her hands on her?" Simon had astonishment written all over his face. "Dear God, she's only been in London two weeks. What the hell were you thinking?"

Normally Daniel would have come to his grandmother's defense in the face of such an obvious insult, but Simon had firsthand knowledge of her acid tongue. The Dowager Duchess of Stratton usually took him to task whenever the opportunity presented itself.

"I should never have left her alone." Daniel dropped his head into his hands.

"I was not earnest, Daniel. While your grandmother may strike the fear of God into me, I know she never means any harm. Well, nearly never means any harm."

Daniel climbed to his feet and began to pace, his grey eyes becoming cloudier with each step. "She is not used to the ways of society, Simon."

"I came by to tell you there is talk. Eva has been in London for over two weeks, yet no one has actually seen her. It's time for her to make her appearance, my friend, before the rumors escalate."

"Who's talking about her?" Daniel lowered his brows. "And what are they saying?

"That your duchess has an eye on her forehead and ten fingers on one hand." Simon sat back, watching his friend pace.

"I should have realized society would conjure up several nasty inflictions for her if she didn't make an appearance straightaway."

"So you will go to the next ball?"

"I believe so." Daniel moved to the window and looked down at the street below.

"A carriage has arrived, your Grace," Wernham said, bringing a tray into the room.

"About bloody time!" Daniel declared, stalking from the room, leaving Simon behind, grinning.

Daniel saw Eva leaning on the now closed door with her eyes shut as he reached the front entranceway. "Did she upset you?"

Opening her eyes, she watched him approach.

"I am fine. Just tired, Daniel."

"You must have been terrified when she demanded you

accompany her. Old Besom. I've always said the English were not using their strongest weapon against the French."

She tried not to laugh but her eyes twinkled. Daniel looked her over, just to check she was in one piece.

"It would be untruthful of me to lie so I will say that your grandmother was initially terrifying, yet I did enjoy myself once we established a few rules."

"Rules?" Daniel took the three packages she held against her chest and then, slipping a hand around her waist, he guided her toward the stairs.

"I realized straightaway that if you don't stand up to your grandmother, she will stomp all over you."

He laughed at that.

"She told me she would not clothe her servant in my dress."

Looking her over again, Daniel disagreed. The pale blue was perfect with her dark hair and creamy complexion.

"Simon has called." Daniel directed Eva into the front parlor where Simon was seated, or rather, lounging, in a comfortable chair. In one hand he held a cup of tea and in the other a huge piece of cake.

"Make yourself at home, Kelkirk," Daniel drawled, lowering his wife into a seat before taking the place beside her.

"Always have excellent cake here," Simon said. "Hello, Duchess, you are looking fetching today."

"Thank you, Simon."

They drank and talked and Eva told Simon about Reggie going away to school and what they had seen since she arrived in London.

"So London is not the horrible city you envisaged it to be, Duchess?"

"I shall reserve judgment until I meet some of its inhabitants."

"Fair enough," Simon said, standing. "And now I am full, I shall leave you. Goodbye, Duchess." He gave Eva a kiss on the cheek, which made her blush.

"Lord Kelkirk is a very nice man, Daniel," she said when he had left.

"He has his moments." Daniel got up to shut the door.

"I'm glad he's your friend."

Taking her cup, Daniel placed it on the tray and then he opened the buttons of her pelisse and slipped two fingers into the neckline of her dress to caress her soft flesh.

"Daniel!"

He took her lips for a thorough kiss that left Eva breathless and wanting more. He then buttoned her pelisse back up and placed her on the chair opposite his.

"Tell me of your shopping exhibition, Eva," Daniel said, drawing in a deep, steadying breath. The woman was a walking siren.

"Sh-shopping?"

He laughed as she struggled to compose herself. It was no different for him - just breathing her scent had him hard as a table leg.

"With my grandmother...today," he prodded.

"Oh, yes, of course," Eva smoothed her hair and skirts. Daniel had never touched her like that in daylight. She wondered why he had now. "Your grandmother told me I had a responsibility to the dukedom and dressing like a maiden aunt was not taking that responsibility seriously. She then dragged me from shop to shop until she was satisfied

I would be dressed as befitted a duchess."

"Did she? Never has had any tact. Half of London is terrified of her, you know." Daniel swallowed a small piece of cake and immediately reached for another.

"She talked of balls and dances and what I would need to learn." Eva sighed. "And corrected me constantly over my bearing and address."

"Shall I tell her to leave you alone?"

"Of course not!" Eva looked indignant. "It was rather sweet having someone care about those things, even if she is a little brusque."

Daniel choked on his cake.

"A small, rosy-cheeked child is sweet, Eva, not my grandmother."

"She is my grandmother now, too," Eva picked up her parcels, preparing to leave the room. "And as I do not have another yardstick with which to measure her, I will call her sweet if I wish to."

"That is, of course, your prerogative, however misguided." Daniel rose as she did. "I will be in my office with my man of affairs for awhile, Eva. Apparently I have been neglecting things since my return to London."

"Then I shall finish the letters I started before your grandmother descended and will see you later, Daniel."

He watched her leave the room. The changes in her over the past two weeks were vast. She now felt comfortable around him, she laughed more freely and he believed she no longer feared him. However, it was only because of her upbringing that she could believe his grandmother was sweet.

# CHAPTER NINE

*W*ernham intercepted Eva as she took her parcels to her room. "A note has arrived for you, your Grace."

Taking the missive, she thanked him. Hopefully, it was from Claire. Eva would love to speak with her new friend because she knew so much about society. She was aware that Daniel was not pushing her to attend any functions, yet she also understood that speculation was mounting about her. His grandmother had told her that in no uncertain terms today.

You need to get out there, gal. Your husband will become a laughingstock if you don't!

And because her husband had been so generous to both her and Reggie, she did not want that to happen. Therefore she would go to a function soon. She just wanted to have a bit more coaching from Claire first.

Opening the note, she quickly scanned the contents.

Come alone to the park across the road now or I shall be forced to journey to Edinburgh to collect my son.

Pushing aside the instant wash of icy fear as she read the

words, Eva quickly pulled on her gloves and bonnet and hurried from the room. The note was from her father and she knew he would do as he stated and she could not allow that, would not allow Reggie to be hurt anymore. Heart thumping, she reached the front entrance.

"You are going out, your Grace?"

"Just to the park, Wernham, a friend is awaiting me there," she lied. "I shall return soon."

"His Grace would be displeased if you did not take someone with you, your Grace."

"Molly is coming, Wernham, she will be along shortly so do not fret and please do not bother my husband as he is very busy."

Reaching for the door, Eva forced a bright smile onto her face as she opened it herself and ran down the steps before he could stop her.

The day was warm and under different circumstances she would enjoy the walk. Hurrying along the path she reached the park. Pushing open a small gate, she held it for a lady holding the hand of little girl.

"Lovely day for a walk, don't you think?"

Eva nodded and mumbled a reply and then found the path that ringed the park. Plenty of people were here. Some had dogs; others, children, and all were enjoying the sun and the simple act of being outside.

"Hello, daughter."

All the old uncertainties resurfaced as a hand touched Eva's back and she struggled to remain a duchess and not the scared girl she had been.

"What do you want, Father?" Eva stopped walking and

turned to face the man who had sired her.

He was big - not as big as Daniel, but still, he could and had hurt her without too much effort. Large and broad-shouldered, he and his two elder sons shared the same unfortunate pale skin which tended to turn pink in the sun. His hair was now grey, freckles dotted his face, and as usual, his brown eyes held a belligerent expression.

"Adjust your tone, Daughter." Eva didn't flinch as his fingers pinched her arm.

"What do you want, Father?" she repeated, fighting to stay calm.

"Lord Huxley and I have had a bad run on the tables lately and need a bit of blunt to turn things around."

"You would dare to ask me for money after the life you subjected me to!" She couldn't breathe. Her chest felt tight and she struggled to force air into her lungs.

"Think you're better than me now, Duchess?" He spat the words at her. "You're still the worthless girl you always were and no clothes or title can change that! You should be thanking me for giving you the life you now live."

"I know I'm better than both you and Lord Huxley." Eva kept her voice low.

"If you don't give me money, I'll go to Scotland and make your brother's life hell."

"No! Leave Reggie alone." The sense of despair that she could not fight him returned. How had he found Reggie so soon?

"Then you better do as I ask, girl, because if you thought Scotland was far enough to hide him, you were wrong. You're the only one now who can keep Reggie safe."

"Do you care nothing for your son?" Eva rasped.

"You're both as weak as your mother was. Should never have married that woman. My first wife was much stronger. Shame she died of that rotted tooth."

Eva didn't speak, just stared into his hated face. Why had she believed she would ever be free of him?

"And don't think about asking your husband, either. I can have him hurt just as easy as your brother."

"You can't touch the Duke of Stratton, Father. He is both stronger and smarter than you." Eva felt better just saying the words. Daniel would help her if she went to him, help rid her of her family once and for all.

"If you don't pay up, girl, then Lord Huxley will challenge the duke to a duel and we both know the outcome now, don't we."

Eva felt a physical pain at the thought of anyone hurting Daniel.

"Lord Huxley has never been defeated, Eva, and he loves to fight. He told me to tell you he hates the duke enough to want to see him dead if you don't do as I say."

Eva knew she was trapped. She could not allow Daniel to fight Lord Huxley, but knew if the man challenged him, he would not back down. She would have to pay her father or see her husband dead or maimed.

"I want the first payment tomorrow. One of your brothers will be in this park at two. Be here or I will be on my way to Scotland before your brother has settled into his new life."

He was gone before she could say anything further and numb Eva began to walk home. She had no money of her own – well, not enough to appease her father, anyway. She would have to give him the ring her husband had given her when first they married. It was big and ugly and surely Daniel would not miss it or ask for it back. So much had changed between them lately and she had even begun to believe that they could share a life together. Have children and a family. Eva struggled to hold back the tears as she approached the townhouse. Damn her father for forcing her into the one thing she had always vowed she would never do to her husband, no matter the provocation. She was about to betray him and now everything between them was about to change.

"Will you play for me, Eva?" Daniel looked across the table to his wife. She had been quiet this evening, her face pale and drawn. He'd asked her what was wrong and she had used missing Reggie as an excuse. She was lying. He knew it by the way her eyes dropped when she answered and he wondered what had taken place between him spending a few hours in his office and now.

"I have not had a lot of practice on the new piano, Daniel. Indeed, I will sound almost rusty when compared with some."

"Then I shall listen and point out your mistakes."

His taunt did not even produce a smile.

"Eva, has something upset you?"

"No, I am well, your Grace, just missing my brother."

He was suddenly 'your Grace' again.

"I would like to thank you again for my beautiful piano, Daniel. Will you play it also?"

"I'm not sure I remember how," Daniel said. Memories of his mother always surfaced when he played so he had just stopped. "Eva, we are to attend the Stratton Ball tomorrow."

Any color she had in her face had just leeched away.

"Must we?"

"Yes, we must. I am a duke and you, my duchess. Therefore, there are expectations upon us."

She looked ready to faint. Where the hell had the woman he had kissed this morning gone? He would speak with Wernham and see if she had had any visitors. Something had unsettled her and he wanted to know what.

"I have no gown." She was digging deep for any excuse.

"Eva, it is decided and tomorrow night you will go with me to the Sutton ball. Claire and Simon will both be there, as will my grandmother. For all the good she will be."

"Excuse me. I…I will go and choose some music."

He watched her bolt, then picked up his wine. He had no doubt it would take only a short time for her to win over society and he predicted the ton would have a new darling by the end of the season.

Daniel slipped into the music room and seated himself in the big chair he had placed before the fire. It was angled perfectly so he could see Eva's face as she played. Her hands flew over the keys and her eyes were fierce as she followed the sheets of music. He could almost feel her passion as she poured everything into her playing. She made love with the same intensity and she was his - every delectable inch.

He let her play for some time, then rose and went to stand beside the piano.

"Will you play with me?"

Eva saw that her words had surprised him. Reaching for his hand, she urged him down onto the seat beside her.

"It has been many years since I have touched a piano."

He was nervous, his fingers stiff as he ran them down the keys. He looked suddenly unsure, almost vulnerable, and she pushed aside her worries to comfort him. "Did your mother play for you?"

She saw the answer in his eyes as he began to play. "She played like you, from the heart."

Eva joined him as he began a slow ballad. He was good, very good, and she enjoyed the feel of his strength sitting beside her, his warmth surrounding her. When the ballad finished, she started another and he followed. They sat there side by side through many more songs until finally their fingers tired.

"I had forgotten how much I loved to play. Thank you for reminding me."

She heard the emotion in his words. Playing had stirred the memories inside him. "Did your mother teach you to play, Daniel?"

Absently, he took one of her hands in his as he thought about what he would say. "Yes, she taught me to play. She also taught me to love and laugh. She was my life."

She didn't know what to say to that so Eva just squeezed his fingers and laid her head on his shoulder.

"Where she was everything that was good and kind, my father was everything that was evil and in the end he killed her."

"Dear God!"

"It seems we have that in common, Duchess. Fathers who hated us."

"How did he kill her?" The devastation in his eyes had her reaching for him. Wrapping her arms around his neck, Eva held him.

"He was punishing me and she died as a result."

His scars were just as painful as hers but buried deeper.

Slipping one arm under her thighs, he lifted her against his chest and strode from the room. Neither spoke again as they undressed and then he kissed her, his mouth seeking something that tonight only she could give him and when he drove deep inside her, she wrapped her arms and legs around him and held him close. For tonight she would give him her comfort and love and tomorrow she would betray him.

. . .

"Ooh, don't you look lovely, your Grace."

Eva stared at the lady in the mirror. "Good Lord, it is me!" Molly had piled her hair high, leaving a few curls to lie on her bare shoulders. Several small diamond clips held it in place. "Molly, you can work magic!"

Ignoring the comment, the maid bustled Eva into her dress. Madame Monterio, her grandmother's dressmaker, had obviously worked her seamstresses into the ground all afternoon, Eva thought with a tug of guilt. The dress was quite simply the most beautiful thing Eva had ever worn. Made of sky blue satin, it clung and swirled in all the right places, falling in soft folds to the floor. The overskirt made of deeper blue was sheer, and opened at the front to show the beautiful rose satin skirt beneath. The bodice was fitted and her breasts swelled above the neckline once Molly had tightened Eva's corset.

"Is the neckline not too low, Molly?" Eva chewed her lip, eyeing the expanse of exposed bosom.

"No more than many and a great deal less than some." The maid moved to do up the tiny buttons that ran the length of Eva's spine.

The sleeves were fitted to the elbow and Eva slipped on a pair of ivory gloves, while on her feet were matching slippers. Molly draped a gossamer blue shawl around her shoulders and then urged her from the room as Eva thanked her profusely.

"Daniel."

He turned as she walked into the parlor and the look in his eyes told Eva everything she needed to know.

"I have no words to describe your beauty, Duchess."

She felt beautiful with his eyes on her as she walked toward him.

"You take my breath away."

"Thank you, it is the loveliest dress I have ever owned."

"That neckline is very low."

Eva felt a flush color her skin as he looked at her breasts. "No more than others, Daniel," Eva solemnly quoted Molly.

"God help me, it will be a long evening," he muttered, handing her a long, velvet case.

Eva opened it and stared at the sapphire and diamond necklace and bracelet nestled inside.

"It is so beautiful and you have already given me so much."

"These have been worn only by the Duchess of Stratton." Daniel lifted the necklace and obediently, Eva turned. "I have one more gift for you, Duchess," he added, releasing her to remove a small box from inside his jacket pocket once the necklace was fastened.

The ring nestled amongst the red velvet folds was a delicate gold band with a perfectly formed diamond flanked by two smaller rubies.

"I have never seen anything so beautiful, Daniel."

"It was my grandmother's." He took the ring from the box and lifted her hand. "The one I gave you before was my grandfather's," he said ruefully.

Eva watched as he slipped it onto her finger. The fit was perfect. "Thank you." She placed a shy kiss on his cheek.

"You can now return my grandfather's ring, which I am ashamed to say I should never have given you."

No, I can't, because my father has it! Guilt, thick and heavy, settled on her shoulders.

"Well, Duchess, shall we head to your first ball?"

She nodded and put her hand on his arm and thankfully he mistook her silence for nerves.

Lord and Lady Sutton lived ten minutes from the Stratton townhouse but the journey took over thirty minutes, due to the traffic. By the time their carriage finally pulled up outside the ball venue, Eva was beyond nervous.

"Eva, I will be with you, as will Claire and Simon. Surely you can see we will let nothing happen to you?" Daniel took the small reticule from her hands and untangled the silk ribbons. He had tried to talk to her and take her mind off her fears but she would not be soothed.

"I know all you say is true, Daniel, yet I am not one of these people by birth, only by marriage."

"And you are now a duchess. Never forget that fact, wife."

"I will not forget."

"Before we go in, there is one more thing I wish to discuss with you, Eva, and I must ask you to honor my wishes."

She nodded focusing on his face.

"I have asked that Lord Huxley not be invited here tonight, but if he does get in then you must stay away from him or come directly to me or Simon. Do not engage with him in anyway, Eva, I need you to promise me this."

"He will not attempt to seek me out."

Daniel wasn't happy with her answer but as the door had just been opened there was little more he could say about the matter.

Light blazed from the Sutton house as Daniel and Eva walked inside and joined the receiving line. Her fingers dug into his arm, yet her face betrayed none of her tension and he wondered if this was also a remnant of her childhood.

"The Duke and Duchess of Stratton!"

"Oh dear Lord, my dinner is about to make a reappearance," Eva whispered, then tried to turn and run.

Daniel, however, had other ideas. Placing an arm around her waist, he walked her forward until they stood before Lord and Lady Sutton. "May I introduce my duchess?"

Daniel shook Lord Sutton's hand. Eva's smile was at best a grimace as she dropped into a curtsy.

"It is indeed a pleasure to meet you, my dear."

Eva stuttered something and then smiled.

Daniel, who was most often the recipient of Eva's smiles, watched the old lord smile back. She had a very sweet, disarming quality about her that made a person want to respond. He could see in Lord Sutton's rheumy eyes that the elderly man had taken an instant liking to her.

"My lady." Daniel placed a hand on Eva's back and moved her to meet Lady Sutton. Not as easy a nut to crack as her husband, Eloisa Sutton had a reputation for putting the fear of God into young ladies.

Daniel watched as Eva withstood the chilly stare from Lady Sutton's eyes. Like his grandmother, this was one of the more formidable society ladies who would not think twice about saying what she thought.

"It is a pleasure to meet you, my lady." Eva's curtsy was perfect.

"I hope God assembled you with a few wits, gal, unlike half the woman of society."

"I believe I was given my share of them, my lady." Eva lifted her chin.

Daniel wanted to applaud as Lady Sutton's mouth twitched. It was a rare talent that produced any emotion in the old woman.

"She'll do, Duke." Lady Sutton turned her back on the duke and duchess and moved onto the next guest.

"I had believed society would be all charm and sophistication. It seems I was mistaken," Eva whispered as they wandered through two huge doors where she could hear the murmur of voices and music drawing closer.

"You did not get that idea from me, wife. If you had

asked, I would have set you straight. Society has more teeth than old Lord Bristow. Now smile, my sweet duchess - we are about to launch you into it."

"You make me sound like a large seafaring vessel." Eva gripped Daniel's arm.

"Large? Surely not. More like a sweet little vessel with a rounded stern and two perfect —"

"Daniel!"

"Eva?" Daniel looked at her with all the innocence of a schoolboy.

"The Duke and Duchess of Stratton!"

"Dear Lord!" Eva whispered as every face below turned to look to the top of the stairs. Huge chandeliers threw light over the guests, and everywhere they looked there was color, from the beautiful dresses to the sparkling gems adorning the women. It was a riot to the senses, and Daniel was sure Eva's knees were trembling beneath her gown.

"Look." Daniel patted the hand that clenched his sleeve. "There, below. Lady Rutledge has a small forest on her hat, and I am sure I saw a bird just seconds ago. It is a stroke of luck our very own Mrs. Potter is not here - she would be most put out to be upstaged by such a confection. Although perhaps the furban could create a stir."

"Where?" Daniel knew Eva was more than happy to be distracted as she searched through the unfamiliar faces below.

"To the left, beside that man who has forced himself into the puce satin coat. Promise you will not let me make a fool of myself like that in my dotage. Do you know I have changed my mind on that gown," he added as they neared the bottom of the stairs. "Being taller than most, I get to look right down your neckline."

"Daniel!"

He smiled into the shocked face of his wife, keeping his expression innocent, his eyes however were another matter entirely.

Thus, society's first real glimpse of the Duchess of Stratton was of her looking adoringly up at her duke, her face alight with laughter.

Daniel placed his hand over Eva's fingers as he made his way around the room, keeping up the small talk, telling her silly little stories about several of the guests they encountered, until slowly the tension in her eased.

"The old windbag before us is Lord Diproth. He will insist I introduce you. Just smile and nod, then tell him you like his waistcoat."

She shot him an uncertain look to see if he was having fun at her expense but could see he was serious.

"Lord Diproth," Daniel said bowing, "please allow me to introduce my wife, the Duchess of Stratton."

"Your Grace," Lord Diproth wheezed.

Eva's hands fluttered over the elderly gentleman as he sank into a bow that took a great deal of effort and time, however he soon righted himself.

"Good evening, Lord Diproth. It is an honor to meet you." Eva's curtsy would have pleased the king.

"Your father would be proud of her, boy."

"It is my fondest wish, my lord," Daniel lied smoothly.

"That is a very handsome waistcoat, my lord." Eva looked at the multi-colored front panels and was rewarded with a smile as the elderly gentleman puffed out his chest.

"The gal obviously has style, Stratton," Lord Diproth said, then wheezed off to the left.

"You now have his undying devotion," Daniel said as they once again started moving. "Perhaps I should rethink my waistcoats," he added, looking at his chest.

"I would give it some thought, your Grace." Eva whispered.

"You have a smart mouth, wife."

"Yes, I believe I do."

Her teasing delighted him. She was growing in confidence daily.

"Dear Lord, Grandmother has seen us." Daniel groaned as she signaled that she wished their presence at her side. "Brace yourself, wife, we must obey."

"Oh dear, must we?"

"I fear it is inevitable," Daniel whispered. "She is not above shrieking my name across a room filled with guests if the mood strikes her."

The Dowager Duchess was seated with two other women, both elderly and equally sharp-eyed. As Eva and the Duke approached, it was clear she'd been the subject of their conversation because - unlike a younger lady who would drop her eyes, blush and immediately and cease talking – each of these three tartars kept on eyeing her up and down and even continuing to discuss her.

"I did not request that material in that style!" the Dowager Duchess snapped as Eva curtsied.

"Thank the Lord for small mercies," Daniel whispered in her ear after he had bowed deeply before the three elderly matrons. Then, holding her close, he made the introductions. "Lady Fairlie, Lady Dunbar, allow me to introduce my wife, the Duchess of Stratton."

Eva curtsied.

"Leave the girl alone, Beatrice, she looks lovely. Had you stuffed her into one of your ill-fitting, old-fashioned dresses, she would have looked frumpy." Lady Dunbar's faded brown eyes twinkled with wicked laughter. "It is lovely to meet you, my dear."

Eva looked at the Dowager Duchess, awaiting her scathing reply, but she merely glared and said nothing to reprimand Lady Dunbar.

"Run along, Daniel, and fetch us something to drink while we have a visit with your duchess." Lady Dunbar dismissed Daniel as though he were an errant schoolboy.

Dear Lord, they would eat her alive, Eva thought as she allowed a paper-thin hand to pull her down onto the already full chaise. She kept hold of Daniel's arm until the last possible minute but knew that unless she wanted to cause a scene, she would have to release him.

He looked down at her and she could see the uncertainty in his eyes.

"I'm parched, Grandson, yet still you stand there!"

His bow was insultingly brief this time, as was the word he hissed and then he was leaving her. Eva watched his long, lithe form disappear from her view.

"My husband had a set of shoulders to rival those." Lady Fairlie sighed.

"And a rather nice pair of legs, if I remember correctly," the Dowager Duchess added.

"And the curls of an Adonis. Do you remember, Agatha, how they used to curl under the brim of his hat?" Lady Dunbar said.

Eva's surprise must have shown on her face because Lady Fairlie remarked, "We are old, dear, not dead."

"Indeed, the younger set forget that we have been around a long time and there is nothing that surprises us." Lady Dunbar surveyed the guests before her.

"They think that with age comes stupidity, yet with age merely comes cunning, my dear granddaughter, and it would pay you to remember that."

Granddaughter. How wonderful that felt. Eva looked at the elderly trio. Anyone foolish enough to think these three were not awake on all fronts was an idiot, indeed. Their bodies may have been old, but their minds were as sharp as ever.

"Now we must discuss your ball, Granddaughter. I will, of course, have it at my house as your husband's is not large enough."

"Ball?" Eva felt that uneasy feeling return at the prospect of hosting anything bigger than a tea party for Claire.

"Yes, a ball, dear, showing society that not only did you snare one of the most sought after bachelors in England but that you are more than equal to the task of playing his duchess. We must show them all that you are a sterling hostess and not some shy country miss."

"I would like to point out that I did not trap the duke into marriage, Lady Fairlie. Indeed, I had little say in the matter," Eva lifted her chin. "And I see no fault in being a country miss."

"You won't last five minutes in society if you get upset at every comment you do not like, dear" Lady Dunbar patted her hand. "Granted, we are more forthright than most…"

"Some call us vicious, Agatha," the Dowager Duchess added calmly, which made all three ladies chuckle.

"Yet we are here to help you, my dear, and believe me when I say we have a wealth of experience at our fingertips." Lady Fairlie added.

"Of course." Eva nodded, although what she was agreeing to she had no idea.

"Excellent. I will expect you at eleven a.m. tomorrow - and be prompt," her grandmother barked. "We have much to organize."

"Yes, your Grace," Eva felt her newfound confidence erode.

"Where is your wife?" Simon enquired as Daniel approached him.

"She is with my grandmother and Ladies Dunbar and Fairlie."

"Dear God, what were you thinking? Those three will eat her whole without pausing to draw breath. For shame, Daniel, this is her first social engagement and you cast her to the wolves." Standing on his toes, Simon looked for Eva.

"I'm fairly sure I should be insulted over that statement about my grandmother, Kelkirk. You have no need to fear for Eva - they will let no harm befall her," he added defensively. After all, what could possibly happen in a crowded ballroom? Hell, now he was starting to get nervous.

"Those three could have interrogated for Wellington, Daniel. I have suffered their tactics often. Give me Napoleon any day."

"Christ what was I thinking?" Daniel started retracing his steps.

"For pities sake run!"

Daniel ignored his friend's words, but his feet did not slow until he heard the twinkle of Eva's laughter. That was a good sign, surely?

"Where are our refreshments, Duke?"

"A servant will bring them shortly." Daniel held out his hand to Eva, who instantly took hold of it and allowed him to pull her to her feet. "Come, we will dance. Ladies," he added, acknowledging the three elderly women who were watching him avidly.

"Are you all right, Eva?"

"Yes thank you, Simon." Eva smiled as Simon walked past with a pretty lady on his arm.

"He took me to task for leaving you with my grandmother and her cronies," Daniel said.

"I did feel like the last man on a sinking ship for a moment there."

"But you are stronger than you realize, Duchess, and I think it is only you who is not aware of that fact yet."

Was she? Eva thought that perhaps he was right. Looking around her, she became aware of just where she was and what she was doing.

"I'm waltzing in a ballroom."

"So you are, Duchess, and you dance very well for

someone who has not had much practice." Daniel gently led her through a turn that she managed without tripping over his feet.

"Yes -" she gave him a shy smile "- I do." Eva looked up at him and even though they were surrounded by hundreds of people, she was aware of only him. His intent grey eyes were focused on her also. "Thank you."

He understood that the thank you was for so much more than the waltz.

"The pleasure is all mine." Daniel's eyes were on her lips. Eva could almost feel his kiss. She longed to rise to her toes and press her mouth to his.

"You're beautiful," he said, sounding as if the admission was causing him pain.

"So are you."

He snorted. "Men are not beautiful, Duchess. Handsome, yes, even pleasing, but beautiful, no."

"The music has finished, your Graces."

"Eva looked into the smiling face of the lady who was walking past them with her partner.

"Thank you, Lady Tilbury."

"Is something wrong, Daniel?" Eva questioned as she noted he was now scowling.

"Come, Duchess." He did not answer her question, instead grabbing her hand and towing her from the dance floor. They did not stop until Claire stood before them.

"Good evening, Daniel, Eva."

"I shall leave my wife in your hands, Claire."

"You're leaving?" Eva hadn't meant her words to sound desperate, but the thought of being in this room filled with strangers, without him at her side, was daunting.

"I will return for the second waltz, Duchess."

"Of course." Eva straightened her shoulders. "I shall be fine here with Claire." That sounded better, stronger, as if she was in control and not quaking with nerves inside.

He gave her a last, intent look before walking away.

"You look beautiful, Eva." Claire took her hands, holding them wide. "It is a far cry from the dress I first saw you in."

"'Not quite the thing', I believe you said." Eva remembered that day clearly, because after Claire left, she had been attacked by Gilbert Huxley. Was he here? She hoped not.

Thinking of Lord Huxley brought her father to mind. How could she have given him Daniel's grandfather's ring? Dear Lord, what would her husband think of her if ever he found out? It had been desperation that had made her hand it to Bartholomew. She'd had nothing else to give at such short notice. If pushed by Daniel to hand it back, she could say she had lost it or it had slipped off her finger. She hated betraying him now, when they seemed to be bridging the gaps that had kept them distant from each other, yet she had to if she was to keep both he and Reggie safe.

# CHAPTER TEN

"Two of the most beautiful woman in the room and standing together. I am blessed, indeed."

"Simon, how are you this evening?" Eva placed her hand in his as he joined them. He looked handsome with his silver hair and black evening jacket.

"Very well, your Grace. Good evening, Miss Belmont," he added.

"Lord Kelkirk." Claire sank into a curtsy with great reluctance.

"Will you dance with me soon, Eva?"

"I would love to."

"And you, Miss Belmont, would you dance with me also?"

"My card is full, Lord Kelkirk."

Eva watched his mouth draw into a thin line before he relaxed once more. "I shall return for you shortly, Eva."

"That man is insufferably rude," Claire snapped, glaring at Lord Kelkirk's retreating back.

"Simon? Surely not. I think he is one of kindest gentleman I know," Eva stated. "Not that I know many gentlemen, but he has always been so lovely to me, Claire."

Claire didn't speak straight away, her eyes on Simon's retreating back. She looked pretty in soft apple blossom, her hair pinned into place with tiny diamond pins that sparkled as they caught the candlelight. "I am sorry, Eva. It is just that I...he seems to annoy me for some reason that I cannot identify."

Eva thought she knew why Simon annoyed Claire but was not about to enlighten her friend. In time, they would work it out for themselves.

"We can't like everyone we meet and I am sure one day you and Simon will be friends."

Claire made a scoffing sound but said nothing further.

"The Dowager Duchess has informed me that I must host a ball which she will hold at her home," Eva said, changing the subject. "I am to present myself there promptly at eleven a.m. tomorrow to discuss the preparations."

"Did she, by God. Old tarter. Still..." Claire chewed her lip thoughtfully. "She is right - you do need to launch yourself into society, and hosting your own ball will be just the event to assure your name sits on all the right lips. And as much as I do not relish spending time in the dowager's company, Eva, for you I will offer any support you need." Claire looked like she had swallowed something vile.

"She is really not all that bad. In fact she and the ladies Fairlie and Dunbar were rather sweet when I sat with them earlier."

"Sweet!" Claire shuddered.

"Now, brace yourself, my friend. You are about to dance until your feet are weary."

"Pardon?" Confused, Eva looked at Claire.

"You are the new Duchess of Stratton, the latest curiosity, and now they will want to get to know you."

"They?"

"Them." Claire nodded toward the throng of people.

"Surely not all of them?" Eva said, only half joking.

"Not all, but quite a few and here comes your first."

Eva watched as a tall, elegantly dressed man made his way toward her.

"And I am to accept all these requests to dance?"

"Yes." Claire smiled at the man as he stopped before them. "Lord Culliver, how do you do this evening?"

"Very well, Miss Belmont." Lord Culliver bowed before them. "I wonder if you would be so kind as to introduce me to the Duchess of Stratton."

Eva looked confused as the man spoke to Claire and not her when it was she he wanted to meet.

"Your Grace, allow me to introduce Lord Culliver to you." Claire turned to face Eva, as Lord Culliver did.

"How do you do, your Grace? May I have the honor of this dance?"

Claire nodded and then widened her eyes, which Eva thought meant she was supposed to return the greeting.

"Good evening, Lord Culliver, and thank you, I would love to dance."

Placing the tips of her fingers on his sleeve, she nodded to Claire and then they made their way to the dance floor. The music started and taking a deep breath, she searched her memory for the steps to the Cotillion. It did not take long to master the dance and soon Eva was enjoying herself.

It was unsettling at first to be holding hands with complete strangers and yet they thought nothing of it; therefore, neither would she.

"Had I known that a delicate flower such as yourself was secreted away in the country, your Grace, I would have moved heaven and earth to reach you before the duke."

Eva smiled to Lord Culliver as they joined hands once again. "Thank you, my lord."

When the dance finished, he returned her to Claire, where another awaited her introduction and so the night went. Eva soon realized there was not much to learn about social chitchat. You answered with a thank you and a name when complimented and usually the recipient was happy to take up the reins and talk about either himself or the latest piece of gossip. She didn't like the leering or touching and in some cases the foul-smelling breath, but for the most part, she coped. Many made pointed suggestions about her rushed marriage to Daniel but those she avoided with a smile or a murmur.

She saw Daniel dancing with other women and refused to acknowledge that the sharp pain inside her was jealousy. These people had been part of his world for a long time and unlike her, he was comfortable in this setting. Occasionally, he caught her eye and tilted his head but he did not come near her again.

"Well, I declare the first social outing for the Duchess of Stratton a huge success," Claire said when Eva returned from yet another dance.

Too tired to say anything, Eva just nodded and slipped into the seat beside her. How did these people dance for so many hours every night?

"There is hardly a man present who has not approached you, Eva."

Eva's feet throbbed as she looked around her. Surely it was well past midnight and time to go home? "And I must do this again soon?"

"Yes. Possibly tomorrow night, depending on what invitations Daniel has accepted."

Eva groaned as she slumped into the uncomfortable chair. She would never survive the remainder of the season.

"My dear Berengaria."

Both she and Claire stiffened as Gilbert Huxley approached. His smile was a mere curl of the lips and his smooth looks, to her mind, made him appear reptilian.

"Lord Huxley. Good evening." Eva stood and took Claire's arm as she did the same.

"I did not realize you knew the Duchess of Stratton, Lord Huxley." Claire's tone could have frozen the Thames.

"Berengaria and I are old friends, Miss Belmont, aren't we, my dear?"

His words made their association sound intimate and Eva prayed no one else heard them.

"Lord Huxley is an acquaintance of my father's, Claire." His eyes narrowed as she clarified their relationship.

"I am friend to all the Winchcombs, Miss Belmont. An acquaintance of long standing, you understand. And to that point, Berengaria, how are you enjoying your first foray into our ranks?"

"As a duchess, I have, of course, been welcomed with open arms, which should not surprise you, Lord Huxley, considering who my husband is."

Claire squeezed her arm in support but remained silent. Perhaps she sensed the tension between Eva and Lord Huxley.

"Yes, you have undergone quite the transition from country maid to duchess, Berengaria."

Eva withstood his eyes raking over her body.

"And now we shall dance for old time's sake." He held his hand toward her and Eva fought the urge to slap it aside.

"I had thought to sit this one out, Lord Huxley. I fear my feet are not yet accustomed to such vigorous exercise." Eva did not want Daniel to see her talking or dancing with Lord Huxley, especially when he had expressly told her not to in the carriage on the way here.

"It is merely a gentle waltz, my dear Berengaria - nothing overzealous, I assure you." He smiled at her, although the gesture failed to reach his eyes.

If she refused him would he cause a scene? Eva could not afford that to happen with so many eyes upon her. Perhaps she could dance and return to Claire before Daniel noticed she was with Lord Huxley.

"Eva, if you –"

"I'm going to dance with Lord Huxley, Claire. I shall return soon."

How could she suddenly feel so alone surrounded by so many people? Lord Huxley swung her into his arms, his fingers gripping hers so hard, she wanted to wince. But Eva knew how to hide what she felt.

"I knew you would dance like an angel, my dear. I hope to have the honor of partnering you often."

Eva tried to keep the correct distance as he pulled her

closer. It was the second waltz she realized, the dance she had promised to Daniel. If only her husband had come sooner to claim her then Huxley would not have approached and she would now be in the duke's arms.

"I have no wish to dance with you again, Lord Huxley, and would ask you to keep your distance in the future."

He laughed in her face. "I think not, Berengaria. In fact, you and I will be spending a great deal of time together. Otherwise, I may have to tell your husband how you gave away his grandfather's ring."

"My father told you what I gave him?"

"Of course. We are partners, your father and I, and you are now our most prized investment. We have quite a few plans for you."

Eva tripped and Huxley pulled her briefly into his chest before setting her back on her feet.

"I will not allow you to threaten me, Lord Huxley, my husband will hear of it if you do," Eva bluffed.

"Now, Berengaria, we both know that you will tell your husband nothing or I will slice him into pieces and return them to you in a small box, and that goes for your youngest brother, too."

"You will never touch them!"

Her words were a venomous hiss, which made Huxley's eyes widen briefly and then he chuckled. "Don't tell me you actually care for your husband, my dear. How terribly uncivilized of you."

Fear for Daniel's safety had forced her to hand over that ring and she knew that in doing so there was no way to turn back now even if she had wanted to. Daniel would never understand why she had done it and he would see it as a betrayal, especially as he had told her he would protect her from her family.

"Now, in future, Berengaria, you will be a very good girl and do exactly what we tell you."

She didn't speak again and was relieved when the music finished. Looking to where Claire stood, she saw that both Simon and Daniel were now at her side. The duke was scowling but not at her; his eyes were directed at Lord Huxley.

"Your Grace, your wife dances like an angel," Lord Huxley said when they drew near.

Daniel said nothing, instead taking her fingers from Huxley's arm and replacing them on his.

"I will call for you tomorrow, Berengaria, and we shall take my carriage for a jaunt around the park."

"I fear there you are to be disappointed, Huxley. My wife drives solely with me."

"Perhaps we shall go for a walk then, your Grace." Lord Huxley looked from Daniel to Simon and his smiled slipped.

"Of course -"

"I think not." Daniel interrupted his wife, impaling Lord Huxley with his eyes until the other man lowered his.

"Until next time then, Berengaria."

Eva watched the loathsome man turn to leave.

"In future, Huxley, you will call my wife by her correct title."

He didn't stop at Daniel's words but Eva knew he heard them.

"The man is a pig." Claire came to stand in front of Eva and ran her eyes over her friend to ensure she was unharmed.

"Did he upset you, Eva?"

"No, Daniel, Lord Huxley was everything he should have been. Please, there is no need to worry."

"I told you to alert me if he approached you, yet instead you danced with him."

She knew he was angry and could read the disappointment in his eyes. Yet how could she have done anything differently, her hands had been tied.

"Surely he was no harm to me here in front of so many people?" Eva said.

"We will discuss this no further here. We are leaving."

Eva didn't argue with Daniel's words. She was exhausted, and dancing with Gilbert Huxley had unsettled her. She hugged Claire, then kissed Simon's cheek and allowed Daniel to lead her from the ballroom.

Eva was sitting on the rug before the fire when Daniel entered her room later that night. She was staring into the flames with an intensity that told him she was deep in thought. Closing the door loudly enough for her to be aware of his presence, he walked barefoot toward her. Her hair hung like ropes of silk around her shoulders and she wore a pale cream nightdress with a sheer wrap over the top that hinted at the sweet body that lay beneath. He could see the arch of one slender foot crossed over the other, and her hands were wrapped around her knees.

"Did you enjoy your first ball, Eva?" Daniel moved to sit in the chair to her left. He was still angry over her dancing with Huxley therefore he did not follow through with his first impulse - to lay her backwards on the rug and lose himself in her soft curves.

"Yes and no."

"Care to elaborate?" Daniel enquired, striving for calm when all he wanted to do was ease the ache in his loins. He studied her profile: the sweep of her spine, the sweet curve of her nose, the thrust of her chin. Every inch intrigued him and she belonged to him. No other man would ever have her, he vowed silently. Just thinking about it made his fists clench. He knew after tonight that other men would want her but he'd never allow that to happen. Sometime in the past few weeks she had come to mean something to Daniel. He wasn't sure what, yet they were now bound together.

"Yes, I enjoyed dressing in that beautiful gown and talking to my new friends and yes, I enjoyed dancing…with some of my partners."

She still would not look his way and Daniel wanted to see her eyes as she spoke and read the expression in their blue depths.

"No, I did not enjoy being the focus of so many prying eyes." Eva dropped her chin to her knees. "And no, I did not like the loud whispers I heard behind my back, or the men who leered at me."

The hiss of flames was the only noise for several seconds. Daniel sighed as she finally looked at him and he saw the confusion.

"With society comes both good and bad, Eva. There are some I count as friends and others who are not and in time you will learn the difference."

"And I must learn these differences myself with no help from you?"

He knew she had been confused when he walked away but he had done so for her own good. Holding out his hand toward her, Daniel was pleased when she placed hers in it and moved to kneel before him. "Married couples are not supposed to spend too much time together or show undue interest in each other." Daniel opened her hand and traced the fine lines of her palm.

"I do not yet understand society. It is filled with nuances and intrigues, all carefully masked behind a smooth, polished façade."

"Very aptly put, Duchess."

"But I think any rule that does not allow a husband and wife to spend time together is a very foolish one, indeed."

"As do I," Daniel said, realizing he meant every word. Leaning forward he touched his lips to hers. "In future, I think we shall forgo that particular rule and make up our own."

"I would not have you change just for me, Daniel. It will take me time to understand all the rules, but I am sure with guidance from you, Grandmother, Simon, and Claire I will catch on."

"I do not want you to change, Eva" Daniel said, knowing it was the truth. "And I do not want to spend the night avoiding you, either, so we will create our own rules."

"Yes, I would like that."

Her skin was beautiful in this light. So smooth, he thought, running a finger down her cheek.

"We need to address the issue of Huxley, Eva. I do not

want him near you again, not after his behavior at Stratton. He is a threat to you and if he does not keep his distance I will take measures to ensure he does."

"Please —" she pressed a finger to his lips "- I do not want to talk of Lord Huxley tonight."

Usually he could read her like a book; every thought that came and went through her head was there for Daniel to see. However, as she lowered her lids and a soft smile formed on her lips, Daniel realized he was at a loss to understand what was going through her head.

"Very well we will leave it for tonight, but we will talk further soon."

Eva wanted to forget about Gilbert Huxley and her father and the things they would demand of her. Tonight she would think only of Daniel and how he made her feel. She knew he was naked beneath the black robe because he slept that way. She'd felt the heated planes of muscle on his chest as she kissed him. The contact with her breasts made her shiver. But he made no move to touch her. His hands lay on his thighs - big fingers splayed on the fabric of his robe.

Eva had never taken the lead in their lovemaking; he had always made sure she found her pleasure before finding his own. She had never seduced him, touched him as he had touched her, kissed him as he...dear Lord, she thought, keeping her gaze on his. Did she dare kiss him...everywhere? Still on her knees she touched her lips to the strong line of his jaw. Slowly she kissed and nibbled the length of his ear, tracing its shell with her tongue.

"Christ, Eva!" Daniel moaned as she blew softly on his

now damp lobe, as he had often done to her. Ignoring his words, she moved to his neck and down to his chest. Pushing his robe aside, she kissed the small indentation under his throat.

He was burning alive. Each touch of her lips made his body tighten. She was a siren, a goddess of pleasure sent to torment him, and she'd only started on his neck. He would be dead by the time she reached his... Dear God, surely she wouldn't...

Stroking the heated flesh, Eva moved her lips to his nipples, then took one into her mouth. His body was clenched beneath her. She felt bold as she touched and stroked him, her body responding to his as he became more aroused. Untying the belt at his waist, she then pushed the material aside.

"I... It would not be wise to... Mother of God!" Daniel groaned as she took his aching length into her hands and began to kiss her way down his stomach. Her fingers enclosed him softly, and then she started to stroke him. Her tentative touches drove him to the brink. "I think that is enough..."

Eva kissed the smooth tip between her fingers, stroking her tongue over the swollen flesh and around the silken head.

Daniel couldn't see; he was sure for the first time in his adult life he had blacked out, so exquisite was the pleasure of her mouth on him. He was going to disgrace himself if he didn't find the strength to take control soon. Her mouth eased over the throbbing head and down the shaft where she glided her lips up and down the taunt length, once, twice…it was pure pleasure bordering pain. Daniel bore it as long as he could then reached for her.

"But, Daniel…" Eva cried as he lifted her to stand before him.

"But Daniel, nothing, woman! You would have found little enjoyment this evening if I had let you carry on."

"But I was enjoying myself." She looked coy and sensual, glancing up at him beneath her lashes.

"Where the hell did you learn that look?" Daniel demanded as he stripped the clothing from her body.

"What look?" Eva pouted.

"I've created a jezebel," he hissed. Pulling her into his arms, he crushed her mouth with his.

He ravaged her, his heated body urging him to find his fulfillment. He would terrify her if he did not pull back. Holding himself still, he tried to slow things down, give her some room, but she was having none of it. Her hands tugged at his hair, pulling him closer, urging him on.

"Easy, Duchess." He rested his forehead on hers while he struggled to fill his lungs with much needed air.

"I don't want to go easy, Daniel." Only he could ease the ache inside her, make her writhe and scream in ecstasy and banish the horror of Gilbert Huxley and her father.

He needed no further prompting. Cupping her breasts, he kissed the swollen flesh, then took one aching peak deep into his mouth. The small noises she made in her throat told Daniel she was as deep under this sensual spell as he. Slipping one hand between her thighs, he stroked her damp flesh. She was ready for him, but he wanted to hear her beg.

Dropping to his knees, he lifted one of her legs. Draping it over his shoulder, he then set about tormenting her, stoking her fires, bringing her again and again to the brink, only to ease back. Eva was sobbing his name, her fingers tugging handfuls of his hair, begging him to release her. Finally he did, plunging his fingers inside her as his tongue swept the small swollen bud. She shattered above him, her body arching toward him. Regaining his feet, he clasped her waist and lifted, then lowered her onto his shaft.

"Wrap your legs around me."

She instantly complied. It was as if her body was his to command. Holding his shoulders, she called his name as he slowly withdrew then re-entered her. The feelings he was creating in her were beyond belief; she couldn't think or draw breath. His hot breath whispered wicked words into her ear as he drove into her again and again, until finally she could take no more.

He felt the beginnings of her release and knew that within seconds she would climax in his arms. Thrusting harder and faster, he joined her. They rode the waves of pleasure, every last drop wrung out of them until Daniel staggered backwards, collapsing into a chair.

The trickle of her tears roused him. Pulling her head from his neck, he used the pads of his thumbs to wipe them away. "Did I hurt you, sweetheart?"

Eva shook her head. "Oh no, Daniel, I… I… It was just so wonderful, I…"

"Ssssh," he whispered against her lips. "I understand." Dear God, he did. Every time he made love to her, his emotions ended shredded at his feet.

With Eva in his arms, he walked through the connecting doors and into his room. He lowered her to the bed. She lay unmoving, limp and thoroughly sated. Pushing the covers aside, he settled them both on the sheets. She murmured something, then wriggled backwards until she was nestled in the curve of his body.

"Goodnight," she sighed.

Daniel pushed her hair aside and kissed a warm cheek. "Goodnight, Duchess."

Eva groaned, rolled over and buried her head under the pillows as her maid opened the curtains.

"A Mr. Winchcomb has called to see you, your Grace."

Eva sat upright. Instinctively her hands clutched the pillow closer.

"Which Mr. Winchcomb, Molly?"

Molly picked up Eva's nightdress where it lay beside the fireplace. "I am not sure, your Grace. Mr. Wernham did not say."

"I…is my husband at home?" Eva asked, praying fervently that he was not.

"No, your Grace, he left early but has organized for two grooms plus myself to accompany you on your visit to the Dowager Duchess's house.

It would be her father. Dear God, why had he come here?

"I have your bathwater ready, your Grace."

Eva, who was usually fairly independent when it came to dressing and bathing, allowed Molly to assist her because her mind had suddenly gone blank.

"Is there a problem, your Grace?"

"Oh…uh, no, Molly." Eva tried to focus on her maid as she arranged her hair. She must gain control of herself - she was now a duchess, and would deal with whatever her father wanted. Her eyes fell on the beautiful sapphire bracelet and necklace Daniel had given her last night. Surely he would not want more from her so soon.

Wernham was waiting for her at the bottom of the stairs. His face wore its usual impassive expression.

"Good morning, Wernham."

"Good morning, your Grace. I have put Mr Winchcomb in the rosewood parlor."

"Thank you and please send a note to the Dowager Duchess of Stratton to say that I will be on time for my eleven a.m. appointment this morning." Eva then took a deep breath and followed the butler. He opened the door and she lifted her chin and walked inside.

"There she is," her father said, climbing to his feet and coming toward her. "My daughter, at last we are again reunited."

"What do you want, Father?" Eva took a step to the side as he reached for her. "Surely you have not come for more money so soon?" This last she whispered so Wernham did not hear.

"Is that any way to greet your dear papa?" Spencer Winchcomb did not look happy at her words. "Dismiss your servant, child, and come and sit with me," he coaxed.

"I have instructions to stay with the duchess when she has visitors, sir, especially male visitors," Wernham added and Eva wondered if her husband had made that decision after last night and her dance with Huxley. Moving to stand beside the door they had just entered, the butler nodded to her and she knew there was no possible way she would be able to move him, even if she wanted to.

"I am no visitor," Winchcomb roared. "I am her father!"

"You will not speak to my staff that way, Father. They are not yours to dictate to." Eva was still standing although her knees were quaking.

"Have you forgotten our discussion so soon, Daughter?"

Eva watched her father struggle to control his temper and then followed him as he moved to the rear of the room out of Wernham's hearing. A muscle had begun to tick in his neck and had they been alone, he would have struck her and she did not rule out the possibility that he would when next they met.

"Why have you come here, Father?"

"I have merely come to see if the duke is looking after my little girl," he said through his teeth. "And to remind her where her duty lies."

So that was it. This was just a visit to intimidate her in her own home. His show of strength to let her know there was nowhere she was safe.

"Lord Huxley was not happy with your behavior last night and urged me to pay you a visit to remind you where your loyalties lie."

This man had tormented her and Reggie most of their lives, and he dared to question her behavior.

"I will do as you say, Father, because the consequences are not worth the risk of disobeying you. However, I will not allow you inside this house again, nor will I allow your revolting friend to torment me."

His lips curled as he grabbed her hand and squeezed it hard.

"We have plans for you, daughter, plans for your future. So we can wait, but in the meantime you will supply us with the funds to continue living like gentlemen."

He pinched her cheek and then he walked from the room, whistling.

"I will show your father to the door, your Grace."

"Thank you, Wernham, and I would ask you not to inform my husband of Mr Winchcomb's visit." Sinking into the nearest chair, Eve then put her head in her hands and tried to think. How was she to escape both her father and Lord Huxley's clutches?

# CHAPTER ELEVEN

"The carriage has arrived, your Grace, and Molly is ready to accompany you," Wernham said, re-entering the room a short while later.

Eva spent the short trip to the Dowager Duchess's townhouse wondering when her father would strike next and trying to work out what he meant by future plans for her. He could blackmail her into giving him money but what else did he have in mind? Pushing the thoughts aside, she focused on the upcoming interview. Like her husband, the Dowager Duchess had her own brand of intimidation and she would need her wits about her.

London was bustling as usual, and Eva realized she was growing accustomed to the strange sights and smells as the carriage rolled through the city streets.

"Mr. Wernham has asked me to stay by your side, your Grace," Molly said, looking determined yet frightened by the prospect.

"That will not be necessary, Molly - the Dowager Duchess will not harm me."

"As to that, your Grace, Mr Wernham says that she can terrify most people into a fit of hysteria."

"Surely not. She is but one old lady, Molly, and my husband's grandmother. I am sure there is nothing to worry about." Eva could tell the maid wasn't convinced, yet she held her tongue, and by the time they arrived, Eva's already taunt nerves were stretched tighter.

She were shown into a small parlor. The walls were dark, the furniture large and austere. She searched for a few lace covers or pretty flowers but could find none.

"At least you are prompt!"

"Thank you, your Grace," Eva sank into a curtsy.

"For pity's sake, girl, call me Grandmother!"

"Really?" Eva felt her cheeks flush with pleasure.

"Really what?" the dowager snapped, taking a seat.

"I may call you Grandmother?"

"I have said so, have I not?"

"Thank you, Grandmother, it will be an honor." Eva moved to the elder woman's side and brushed a kiss on her cheek.

The dowager harrumphed and muttered something about it not being the done thing to be so demonstrative, but secretly, Eva felt the old lady was pleased with the attentions and suddenly she was not so afraid. Daniel had given her a grandmother.

"Come, I will show you the ballroom."

Before she could offer her assistance, the woman had stalked from the room. Eva quickly followed. They walked down stairs, along halls and up more stairs until Eva was thoroughly lost.

"We will have a formal ball. None of this silly theme and mask-wearing carry-on, Granddaughter."

"Of course." Eva looked around her. The ballroom in the dowager's home was huge - surely it could house hundreds of people without them even touching each other. The floors were of beautiful polished wood, and along one side, a row of white doors led to a large balcony.

"My husband and I entertained often when first we wed."

"And of course you were one of those hostesses everyone speaks of," Eva said wistfully as she walked slowly down the room.

"Yes, I was a grand hostess - everyone begged for an invitation to any party I hosted."

Eva sighed as she touched one satin curtain. "I fear I shall fail," she whispered.

"You most certainly will not fail!" the dowager declared. "We shall ensure that, in fact, you are a great success."

Eva looked at her new grandmother. Their eyes held, steely determination in one set and uncertainty in the other. Something passed between them in that moment and Eva wondered briefly if this was what having a mother felt like. Someone who looked out for you, took you to task when required, but cared if you succeeded or failed. She saw acceptance in the elderly woman's gaze.

"In that case, Grandmother, tell me what you wish me to do."

"I will have my staff clean and polish this room till it sparkles. Plenty of flowers I think. I will also have the menus drawn up, since you will have no idea what is required yet."

Eva nodded.

"We will take tea now and work on the guest list."

"Well, I have two friends to put on the list," Eva said wryly.

"Perhaps I will have your husband look over it." The dowager snorted.

Eva followed her as she strode around the room, pointing out this and that. Daniel was so like his grandmother. They were both big and blessed with the belief that wherever they walked, others would follow.

"You will need a new gown for the night and I shall leave that in your hands. Just make sure it is not too revealing - I will not tolerate the new Duchess of Stratton looking like a trollop."

"I shall make sure that is not the case," Eva vowed solemnly.

"Tea is served, my lady," a servant then announced.

Eva took the dowager's arm as they retraced their steps through the huge mansion. After taking her seat, she watched, enchanted, while her grandmother prepared the tea in a long, drawn-out ritual she had obviously undertaken many times.

"The Duke of Stratton, my lady."

Daniel had been on his way to the club when he'd found himself outside his front door. Thoughts of Eva had consumed him all morning. The need to touch her, see her and make her smile had taken precedence over anything else. When Wernham had told him she had gone to visit his grandmother already, he had followed. He would not allow the old woman to censure her. Eva was just starting to gain confidence in herself and he would let no one hinder that.

Walking into the parlor, he stopped. Dear God, his grandmother was laughing. In fact, if he was not mistaken, she had tears raining down her cheeks. His wife was giggling, a husky little laugh that rolled down his spine and made his stomach clench.

"Daniel!"

"Hello, Duchess." Eva came toward him, her smile spontaneous and genuine. Taking the hand she held out to him, he kissed the palm.

"Such an unseemly display in public," the dowager huffed.

"Surely not unseemly, Grandmother," Eva protested. "After all, you are not public - you are family. Therefore, the rules do not apply."

Daniel waited for the set-down from the older lady and then he would step in and defend his duchess.

"She has spirit, Grandson," his grandmother said, to his surprise. He could see the laughter in her eyes as she looked at Eva; it seemed his wife had enlisted the dowager to her ranks of devotees.

"May I steal her away, Grandmother?"

"Yes, go. I have much to do. But I will see you again on Thursday, Granddaughter."

"I will be prompt, Grandmother." Eva bent to kiss her cheek, something Daniel rarely did. It seemed Eva was breaking down barriers and not just inside him.

Daniel moved to kiss his Grandmother, too. "Thank you for making her welcome."

"Look after her, Grandson, or you will have me to answer to," the dowager whispered back.

"With my life," Daniel vowed.

"Where are we going, Daniel?" Eva asked him when they were in the carriage.

"Be patient and you shall soon see."

A short time later, Daniel helped Eva from the carriage after it drew up outside the British Museum.

Two days earlier, he'd told her in an offhand way that he intended to visit a new exhibit of Parthenon sculptures that had recently been put on display. To Daniel's surprise, Eva had immediately said, 'Not the Elgin Marbles?' to which he'd replied in a stunned voice, 'Yes.'

"So how do you know about the Elgin Marbles?" he asked now, watching her face intently as she looked up at the building before her. Her eyes were sparkling and her body quivered with excitement.

"I read about them in the newspaper. It said Lord Elgin acquired a collection of stone objects when he was ambassador to the Ottoman Court of the Sultan in Istanbul, plus there were some items from Athens. I understand the British Museum has only just purchased them from him."

Surprised that his wife knew of such things, and stunned that she might actually share his passion for old artifacts, Daniel could only manage to nod.

"I have always wished to visit here." She stood beside the carriage with her hands pressed together, looking up at the museum. She looked sweet and tempting in her long blue coat and bonnet and Daniel wondered at her allure. Was it the innocence of a woman raised outside society or the vulnerability due to how she had been raised that got to him? She had no false side, no arts or allurements and he would do his damndest to ensure she stayed that way.

"Then let us grant that wish, Duchess." Daniel held out his hand and she took it, slipping her fingers between his.

She dragged him everywhere, to see every vase, every Egyptian artifact, exclaiming while studying each from every angle. A poor hapless curator was often asked to explain what Daniel could not, although he acquitted himself quite well.

"Do we get to stop for tea?" Daniel brushed a smudge of dirt off Eva's cheek as she turned to look up at him.

"This is your place, Daniel, isn't it?"

"My place?" he questioned, studying his disheveled wife. He had never known anyone who studied an artifact as thoroughly as her. Several long curls had escaped her bonnet, her pale lemon-and-white dress was smudged in places, but her eyes were alight with an energy that he could not help but share.

"Where you go to be on your own and escape all the pressures your position places upon you."

How had she known that? "Yes. When I'm in London, I come here when I need to think or be alone."

She turned back to the cabinet to continue inspecting its contents.

"Everyone needs a place like that."

"Where was your place, Duchess?" Daniel moved behind her to look over her shoulder.

"A small shed tucked in the forest behind my father's home."

She had a shed to hide in while he had a whole museum. "Well, now you can share my museum."

She didn't look at him but he heard her softly spoken words. "I'd like that."

"Now I think we should leave the rest for another day." Daniel took her arm and started propelling her toward the exit before she found something else to inspect.

"Must we? I am sure there is still time before closing, and I wanted to see everything," Eva batted her eyelashes at him, then licked her lips for good measure.

"That only works in the bedroom, and yes, we must," Daniel ignored her pleading, instead taking her hand in his. "We will stop at Gunthers for an ice and you can have another first," Daniel said, which mollified her slightly.

She'd lost her inhibitions in the museum and chattered like a small child the entire carriage trip, telling him all the things she had seen, which, naturally, he had also seen, but Daniel did not remind her of that fact. Instead, he simply listened. She made him feel young again, less jaded. Here and now the shadows he often saw in her eyes had vanished and the secrets he was sure she still hid from him were, for a while, forgotten.

"You should probably draw a breath before you pass out, wife," Daniel drawled as she launched into another detailed description of a statue.

Hers was lemon; his, rum, and they ate their ices seated at a small table in the shade of a tree. Around them, other people were engrossed in the same activity. Only the occasional hum of conversation could be heard as everyone enjoyed their delicious treats.

"This is surely the food of angels, Daniel." Eva sighed as she took another lick of the treat.

"I fear I am setting you up with several vices, Duchess."

"Ahhhh, but what a vice, Duke."

"Did you have any visitors this morning?" Daniel watched the smile fall from her face and her eyes flit away. She lowered her lashes to hide her expression from him. Damn her bloody family. Wernham had told him about the visit from her father and how Winchcomb had threatened Eva. His first instinct had been to go round to the man's house and beat him to a pulp, but he had restrained himself and decided to speak with her first.

"Visitors, Daniel?" Eva was looking everywhere but at her husband.

"Namely your father."

"Wernham promised me he wouldn't tell you."

"He didn't. I just knew he had something to say because he followed me around the house talking incessantly until I threatened to thrash him if he didn't tell me what was on his mind."

"My father simply called on me to see if I was all right."

They both knew that was a lie and Daniel wondered why, as she had last night with Huxley, she was protecting her father now.

"I'm not sure why you're defending him or Huxley, Eva, but it does not sit comfortably with me."

Her eyes shot to his and then back to her hands.

"Th-they are no threat to me now."

Neither of them believed that, either.

"Your father and Huxley will always be a threat to you if

you let them, Duchess. Therefore you must come to me with any attempts from either of them to hurt or threaten you."

She didn't respond to that comment, but he saw the tension in her shoulders. She was no longer the laughing, relaxed companion of minutes before.

"I should not have found out about your father's visit from our butler, Eva. You should have told me," he said, giving her a look that spoke volumes about his disappointment in her.

"I have no wish for you and my father to confront each other, Daniel."

Not many people had ever offered Daniel protection in his lifetime and it humbled him that Eva wanted to.

"I understand you are used to dealing with your family by yourself, Eva, but I must have a promise from you that you will tell me at once if in future any of them try to contact you again. I promised to protect you when we left Stratton, but I cannot do so if you do not let me."

"They will not contact me again."

"Promise me, Eva."

They looked silently at each other for several seconds and it was she who spoke first. "Please do not go and see either my father or Lord Huxley, Daniel," Eva begged. "They are not to be trusted and I want you nowhere near them."

"Tell me why you fear them so much? What do they hold over you?"

"Nothing. They hold nothing over me." Daniel heard the lie in her shrill words and decided it was time to take action. He needed to start digging deeper. Something was wrong and if she would not tell him, he would find out through other means.

"I cannot make you tell me what is wrong, Eva, and I had hoped you would come to me when you were ready. However -" he lifted one hand as she tried to speak "- I want you to remember that I am a duke and you a duchess and it is Huxley and your family who should be wary of us, not the reverse. If your fear is for Huxley's reputation with a sword then I would ask you again to have faith in me, I am a skilled swordsman also."

"Promise me you will not approach them, Daniel! I cannot bear to think of you anywhere near them."

"I will only promise not to seek your father out this time," Daniel said. "But if he or any of his sons continue to threaten you in any way, my promise will no longer stand."

"Thank you."

"You're welcome." Daniel offered her his hand as he stood.

"The Duke and Duchess of Stratton. Look, Miss Myers, do they not make a lovely couple?"

Daniel knew who the voice belonged to but did not turn to face him until he had helped Eva from her seat. She stiffened and moved closer to his side. Slipping an arm around her waist, he squeezed her gently before turning.

"Miss Myers, Lord Huxley." Daniel offered a short, insulting bow while still holding his wife close to his side.

"Your Grace." Huxley took Eva's hand in his and lifted it to his lips and Daniel felt the sudden tension in her as she snatched it back.

"Are you well, Miss Myers?" Daniel looked at the young

lady as Eva questioned her. She did look a bit distressed. Had Huxley done something to her?

"I wonder if I may impose on you to look at my hem, your Grace. I fear it is torn and trailing behind me."

"Oh, of course."

Daniel reluctantly released Eva as she patted his fingers. He watched as she bent over to inspect the fabric of Miss Myers's hem.

"My congratulations, Duke."

Daniel looked at Huxley but the man's eyes were on Eva. "Congratulations?" Daniel queried in that soft voice that usually made people stand to attention.

"On finding such a rare gem. I have known her for many years and had hoped..."

Daniel watched as Huxley gave Eva a final look before facing him. The man was a parasite whose very existence was to feed off others. He slept with other men's wives and preyed on young, rich men, often luring them into gambling, which caused some to lose their fortunes. He had fought numerous duels and rarely, if ever, lost. Daniel and Huxley did not often meet - their circles were made up of different men - but Huxley had obviously fixed his intentions on Eva some time ago. Daniel would have to un-fix them, permanently.

"One thing you should know about me, Huxley," Daniel said in a conversational tone so Eva was not alerted, "is that what is mine I protect, and if you cross me, be very clear on who will be the winner."

Huxley paled and took a step backwards.

Daniel followed. "If you ever subject my wife to your

unwanted attentions or your eyes pass over her in that insulting manner again, I will take that as a direct insult and my seconds will be upon you in minutes...that is, if I choose to wait until dawn," Daniel added. "I know you visited her at Stratton but as yet I do not know what took place, but I will, and if through some misguided belief, you think I will not protect her or deal with any threat against her, then I advise you to strongly think again."

"Sh-she has always welcomed me with open arms."

"She loathes you, Huxley, and you are deluding only yourself in believing otherwise."

"Y-you misunderstand me, your Grace."

"I think not, my lord, but now I think you understand me and be very careful where you step from this moment on, because if I ever find out that you are threatening or intimidating my wife, there will be nowhere for you to hide, and remember this, Huxley. I am not scared of you like so many others."

Turning his back on the man, Daniel took Eva's arm again, bowed to Miss Myers and led his wife back to their waiting carriage.

. . .

"We are to go to the theatre tonight, Eva, with Claire and Simon," Daniel said over his newspaper the following morning. "And I cannot believe I'm saying this, but my grandmother and Lady Dunbar are attending also."

Eva, who was spreading strawberry conserves on a muffin, nodded. "You invited your grandmother? That was very nice of you."

"Actually she invited herself and I simply agreed."

"What does it say on the back bit there?" Eva leaned over to tap the back of his paper. "About a new exhibition on Egyptian artifacts?"

"If you have just put strawberry conserve on my paper, I will not be pleased, wife."

"Then perhaps you could just give me that back piece," Eva said, reaching over to tug it out of his grasp.

"If I remember correctly, you vowed to honor and obey me," Daniel muttered.

"Lord Kelkirk, your Grace," Wernham said, opening the door.

Eva smiled as Simon strolled into the breakfast parlor. As usual, his face wore a calm, unruffled expression and he was dressed in the height of fashion. "Simon. How lovely to see you. Would you like something to eat?"

"He has his own home. Can he not eat there?" Daniel retrieved his newspaper.

"I was reading that." Eva frowned as he pulled it from her hands.

Daniel looked at Simon, who in turn looked at Eva.

"If ever there was a reason to re-enforce my current unmarried state, having to share my morning newspaper would be it." Simon said, lifting a silver lid on the sideboard and peering beneath. "May I suggest you read it in your study? Surely in there you will be safe."

"Now there's a thought." Daniel once again buried his head in the newsprint.

"Lord Lucien has four greys that he is selling, Daniel, and I want to be the first to see them." Simon stole the last muffin and slathered it in honey.

"And this concerns me because…?"

Simon placed one hand on top of the paper and pushed it down. "Because, and I say this reluctantly, you are a very fine judge of horse flesh and I value your opinion."

Eva noted that Simon looked like he'd sucked on a lemon as he spoke.

"I'm flattered." Daniel folded the newspaper and passed it across the table to his wife. "And as you have begged so nicely, I will, of course, accompany you."

"I did not beg - I asked. There is a subtle difference," Simon said.

"Will Claire be here shortly, Eva?" Daniel enquired.

"Yes, we are to visit the bazaar - it is for the orphans and widows."

"My God! Come, let us leave, Stratton, before that virago arrives." Simon shuddered.

"Claire is not a virago!" Eva declared.

"Methinks the man protests too much," Daniel said with a sly smile. "Have a nice morning, Duchess, and be sure to kept Molly at your side. I will instruct two of the footman to accompany you at all times also, he added, kissing the top of Eva's head. Eva lifted her face so he kissed that, too.

"I protest too much about what?" Simon demanded as he and Daniel left the room.

. . .

"I always attend the bazaar during the season." Claire slipped her arm through Eva's as they began to stroll through the stalls. "I like to support the widows but in all honesty there is always a wonderful array of things on display."

Eva felt a flush of warmth. She had still not gotten used to the fact that this woman actually liked her. Her life seemed to be filled with moments of extreme happiness and dark despair. Happiness when she was with Claire or Daniel - especially Daniel. He made her forget about her father and the terrible thing she had done. He made her laugh and sigh, but most of all he made her believe in the future, a future for them.

Her father had approached her twice more and she had given him the spending money Daniel had given her the first time, and the small pearl pendant, which he had gifted her recently, the second time. It had nearly broken her heart to hand it over. Spencer Winchcomb had simply laughed at her distress and said there would be plenty more where that came from and surely keeping her husband's health intact was more important than a few baubles. Eva had realized then that unless she took a stand, they would never leave her alone. She had brought herself some time when her father had approached her again, telling him she had nothing else to give at that moment and if he wanted her to continue supplying him things he would have to wait awhile. So far, he had kept his distance. Lord Huxley had not approached her again, either, but wherever she and Daniel went at night, she could feel his eyes on her. Watching and waiting, but for what she was not sure. She was terrified of the threat against Daniel, terrified Huxley would challenge him, but she also knew she had to find a way to break all ties with both her father and Lord Huxley or she would never be free to live her life.

Her next letter to Reggie had contained the truth. She had told him everything and warned him of their father's threats and begged him to be vigilant. That was all she could do for now. She had told him that Daniel did not know and pleaded with him not to tell him until she was ready to do so herself.

"Do look at this blanket, Eva."

Inspecting the soft, white wool, Eva pushed her dark thoughts aside. "I received a letter from Reggie this morning and he is settled and very happy. His studies are keeping him busy, as are his new friends."

"Even though you miss him, you must be relieved, Eva."

"Yes, I am happy for him and yes, I miss him but I have..."

"Daniel," Claire filled the gap when Eva hesitated.

Blushing, she nodded.

"Oh, look! Is that toffee? I have always wanted to try it." Eva cried as they passed another stall.

"You haven't tried toffee?" Claire's face was a picture of horror as she dragged her closer.

"No." Eva eyed the small squares of confection eagerly.

"Sacrilege!" Claire signaled to the lady who was running the stall that they would take several pieces.

After handing several pieces of toffee to Molly and the two footmen, Eva and Claire continued to wander with their mouths full of the delicious sweet. Claire studied knitted shawls while Eva, still chewing her toffee, stood a little to one side. She smiled to several passersby and then a noise drew her eyes behind the tent to where three young men seemed to be handling something, throwing it backwards and forwards between them, and when she heard a yelp, she knew it was an animal of some kind.

"Hold these!" Eva thrust her parcels and toffee into Claire's hands.

"Where are you going?"

"Stop that at once!"

The boys turned to look at Eva as she yelled at them. All wore identical expressions of surprise when they saw who had spoken.

"How would you like me to throw you around?" Eva glared at the boy who held the wriggling puppy.

"How about we throw you around, love, and then we could all have some fun," one of the boys said, moving closer to Eva. His fingers wrapped around her wrist and he tried to pull her nearer.

"Unhand her at once!"

The boy's eyes widened as both footmen suddenly appeared at her side. He dropped her arm quickly as they scowled at him.

"Eva!" Claire arrived seconds later. "What is going on?"

"Give me that puppy now!" Eva demanded ignoring Claire in favor of glaring at the boy who held the dog. A little wriggling body was thrust into her arms and then the boys ran off.

"He's very dirty, Eva." Claire peered down at the puppy in her arms. "And he will cover you with fleas and disease."

Eva didn't care. She stroked one small ear and the puppy looked up at her, his big dark eyes seeming to study her, and then his body shuddered and he burrowed his head into her arm.

"Oh, you clever devil, he knows a soft touch when he sees one." Claire took out one of her newly purchased shawls and wrapped it around the shivering little body.

"I want to keep him." Eva stroked his head.

"Well, in that case, I think this signals the end to our shopping." Gathering her parcels, Claire led the way with Eva following, clutching the puppy in her arms.

"Shall I take him for you, your Grace?"

"No thank you, Molly." Eva was not letting him go.

The duke wasn't home when Eva returned, so with the help of a reluctant Wernham and Molly, she bathed the puppy and fed him, then found a pillow to lay him and his new shawl on. Now that he was clean, she could see his fur was white and grey and he had a black ring around one eye. He was the sweetest puppy Eva had ever seen and she hoped Daniel felt the same. She was very conscious of all the things Daniel had indulged her in and she had no wish to force him into allowing her to keep the puppy just because she had never had one before.

"You called for me, your Grace?"

"Yes, thank you, Molly." Eva looked down at her dress; it seemed she had more water on her than the puppy had. "If you will just help me undress, I wish to rest for a while before getting ready for the theatre this evening."

Daniel had not seen his wife since breakfast and was not about to analyze why that bothered him so much. Entering her room, he found her sitting on her bed dressed in a robe.

"Hello, Daniel, how were the horses?"

"Nags with sway backs and short hocks. Simon has no

idea on horse flesh." Daniel looked down at his wife. "How was your bazaar?"

"Uh...well, it was pleasant."

Her hesitation told him there was more to this conversation. "And did you buy anything?"

"Yes - and Daniel, I have to tell you something."

"Yes?"

"I...I... Oh dear, I think I will just show you." Eva got to her feet and went into the dressing room.

Perplexed, Daniel watched Eva disappear and then re-appear clutching a soft, white woolen shawl in her arms.

"It's beautiful, my sweet, but hardly my color," he teased. She was so serious, a crease had formed between her eyes as she walked toward him.

"The thing is, Daniel, you have given me more than I could ever wish for and I would never force anything upon you or use my past to coerce you into indulging me."

"I know that." And he did. Eva did not have a mercenary bone in her body.

"Really?"

"Really."

"The thing is, Daniel, this puppy was being bullied by three boys and I saved him." She placed the sleeping dog into Daniel's arms.

No one made a sound for several seconds. Daniel looked down at the slumbering animal. Lifting one hand, he stroked its spine, his big hand completely covering the small body.

"If...if you feel you cannot tolerate having him in the house, I thought perhaps he could live with one of servants, or maybe in the garden shed or..."

"Ssssh, Eva," Daniel reached for her, then urged her onto his lap.

"Isn't he cute?" she whispered, laying her head on his shoulder.

"Yes, and he will chew our shoes and no doubt release his bowels on the carpet, but I think we should keep him." Daniel kissed her cheek.

"Did you ever have a puppy, Daniel?"

"No."

"Nor did I."

"So what are you going to call him?"

"Furban."

"Perfect." Daniel laughed so hard, the puppy woke. "But I insist he sleep somewhere other than your bedroom."

"Of course. I shall have Wernham find just the place for him." Eva rose to take the puppy back to his bed. "I had toffee today, Daniel, and I think it may surpass a Gunther's ice as my favorite sweet," she said when she returned.

"Eva, Wernham tells me you have misplaced your pendant."

He watched the color leech from her cheeks as she nodded. "Yes. I'm so sorry, Daniel." Guilt was written all over her face and he felt a chill run down his spine. Why was she lying to him again?

"Eva, where is your necklace?" His words were harsh but he was past caring. This time he wanted the truth.

"I...I have lost it, Daniel, as Wernham told you."

She was hiding something and he was determined to find out what. "Eva - "

"I must get Molly to take Furban outside. Excuse me, Daniel."

He watched her go, eyes narrowed in thought. Tonight she would be in his arms in his bed and he would not let her leave until she told him everything.

# CHAPTER TWELVE

"*S*sh, for pity's sake, Eva, the actors will hear you."

"Sorry, Claire, but you must admit he looks silly," she whispered back.

"Silly? He looks like an overripe peach," Claire added from her seat to Eva's left.

"Sort of all hairy and fleshy, do you mean?"

Eva looked down at the actors again. This was her first play and she could not believe what was taking place around her. Not just the performance - which was actually not all that good - but the antics going on in the stalls below. People were screeching with laughter, some even throwing things at each other. Meanwhile, the actors were taking it all in their stride.

"His head could be the pip," Lady Dunbar said. She and the Dowager Duchess were sitting to Eva's right and Simon and Daniel were seated at the rear. Claire had at first been nervous about sitting so close to Daniel's grandmother but the old lady had been surprisingly pleasant so far.

"Stone, I think you mean."

"Thank you, Beatrice – yes, I did mean stone. However, now I think on it, I have yet to see a peach with a stone on its head."

"May I suggest melon as a substitute?" Simon offered over Claire's shoulder before turning his attention back to a discussion he was having with the Daniel.

Eva heard the word Bonaparte and Wellington then little else.

"No, but thank you, Simon, melon suggests round and smooth," Eva said.

The women turned their eyes to the stage. Round and smooth were definitely not words to describe the actor.

"Orange?" Simon proffered.

"No," the four women said simultaneously.

"Pear?"

"Now you're just being ridiculous, Simon," Claire scoffed.

"Accept my apologies, Miss Belton. I had not understood the gravity of the conversation," Simon replied in a deep drawl.

Eva was pleased to see Simon and Claire had formed a truce and were being scrupulously polite to each other, although perhaps a little too polite, she thought, studying the glint in her friend's eyes.

"Are you enjoying your first theatre experience, Duchess?"

Eva shivered as the deep words tickled her ear. Turning, she looked at her husband. He had known she was lying earlier today when he questioned her about her pendant and guilt had nearly made her confess but fear had kept her quiet. Fear that he would turn away from her, that what they had found would be gone forever, had made her remain silent and walk away from him.

The feel of his fingers on her cheek made tears sting behind her eyes. He deserved the truth from her, yet she was too much of a coward to tell him.

Eva looked at the stage while she listened to her friends discussing and dismissing various varieties of fruit. What had she done to deserve so much happiness? And how would she cope if Daniel was taken from her? Never had she cared for another person like she did her husband and it terrified her to realize that without him she would be lost.

"Don't frown, Eva. Wrinkles will come in their own time - there is no need to aid them."

"Sorry, Claire," Eva ignored the snort of humor from her husband. However, she could not ignore his hand as his fingers lightly brushed the back of her neck. Giving herself a mental shake, she once again refocused on the stage.

"What have you called the puppy?" Claire asked.

"Furban."

Simon laughed and everyone demanded to know the reason, and thoroughly enjoyed the tale of Mrs. Potter and her ferret turban.

"I have it. He could be a selection of fruit!" Claire cried, then clapped a hand over her mouth as all eyes looked at the Stratton box.

Simon groaned but everyone else laughed.

"His head and neck could be the pear," Claire said.

"The body of a peach," Eva added.

"Good Lord! Is that Lady Bethelhume who just threw her drink over the ghastly Mr Priestly?" Lady Dunbar demanded, cutting through their silly conversation.

In seconds, the entire Stratton party was pressed against the edge of the theatre box and peering down at the melee below.

"Nice shot, Lady Bethelhume!" Daniel called as the lady in question swung her fist into the face of a young man.

"Why is she hitting Mr Priestly, Daniel?" Eva queried.

"Priestly took her son gambling and he lost a considerable amount of money. It appears Lady Bethelhume took exception."

On the stage, the actors had stopped and were now also watching the antics below, some even calling encouragement as the argument escalated.

"Look left - I believe another player is about to enter." Simon pointed to an elegantly dressed man walking through the crowd below.

"Good Lord! It's Lord Bethelhume. Now that is interesting. He rarely comes to the theatre. Told me last year he'd sooner have a tooth pulled." Daniel placed his arms on either side of his wife to stop her falling over the edge. "Do you know he's one man I would not be keen to come up against. He's always struck me as someone who means business, even if he is in his fifty-ninth year."

All eyes watched the gentleman in question gently remove his wife's hands from the neck of Mr Priestley and push her behind him.

"I wish I could hear what he was saying." Eva leaned further over the edge.

"Nicely done." Simon applauded as Lord Bethelhume drew back his fist and planted it in the face of Mr Priestley. He then bent down and dragged the man to his feet, shook him like a rag doll, said a few more words and released him.

Turning, he placed an arm around his wife before leading her from the room.

"Ohhhhh," sighed the ladies.

"You will go to your club tomorrow, Daniel, and find out exactly what was said down there."

"Nosey little thing, aren't you?" Daniel laughed, placing a kiss on Eva's cheek.

The actors filled off the stage, signaling the end of the first act, and Claire and Lady Dunbar stood.

"Come, Eva, Lady Dunbar wishes to stretch her legs and we shall accompany her."

"How about you, Grandmother?"

"I shall stay here, child, and annoy the men."

Giving her grandmother's cheek a kiss for no other reason than she could, Eva then left with Claire and Lady Dunbar.

They walked and talked with the other guests and Eva strolled to the edge to look down below as Lady Dunbar and Claire stopped to chat with a friend.

"It was foolish of you to stop ceding to your father's demands, Berengaria. Now your husband and brother must pay the ultimate price."

Eva spun around to face Gilbert Huxley, but he had continued walking without looking back. On his arm, a lady was chatting gaily whilst he bent his head to listen attentively. She hadn't imagined those words or their meaning. Panic gripped her. She had merely hoped to put her father off for awhile until she decided what to do yet it seemed Lord Huxley believed differently. How had he known her intentions were to stop any further payments?

Was Reggie even now in danger?

"Eva?" Daniel appeared beside her. "What has happened?"

"Nothing. I just felt a little overwhelmed with so many people around me."

"Don't lie to me. Your knuckles are white they are gripping the balustrade so hard." Anger flared in his eyes as once again he saw through her deceit. He turned from her to scan the guests around them and Eva had to stop him before he saw Lord Huxley and confronted him.

"Why did you follow me?"

With a final look, he returned his gaze to hers.

"Tell me who has put the fear back in your eyes."

The words may have been softly spoken yet there was steel behind them.

"I…I have no idea what you mean."

He was silent for several seconds, just looking at her, and Eva could not find the strength to pull away.

"We shall not have this conversation here but remember, Duchess, lying is a heavy burden not many can bear for long."

She took the arm he held out to her and they silently made their way back to their seats.

Eva remembered nothing of the second act, as thoughts tumbled around inside her head. She forced a smile onto her face and chatted with the other guests and if anyone noticed her anything amiss, they did not comment. Behind her, Daniel was stiff and silent, and she missed the brush of his hands on her shoulders and his deep rumble of laughter in her ear. Eva was relieved when the play finally closed.

Goodnights were exchanged and Daniel saw his grandmother and Lady Dunbar into their carriage before helping Eva into theirs. She rested her head on the back of the seat, suddenly exhausted from the evening's events.

"Care to enlighten me as to what took place in the interval?"

"I told you what happened. I was overwhelmed."

"You don't lie very well, Duchess. Now tell me the truth."

There was a ping of broken glass as Daniel leaned forward to close the curtains and he fell backwards, reaching for Eva as he did so. He threw her to the floor, then followed her down.

"What's happening, Daniel?"

"Stay down. Someone is shooting at us!" Daniel felt the carriage pick up speed and knew instantly that the driver had either been shot or lost control of the horses. He climbed onto the seat, then lifted the hatch. "Elijah!"

"I've been hit in the shoulder, your Grace!"

Relieved that his driver was at least still breathing, Daniel moved to the windows and wrenched open the curtain. They were not being followed. Whoever had fired that shot was long gone. The carriage was rapidly picking up speed and he caught glimpses through the darkness of familiar landmarks as they flew by. Soon the horses would not be able to take a corner and the carriage could overturn. He could not allow that to happen. Eva was too precious to him.

"Eva, Elijah has been shot in the shoulder. I will have to

climb up through the hatch and help him stop the horses."

"Please be careful, Daniel." Eva gripped his hands.

Daniel crushed her briefly to his chest and then told her to hang on tight to whatever she could. Climbing through the opening, he then struggled against the wind as he fought his way into the driver's seat beside Elijah. He could see nothing ahead and hoped no carriages suddenly appeared through the darkness. Taking the reins from his driver's uninjured hand, he tried to slow the four horses.

"'Tis no use, your Grace, they won't be stopped!"

"Knife?"

His driver removed a long blade from his boot and handed it to him. Clamping it between his teeth, Daniel then climbed down and started cutting the traces that held the carriage. It was a risk, yet it had to be done. He hoped the carriage would stop of its own accord, once freed from the horses. Just as he reached the last strip of leather, the horses veered. He scrambled to find something to hold onto but his fingers found nothing and he was thrown from the carriage. Hitting the ground, he grunted at the impact and then rolled several times, narrowly missing a fence railing. Climbing to his feet, he watched, horrified, as Elijah jumped clear when the carriage teetered on two wheels, then turned over completely onto its side. The last trace snapped and the horses charged off into the night. Daniel ran, trying to reach the carriage as it rolled over once more and then finally came to a rest against the side of a building with a sickening thump. He heard the splinter of wood but no cry from inside.

"Eva!" Icy fear filled his veins as he reached the now

stationary carriage. Climbing onto the top, he tried to open the door, which refused to move. Stomping his foot through the window, he pushed the glass aside and lowered himself down into the carriage

She lay on her back, one arm thrown across her head, the other flung wide; her legs were twisted beneath her.

"Speak to me, Eva." He desperately searched her neck for a pulse, it was faint but there was definitely a beat.

"Daniel!"

"Simon, help me!" Daniel heard his friend's voice drawing near. "It's Eva. I don't know how badly she's hurt." He couldn't think. His heart was pounding so loudly, he feared it would burst right from his chest.

"Is she bleeding?" Simon's face appeared in the hole above Daniel.

"Yes. No. I-I don't kn-know."

"Take a deep breath and focus now, Daniel. You need to check her injuries to see how badly she is hurt."

Daniel latched onto his friend's voice like a lifeline. Drawing in a deep breath, he began to feel Eva's body. Straightening her legs, he noted no broken bones. Moving upwards, he could feel no obvious injuries through her clothes. He ran his fingers slowly over her hair, pulling pins free as he went. "Her shoulder appears to be dislocated and there's a bump above the ear but in this light I can see nothing further." Gently, Daniel lifted her into his arms.

"It's better if she sleeps while we lift her out." Simon's voice was steady and reassuring and Daniel battled the panic that threatened to consume him.

He lifted her upwards and into Simon's hands, then

climbed out and in seconds he had her back in his arms.

"My carriage is here." Simon opened the door for Daniel to enter.

"My driver?"

"Here, your Grace," Elijah said from inside the carriage.

They journeyed in silence. Simon pressed his handkerchief into Elijah's bloodied shoulder to staunch the flow of blood while Daniel held Eva against his chest and continued praying for her to open her eyes.

Simon ran inside as the carriage stopped outside Daniel's townhouse. "Fetch a doctor at once, Wernham! The duchess and the duke's driver are injured."

Daniel carried Eva inside and up to his room where he laid her on the bed.

"Light!" he roared. The fire was lit in minutes and jugs of steaming water and clothes where carried into the room by silent servants. Branches of candles placed around the bed gave Daniel the light he needed.

"Molly, we must get her out of these clothes to see if she has other injuries."

"Yes, your Grace." Ashen faced the maid nodded.

Daniel's eye remained on Eva's face as he and the maid eased her clothing from her body. There were bruises starting to form and he knew they would be the color of grapes by the morning. His fingers were unsteady as he brushed hair from her cheek.

"Open your eyes now, Eva."

"Set her shoulder while she sleeps, Daniel," Simon said, coming into the room.

Lifting her into his arms, he reached for the shoulder and

gently pushed it back into the joint. She didn't even flinch.

"Do you have any smelling salts?"

Molly nodded at Simon and then hurried from the room.

"I won't live without her."

"She is unconscious, not dead, Daniel." Simon said. "Find that calm you are famous for before she wakes and sees the terror in your eyes."

"Christ, Simon, she could have been killed!"

"I know, my friend, but she was not and we will be making bloody sure nothing like this happens to either of you again."

Molly came back with a small bottle, which she handed to the duke. He pulled out the cork and placed it under Eva's nose.

"Again," Simon urged when she did not respond.

This time, she flinched and then her eyes sprang open as she screamed his name.

"I'm here, love." Daniel's hands held her so she could not move.

"A-are you hurt?"

"No, Eva, but you are hurt." He looked down into her eyes. Filled with pain and tears, they smote his heart.

"I was so scared." She grabbed a handful of his shirt and pulled him closer as she began to cry. "I thought you were dead when the carriage turned and I knew you were on top and it is all my fault."

"Ssssh, love," Daniel soothed her. "I am here."

"The doctor has arrived, your Grace."

"Thank you, Molly, please let him in."

Daniel watched as the doctor examined Eva thoroughly,

then pronounced she suffered from a knock to the head and a few bruises. Her shoulder would ache but she would make a full recovery, given time. He gave her something to ease the pain and help her sleep.

"Please see to my driver now, doctor," Daniel said, signaling Simon to see to the task.

"Of course, your Grace, and I will return tomorrow to check on the duchess."

Between them, Daniel and Molly put her into a nightdress. He tried not to flinch every time she winced and moaned.

"Daniel?"

"Yes, love." He ran a finger down her cheek. He could have lost her tonight and he realized if that had happened, his own life would have ended alongside hers.

"Daniel?" She yawned and her eyelashes fluttered shut. "I...I must talk - "

"Sleep now, Eva."

"I-I love you," she said so softly that had the room not been silent, he would not have heard her.

Daniel closed his eyes briefly as her words surrounded him. She loved him.

"I will sit with her for a while until you return, your Grace," Molly said.

Nodding, Daniel stood and quietly left the room.

Simon was pacing around his study when he ran him to ground minutes later. "She sleeps." Daniel took the drink his friend handed him. "I don't know why you were following our carriage tonight, Simon, but I will be forever in you debt," he added, sitting on the edge of his desk.

"Claire went home with her aunt who was at the theatre, therefore I decided to go to my club. It was purely coincidence that I was following your carriage." Simon refilled both their glasses before continuing. "I heard the gunshot and when I looked out the window, I noticed your carriage tearing down the street ahead. Christ, Daniel! My heart nearly gave out when I saw you thrown and then watched as the carriage flipped onto its side."

"Was it deliberate? Was I the target or Eva, or was it just a random act of foolishness by an idiot?" Daniel ran a hand over his face.

"Who are the possibilities?"

"Her family, Gilbert Huxley - dear God, there are plenty of possibilities if I give it thought."

"Claire's sure Huxley spoke to Eva tonight when they went for a walk with Lady Dunbar. She saw him pause briefly behind her, and then by the time Eva had turned around, he had walked on."

"I'm certain he and her father have some sort of hold over her but she will not talk to me about it." Daniel paced the room. "I will not allow her to be threatened or hurt again, Simon. We must get to the bottom of this."

Nodding, Simon rose. "I will leave you for now, but I think in the morning we should send out a few men to enquire over tonight's events."

Daniel agreed. After Simon left, he went back to his rooms. Dismissing Molly, he stood, looking down at his duchess. The gentle rise and fall of her chest was the only movement. Her cheeks were pale and he wanted to take all her pain and make it his own. How was one small woman to shoulder so much anguish? A life spent with angry, abusive men, and then to suffer the unwanted attentions of Lord Huxley and whatever threats he and her father were holding over her. He would get her to tell him and then he would make them pay for her pain.

Removing his clothes, he then washed. After ensuring the laudanum was where he could reach it, Daniel blew out the candles and climbed into bed. As if sensing he was with her, Eva edged toward him in the dark.

"I will protect you, my love." He gathered her into his arms and then, wrapping her hair around his fist, he tried to tell himself she was safe now, but the night's events ran endlessly through his head and it wasn't until the grey fingers of dawn filtered through his window that he slept and finally the tension eased from his body.

. . .

"Hello, Grandmother." Daniel looked up as she stomped into his breakfast parlor.

"You did not send word that my granddaughter was injured!"

"That is not exactly true, Grandmother. I sent around a note saying she was indisposed," he said, climbing to his feet and holding out a chair for her so she could join him, which, of course, she refused and instead, stood glaring at him.

"Being hurled around in a carriage after said carriage was shot at does not constitute being indisposed!" she snapped at him.

"She is all right, I promise. I would have alerted you

instantly if that was not the case, Grandmother." Daniel saw the genuine distress in her eyes and realized that she cared a great deal for Eva and most probably him. He'd just never really taken the time to look before.

"I don't understand, Daniel. Why would anyone want to shoot at either of you?"

Dear Lord, his grandmother had tears in her eyes and her shoulders had slumped. Taking her arm, he hugged her. She resisted at first and then leant against him. He could feel her tremors and realized he had underestimated her and it humbled him to have her love when, in all honesty, he had probably not done a lot to deserve it.

"Come now, I will pour you some tea, Grandmother. We are unsure why we were shot at but I have men investigating it as we speak." Daniel talked steadily until she had regained her composure. "It could just be a random act of stupidity that we were unlucky enough to have been caught up in."

"But you are not convinced."

Shaking his head, Daniel continued, pleased to have an ear to voice his thoughts, thoughts he had tried to hide from his duchess.

"It could be her family or someone else." He went on to explain about Huxley's infatuation with Eva and his visit with Eva at Stratton.

"Scoundrel!" she roared. "I'll ruin him!"

At least the color has returned to her cheeks, Daniel thought as his grandmother proceeded to explain in detail what she would do to Gilbert Huxley.

She swallowed her tea and grimaced. "You did not

follow the correct procedure for pouring tea, boy!"

"Forgive me." Daniel realized her moment of weakness was well and truly behind them.

"Grandmother?"

The breakfast door opened and this time in came his wife, followed closely by Furban, who had not left her since the accident. Dressed in pale lemon with her hair drawn back in a matching satin ribbon, she looked about fifteen. Her movements were slow, which told him she was stiff and sore and she wore a sling, which both he and the doctor had insisted upon.

I could have lost her.

"What are you doing out of bed?" the Dowager Duchess snapped, once again on her feet. "And what is that?" she added, glaring down at the puppy, who was sitting on his haunches, staring up at her.

"I am pleased to see you also, Grandmother." Eva kissed her cheek. "And this is Furban."

Daniel watched as his grandmother wrapped her arms around Eva and gave her a gentle hug. He heard both of them sniff and then pull away from each other and move to join him at the table.

"That dog is not fit for a duke and duchess," the dowager declared, looking at the puppy who had followed Eva and was now seated at her feet.

"He is our dog, Grandmother, and someone I am sure you will come to love in time," Eva said as she reached for the teapot.

"Harrumph," the elderly woman grumbled. "Shall we postpone the ball, Granddaughter?"

"Absolutely not!"

"Are you sure you will feel up to it, love? It is only four days away," Daniel added and how the hell was he to protect her at such an event.

"It is only my shoulder that pains me and I will wear my sling if it tires, I promise."

"I think we should wait." He looked not at Eva but his grandmother. Just thinking about Eva surrounded by so many people made him sweat.

"Oh, please, Daniel, I want to continue with the preparations." Eva forced a smile onto her face. She did not want to delay the ball. Just thinking about it made her nerves flutter and if they put if off she would have weeks of anxiety. Not that she wasn't already anxious. Eva knew that whoever shot at their carriage had to be connected with her father and Lord Huxley, and she had no doubt the bullet had been intended for Daniel. He could have been taken from her and the thought of life without him was not to be borne. Through her own foolishness in trying to protect him, he could have died. Therefore today, when she was feeling stronger, she would tell him everything.

"All right, the ball will go ahead but you will not leave my side on the night."

Nodding, Eva snuck a crust under the table. Daniel lifted one eyebrow but remained silent.

"We have had most people reply, my dear. It will be a fabulous crush," the Dowager Duchess crowed.

"Wonderful," Eva replied with as much enthusiasm as she could muster.

"And now I must leave you both to plan as I am to fence with Simon this morning and then visit Tattersall's horse sales."

"Oh, but Daniel, I need to talk to you." Eva rose to grip his hand.

"Can it wait, sweetheart?"

Eva nodded when she saw the concern on his face. She didn't want him to leave without hearing her confessions but they could wait a few more hours.

"You are not to leave this house today, Eva."

"Of course."

"Good girl." He kissed her softly and then he was gone.

. . .

"Interestingly enough it appears Gilbert Huxley and Spencer Winchcomb have been seen in each others company a lot more of late." Simon flexed his foil several times as he spoke.

Daniel paused in his own preparations to look at his friend.

"Supposedly, they were seen talking with some rather unsavory characters not four nights ago."

Cursing soundly, Daniel swiped his foil through the air, venting his rage. He had left Eva and his grandmother and met Simon at their fencing club. He needed the release of physical exercise - anything to relieve the tension inside him.

"Perhaps we should wait until your temper has cooled." Simon eyed his friend's furious movements.

"Don't be ridiculous. The points are tipped and I would never willingly hurt you!" Daniel snapped.

"Not willingly, no," Simon muttered, pulling on his gloves.

"En garde," Daniel snarled.

Daniel lunged at Simon, who, in turn, managed to parry the attack by jumping to one side with a rather unmanly yelp.

"Fight, you lily livered bastard!" Daniel roared. His vision was suddenly filled with a red haze as he imagined Eva at the hands of Huxley and her father. His patience had finally fled and he wanted to kill someone or, at the very least, maim them and Simon was in his line of sight.

"Ask me nicely," Simon taunted.

Lunging, Daniel slashed and swiped with little skill but plenty of enthusiasm.

"Your fencing master would be most displeased with your lack of grace, your Grace," Simon panted.

"Shut up!"

They fenced until their clothes were drenched with sweat and eventually Daniel struck the winning blow. Simon slumped against the wall while Daniel bent at the waist to suck in several deep breaths.

"How deep is Huxley in debt?" Daniel rasped.

"According to my source -" Simon wiped his face on a piece of cloth "- he is in very deep, owes money to everyone and is gambling heavily to try and recoup his losses."

"But why shoot at us the other night. It makes no sense. What did Huxley or Winchcomb hope to gain out of it?" Daniel queried. "If, indeed, it was either of them."

The men were silent while they thought things over, the only sound in the room their harsh breathing for several seconds.

"The first shot came as I reached forward to close the

carriage curtains," Daniel said slowly as his mind ran through the events of that night.

"So it's possible it was you they were after?"

Daniel looked at Simon as he spoke. "Perhaps with me gone, Winchcomb thinks he can intimidate Eva to give him money or -"

"He could control her completely. After all, he is one of those men who believe all women can be gentled by force," Simon added. "Perhaps he has promised Huxley a share of anything he gets out of Eva or worse…"

"With me gone, he could hand Eva to Huxley," Daniel growled. "It seems he did not take my threats seriously."

"I think we should pay him another call," Simon suggested.

"Yes," Daniel's smile was feral. "After we buy you a decent horse."

# CHAPTER THIRTEEN

*E*va spent the next hour discussing the ball with her grandmother and then when she thought her head would burst from the lists of things she was charged to do, the Dowager Duchess rose to leave. This time, she kissed both of Eva's cheeks and told her to take care and then stomped from the house.

The note arrived that afternoon. Restless, Eva had been reading a book in the library when Molly tracked her down and handed it to her. She knew instantly that it was from her father. Opening it, she read the words.

I have your brother. Therefore, you will come at once and bring money or jewels. We may have failed to kill your husband but we will not fail again. Don't doubt that Reginald is here, or that I won't make him suffer because you, Berengaria, did not fulfill your obligations to me.

With the note clenched in one fist, Eva ran to her room and wrenched off the sling. Ignoring the stab of pain in her shoulder and aches in her body, she pulled on her coat, gloves and bonnet and then grabbed her reticule. Opening a drawer, she found some money and stuffed it inside.

Neither Molly nor Wernham were thankfully in sight as she reached the front door. Slipping out, she ran down the stairs and onto the street. Making her way to the corner, she kept walking until she found a hackney.

"Tattersall's Horse Sales, please, and hurry." Slamming the door, she sat on the seat and prayed. Visions of Reggie at the hands of her father filled her head as they journeyed through London until finally the carriage stopped. Looking around her as she stepped down, Eva saw a group of boys. Signaling to one, she urged him forward.

"Yes, Miss?"

His face was eager, especially when she opened her reticule and handed him several coins. "How can I help you?"

"I need you to go into Tattersall's Horse Sales and find the Duke of Stratton. When he is before you, inform him that his wife is awaiting him outside. Can you do that?"

"Of course, Miss."

"You must hurry. The matter is urgent."

She watched him disappear into the crowd of men before her and then she waited and watched. Daniel would be furious that she had left the house alone but she had had no choice. She had needed to reach him as soon as she could and calling a carriage and finding Molly would have taken up precious time.

It was only a matter of minutes before she saw Daniel striding toward her. Uncaring of who was watching, Eva picked up her skirts and ran to meet him, launching herself at him when close enough. Strong arms caught and held her.

"I told you not to leave the house, wife." His cheek rested briefly on top of her head.

"I had to. Please, Daniel, we must talk now."

Sensing the urgency in her words, he lowered her to the ground, then placed an arm around her waist as they made their way along the row of carriages until they reached his. Opening the door, he urged her inside and then followed. Taking the seat across from her, he placed his hat beside him and then stripped off his gloves.

"Did you bring servants with you? Where is your carriage?"

"I called a hackney and no, I did not bring Molly. Daniel, I need-"

"What!" His roar bounced off the walls. "You were injured and shot at and you left the house unprotected?"

"Daniel, you must listen to me!" Eva grabbed his hands and he stilled, his grey eyes now intent as they focused on hers.

"Are you finally about to tell me the truth, Duchess?"

Oh God, now the moment was upon her, Eva felt her courage waver. Fierce pain lanced through her. Would she lose this wonderful man now? Could he forgive her?

"Talk to me, Eva."

"Yes, I must." The words were as much for herself as him. "I have been dishonest, Daniel. Betrayed you and abused your generosity. And I will understand if you wish to send me back to Stratton, but I beg of you, no matter what you think of me, you must help Reggie."

Leaning forward until their knees brushed, he lifted her chin so their eyes met. "I can do nothing until you tell me everything, Eva."

She did, starting with her father's blackmail notes and the jewels she had given him. She told him of Huxley's visit to Stratton and how he had spoken to her at the theatre and his threat to fight Daniel. She felt purged as she spoke. Finally, the burden was gone. However, she wondered at what price.

"I understand you did not trust me when your father first approached you, Eva, but after the theatre, you should have told me about Huxley."

"I wanted to but I was injured and there never seemed to be the right moment, and I had betrayed you and given my father your ring and the pendant, Daniel." The words tumbled out one on top of the other as she tried to make him understand. "Plus, I was afraid you would challenge Lord Huxley and he never loses a sword fight, so my father told me. He has killed and maimed many."

"You think I care about jewels or money? You think those baubles can hold the same place as you in my life? Christ, woman, I love you! Them I can replace; you, I cannot."

Eva felt the air squeeze from her lungs as she looked at him. "You love me?"

"Of course I do." His anger made the words harsh, yet Eva didn't care. Was it possible he would forgive her for what she had done?

"But the threat from Huxley and my father, Daniel - surely you can see I could not ignore that. Especially after the carriage was shot at. My fears multiplied after that."

"And this is why you have come to me now?"

Shaking her head, Eva pulled the note from her reticule

and handed it to him. "I had decided to tell you, Daniel - you must believe that - but this note made it imperative I do so immediately."

"That was what you wanted to tell me this morning?"

Eva nodded and watched as he read the note before handing it back to her.

"And you know where they are?"

"Yes, I dropped the pendant there."

His mouth tightened but he said nothing further, instead reaching above him to open the hatch.

"Daniel."

"What?" He returned to his seat after barking instructions at his driver.

"I love you, too."

"I know."

"You do?" Eva slumped back on the seat, suddenly exhausted. Her body still ached and her shoulder throbbed but telling Daniel everything had taken the last of her energy.

"You told me the night of the accident."

"I did?"

Opening his legs, he reached for her, pulling her to the edge of the seat until she was trapped between his thighs, his face now inches from hers.

"If you truly love me, Duchess, you will never lie to me again. Do you understand?"

Eva nodded.

"I don't care if someone threatens me or Reggie or our bloody dog, you will never again keep anything this serious from me. Do you understand?"

Eva nodded again.

His kiss was hard and fast.

"I knew you were hiding something and that whatever it was put shadows in your eyes when you thought I wasn't looking. I was caught between shaking you and hugging you because you were carrying these burdens alone."

Her fingers shook as she touched his cheek. The love inside her was so strong it hurt. "The only worthy thing he ever did for me was give me to you."

"I would say the same thing." Daniel's words brushed her lips. "Our fathers in their greed actually did right by us."

"I'm sorry about the ring and my pendant, Daniel."

He cupped her cheeks as his eyes roamed her face. "I will get them back if they mean that much to you, my love, and just for the record, I'm Huxley's equal with a sword."

"You are?"

"I am," he said, opening the door after someone knocked on it.

"What the hell is going on? I was talking to that insipid creature Rockwell and when I turned around you were storming away." Simon's eyes went from Daniel to Eva. "Hello, Eva."

"Get in here, Kelkirk, and close the door. I need your help."

"I've never known a duke and duchess get into so much trouble," Simon grumbled as he seated himself.

"Show him the note, Duchess."

Eva handed it to Simon at Daniel's prompting and then, much to her shame, he relayed everything she had just told him. However, Simon simply squeezed her hand when he had finished.

"It's all right, Eva. We'll get Reggie back safe."

"That's the house." Eva pointed to a brick building thirty minutes later.

"And am I wasting my breath asking you to stay in the carriage and let Simon and I deal with this?"

"Yes, you are."

"Where the hell is your sling?" Daniel then demanded, obviously just noticing it was missing.

"I left it at home."

He sighed but soon they were standing outside the front door.

Pounding on the wood, Daniel tried the handle and when it failed to yield, they had to wait several tense seconds before a servant finally opened it.

"I want to speak with Spencer Winchcomb," Daniel demanded.

"He's busy." The man then tried to shut the door but Daniel placed one boot in the doorway and pushed it open. The force sent the servant stumbling backwards.

"If you value your health, sir, stay out of this." Daniel added, walking past him. Then he heard it - the sound a fist makes when connecting with flesh. Followed by Eva and Simon, he ran to the stairs. Taking them two at a time, he reached the top in seconds. Everyone stopped as Daniel held up one hand. They could hear voices coming from the room located at the end of the hallway.

"You will pay for defending that worthless little bitch over us!"

"I care nothing about what you do to me, father, and will

laugh in delight when her large husband realizes what you have done to her."

"She will pay next for turning her back on her family."

Daniel grabbed the back of Eva's jacket as she tried to run past him.

"I can't worry about you and Reggie, Eva, do you understand?"

She didn't want to but she nodded and then allowed him to push her behind him.

It was unlucky for the Winchcombs that the first sight Daniel had, when he opened the door, was of Reggie taking a fist to the stomach from Bartholomew Winchomb.

"Release him now!"

Montgomery Winchcomb, who'd been holding his brother, lifted his hands straight up in the air and took a step backwards, leaving Reggie all alone. He then looked at the large, angry beast that was his brother-in-law and started sweating profusely. Quickly, he stepped sideways until he stood beside his father and brother.

"Reggie!"

Eva's cry was from the heart as she took in the battered and bruised sight of her brother, and even though Daniel knew it cost her a great deal, she did not take a step toward him. She understood the situation was volatile and one wrong move could harm Reggie further.

Daniel felt Simon move to stand to his left.

Reggie still stood, but Daniel guessed by the way he weaved, only just. One eye was partially closed, one cheek swollen and his lips were split and never had Daniel wanted to punish anyone more than he did Spencer Winchcomb.

The boy had arrived in London a thin, beaten young man and left for Edinburgh confident and smiling. Looking into Reggie's eyes, Daniel now saw a mixture of both. His father had not quite managed to reduce the boy to what he once was and Daniel would make sure he did not finish the job.

"Come here, Reggie."

"Stay, Reginald!" Spencer roared.

Reggie didn't hesitate. Giving his father one last look, he then walked on unsteady legs to meet his brother-in-law. They were, perhaps, the hardest steps he had ever taken and when he finally stood before Daniel, he offered a small smile and then fell forward, his legs giving way.

Daniel heard the sigh as he held the boy briefly, his battered face resting on Daniel's chest.

"You are safe now." Daniel felt a lump form in his throat as Reggie looked at him.

"I knew you would come."

Daniel gave him a gentle squeeze and then pushed him into his sister's arms.

"You are dead to me, Reginald Ransom Hibernians Cyrus Winchcomb," Spencer declared.

Daniel couldn't be sure but thought he heard the words, 'Thank God' coming from both Reggie and Eva.

"Hardly surprising he didn't leave years ago with a name like that," Simon drawled, intent on taunting Spencer.

"Stratton, what is the meaning of this?" Spencer Winchomb bluffed, his face flushed with color. "How dare you enter my house uninvited."

"I came to discuss the matter of blackmail and attempted murder, Winchcomb."

Daniel watched fear chase across Winchcomb's face.

"She lies!" His eyes were wide as they swung from Daniel to Eva.

"I have a note with your handwriting, Winchomb. Do you deny that also?"

"My father does not answer to you, Stratton. So go home with your pathetic little wife," Bartholomew Winchcomb said. The man had always been the dumbest of the pack.

Daniel took the two strides necessary across the room and punched him in the face. The man's head snapped backward and when it righted itself, blood was streaming from his now larger than usual nose.

"Oww!"

"Do it again, Daniel!"

Glaring his bloodthirsty wife into silence, Daniel said. "You will never speak my wife's name in such an insulting manner again."

"How dare you come into my home and abuse my son!" Spencer howled, handing Bartholomew a handkerchief.

"How dare I abuse your son?" Daniel hissed. "You weak-kneed bastard, you have tormented and abused your daughter since her birth and allowed your sons to do the same and you ask me how I dare mete out some retribution." Daniel sucked in a much needed breath. "You could have killed my wife, your own daughter, when you had someone shoot at my carriage."

"That was Huxley, not me!"

Daniel believed that. Winchcomb was an idiot and capable of blackmail, but he could see Huxley committing murder.

"I have no wish for my wife's name to be dragged through the courts. Therefore you will leave England with your sons quietly and never return. Only then will I not see you hung."

"I only took what was rightfully mine. She owed me."

Disgusted, Daniel wondered how something so sweet could have come from such a man. "How my wife has remained such a beautiful person whilst living in your household is beyond me, Winchcomb. She is everything that is good in this world and I will protect her with my life from scum like you."

Daniel heard Eva sniff and Reggie murmur something. "Know that she belongs to me and what is mine I treasure," he continued, once again in control. "You are a bully, Winchcomb, but in me you have met your match."

"Nicely put, your Grace," Simon said.

"You'll not abuse me and walk away without a fight!" Winchcomb declared as he and his sons stood together, forming a wall.

"I hoped you'd say that." Daniel knew his smile was feral. "Eva, take Reggie from the room."

"Not a bloody chance," was his wife's reply.

If anyone deserved to see their family thrashed, it was the two youngest Winchcomb siblings.

"Your father was a man of few moral standards, Stratton, weak to his soul. It was I who saved your inheritance." Spencer played what he believed to be his trump card.

The silence in the room hung heavy as only the harsh sounds of Reggie's breathing could be heard. Then Daniel spoke.

"My father's actions were his alone, Winchcomb. Do not think to visit his sins upon me."

"Damn you, Stratton!"

Daniel met Spencer as he ran at him. He jabbed him in the nose, then landed a blow to the stomach. The man crumpled to the floor at his feet. Simon bent over as Bartholomew Winchcomb ran at him. Catching him in the stomach, he flipped him over his shoulder and sent him sailing through the air to land in a heap against the wall. Montague closed his eyes and did the same. Daniel stuck out his foot and sent him toward his brother. They lay together, a whimpering mass of tangled limbs.

Daniel stood before them, watching as they moaned and writhed on the floor at his feet. It wasn't the fight he had wanted and yet he was conscious of the fact that Eva was in the room and had no wish for her to experience any further bloodshed.

"Now I am going to state some conditions and it would be advisable for you all to listen carefully and heed my every word." He looked at each of the Winchcomb men as he spoke. "Never speak my wife's name again in anything other than reverence. If any of you approach her in any way or upset her, then this -" he swept his arm around the room "- will be heaven compared to the hell I will bring down upon your heads. Do you understand?

The brothers nodded. Their father said nothing.

"Huxley will be dealt with as soon as I catch him. Therefore, if you know his location, it would pay you to tell me now."

Spencer Winchcomb remained mute.

"Do not mistake me, Winchcomb." Daniel leveled him a look that would have wrought fear into a more sensible man. "I will not hesitate to rid the earth of vermin like you and Huxley, if the need should arise."

"Y-you cannot th-threaten me," Spencer blustered. "And Lord Huxley will see you pay for your actions."

Daniel took a step forward, landing directly on his father-in-law's hand. "Heed me, Winchcomb." He held the man's pain-filled gaze. "This is one fight your particular brand of thuggery will not win and as I told your daughter earlier, I, too, can use a sword with some skill."

Lifting his foot, Daniel turned and saw Reggie held upright by Simon and Eva. Replacing it, he added, "Your youngest son is now under my protection also. Therefore, what I have said relates to him, too."

"Bastard! I'll see you in hell for this day!" Spencer roared, spitting out several vile curses.

Before Daniel could react to his father-in-law's words, his wife rushed past him and kicked Spencer hard in the leg. "Never speak to him like that again!"

Daniel didn't stop her, just stood waiting to step in if she should need him. Her hands were clenched at her sides and her body rigid with fury. He could imagine the fire that filled her eyes. It humbled him that it had taken an insult to him before her anger overcame her.

"Bitch!" Spencer howled.

"Stand up, father, and it will be my pleasure to plant you a facer," Eva growled, her fists at the ready. Spencer stayed down.

"You are still hurting, love, and I'm sure he yields."

Daniel wrapped an arm around her waist and lifted her out of his way before delivering a few final words to her family.

"I have a rather esteemed list of ancestors that would suggest I am, indeed not a bastard, sir. My advice to you is to leave London and take a long break in the country. However, if you choose not to follow my advice, then make very certain that where your daughter and son go, you and your other offspring do not."

Simon led Reggie while Daniel collected his wife and together, they then left the room.

Daniel kept Reggie upright as the carriage took them home. Overcome, tears slipped silently down the boy's cheeks. "I...I would l-like to thank you...Daniel."

"For what?" Daniel questioned as his eyes begin to itch.

"F-for rescuing us."

Eva started crying silent tears that rained silently down her cheeks. She reached for her brother, pulling him close and the two siblings wept softly while Daniel put his arms around them both. He murmured words to the tops of their heads - small words telling them both that they were safe. Simon swallowed several times and cast his gaze firmly out the window.

Wernham sprang into action as they entered the house, sending someone for the doctor.

Daniel watched as his wife looked her brother over, checking his face, then prodding his stomach, her face pale with worry. "Careful, love, he is hurting." He placed an arm around her waist as she leaned toward him.

"I am very glad you thumped my father, Daniel."

"Yes," he said, unsure how to respond to that remark.

"I hope their pain is tenfold compared to Reggie's," she added. "I wish my father had stood up."

"Fiery little thing aren't you." Daniel smiled down at her.

She said nothing further; instead, she put her hand into his pocket and retrieved a neat, white square of linen. Dabbing the small cut on her brother's lips, she stopped the trickle of blood. She then turned to order the servants to organize a bath, some food and prepare a room.

Daniel stood, quietly supporting his brother in law, more than happy to watch his wife order everyone around. It seemed her worries about fulfilling the role of Duchess were unfounded

"Eva, Wernham will help you with Reggie as I need to talk with Simon before he leaves."

"Of course, Daniel," she said, moving to her brother's side again and helping him toward the stairs.

Daniel watched until they had disappeared from sight. Only then did he face Simon.

"Huxley must be found."

"Agreed." Simon looked grim.

"Tomorrow I will start making enquiries of my own amongst his acquaintances."

"And I shall do the same, my friend."

"Eva will not be safe until he is found, Simon. I believe he sees her as unfinished business and his arrogance allows him to believe she should be his."

"And you believe he will stop at nothing to get her?"

Daniel nodded. "I do."

"Then we will look until he is found and then you and your duchess will be safe to enjoy the love you both now share."

Daniel gave his friend a steady look before he answered. "Yes, I believe we will."

Simon clapped a hand on his shoulder and then departed the house, leaving Daniel to wonder how he was to protect his wife from the threat of Huxley, when he had no idea how to find the man or when he would strike next.

"Reggie is sleeping now, Daniel."

Eva watched her husband open one eye as she walked into his room. He was submerged in a bath, wisps of steam rising from his large body. His fingers held a glass filled with amber liquid and he looked like a sated beast in his lair.

"Excellent. I am sure he will get through the night comfortably with the aid of the laudanum Dr. Munro gave him."

"He told me that Edinburgh is everything he hoped it would be and more and is eager to return as soon as he is able." Eva felt nervous as she sat on the edge of his bed several feet from the bath. So much had happened between them today. She had told him about her lies, he had confronted her family and suddenly she did not know what to say to him.

"And did you find out how your father got him back here?"

He looked relaxed yet Eva could tell he was watching her closely. "He sent a note saying I was gravely ill and was asking for him."

"Why would Reggie believe I would allow your father to send such a note, or even alert him to any illness you had after the way he treated you?"

"Because I sent him a message telling him of father's

blackmail threats urging him to be careful, as he had also threatened to go to Scotland and harm Reggie."

"So he was sufficiently concerned after receiving your father's note to return, even though he knew I would not let anything happen to you."

Eva nodded. "Reggie knew I had not told you everything. Part of his reason for returning was to force me into doing so.

"At least one of you has sense."

"I have a great deal of sense," Eva defended herself. "But for so long there were just the two of us looking out for each other, Daniel. You have to understand that it takes time to trust another person."

"There is still someone who is a threat to you, Eva. I need you to understand that."

"Huxley."

"Simon and I are looking for him but until he is found you must not leave this house unescorted."

Eva shivered just thinking about the threats Lord Huxley had made against Daniel.

"I promise not to leave without an escort," she said solemnly.

"Come here."

She hesitated.

"Please."

It was the 'please' that had her walking toward him.

Taking one of her hands, he lifted it to his lips.

"I need to know you completely trust me now, Eva."

She touched his hair, running the short, damp curls through her fingers.

"I do, Daniel. There is not another besides Reggie I trust more."

He sighed as her fingers scraped his scalp.

"I can never hope to thank or, indeed, repay you for all you have done for both Reggie and I."

"Your love is enough, sweetheart. You -"

"Shhh, please, Daniel, let me speak." She pressed a finger to his lips. She shivered as he sucked it into his mouth.

"I just wanted to say, Daniel…"

"What, Eva?" he prodded gently.

"The gift I am about to give you is a present for us both."

"What gift?"

"I think we're going to have a baby."

Surprise flashed across his handsome face and then a slow smile tilted his lips.

"You think?"

Nodding Eva giggled as he stood up suddenly and water sloshed everywhere. He reached for her but she stepped backwards, putting herself out of his reach.

"I have no wish to bathe now, your Grace."

"Come here, Duchess."

He looked like a large, sleek god, and she felt her pulse race as he leant forward and clasped her arm, then pulled her closer. His kiss was slow and gentle.

"A baby," he whispered against her lips. "We will be everything our parents were not."

"Yes."

She stood silently as he removed her clothes, his damp

fingers deliberately caressing each patch of skin he exposed. Lastly, he unpinned her hair, pushing the curls behind her shoulders.

"So beautiful," he whispered.

Eva wrapped her arms around his neck as he picked her up, pressing herself against his warm, wet heat.

"I want you very much, my Duchess." Daniel lowered them both back into the bath and arranged her along his length. "I just need to look at you to want you. I smell your scent," he added, kissing her lips, "or touch your skin," he said, stroking one hand down her back and then moving it gently over the soft curves below, "and I am lost - totally and utterly under your spell. Take me inside you, Eva."

If Wernham noticed the vast amount of water sloshed over his master's bedroom floor later, he said nothing, instead setting the maid to mopping it up.

. . .

The ball preparations had gone well. Even Claire had visited the Dowager Duchess's house and declared the setting fabulous, and now, finally, the night had arrived.

"I can't seem to stop shaking," Eva whispered as she looked around the room her grandmother had allocated her for this evening's preparations. She had been insistent that they stay here for the night and although Daniel had grumbled, he had eventually given in. Molly and Hannah, one of her grandmother's maids, were now helping her get ready.

"You will be the belle of the ball, your Grace." Molly picked up her petticoats and shook them out. "And you will have the duke at your side."

Eva rolled her eyes. Like every other female she knew, Molly was now firmly under Daniel's spell.

Hannah dropped the dress over Eva's head and twitched the silken folds into place. "No one will be able to keep their eyes from you, your Grace, in this dress."

Had Eva the choice, she would have chosen one of her old dresses. Anything to keep people from looking at her. Suddenly, she felt besieged with nerves. Hosting her own ball - how could she hope to pull this off?

Hannah opened the door to a knock, then returned, carrying two boxes. "These are for you, your Grace."

Eva's hands shook as she took the first box, a long, slim one. She opened it and found a small golden heart with a diamond and ruby pressed into the centre.

"Oh, my," Hannah whispered, moving closer. "'Tis the most beautiful necklace I have ever seen."

Lifting the chain, Eva studied the heart, her own thudding loudly as she realized there were initials on the necklace, too. The D was entwined with the E, linking them forever.

"There is a note, your Grace," Molly said, pointing to the small square of paper nestled against the white satin.

Eva stepped backwards until her thighs touched the bed, then sank down onto the cover. Opening the note with trembling fingers, Eva saw Daniel's strong scrawl on the paper before her.

I love you, D

"Oh, Daniel," Eva sighed.

"Your Grace?"

"I'm fine, Molly." Eva waved her hand at the maid. She

reached for the second bigger box and opened the lid. Inside was a wooden box. With gentle hands, she lifted it out. The top and one side were glass and inside, Eva could see a small stage. Porcelain figures appeared to be dancing inside a miniature ballroom, each so delicate they almost looked real. Musicians held their instruments as if they were about to play.

"There is a handle to wind, your Grace."

Both Hannah and Molly now stood close, eagerly looking at the box. Molly was pointing to the back.

Eva quickly turned it and the sweet sound of a minuet filled the air. Inside the case, the little figures began to turn as the floor moved beneath them.

"It's the most beautiful thing I have ever seen." Eva couldn't take her eyes off it. Everything was so perfect, each detail exquisite.

"Here, let me put that pretty box on the side table, your Grace. We must finish your dressing now."

Bemused, Eva let the maids help her to her feet. She stood, unmoving, as they finished fussing with her dress, then placed the necklace around her neck. The love she shared with Daniel humbled her and she felt warmth spread through her body. Soon there would be another in their life. Eva placed a hand over her stomach. Their child, created out of love.

"Your gloves, your Grace."

Thank you," Eva did not even glance in the mirror as Molly ushered her out the door. Thoughts tumbled through her head. Only Daniel would know what a musical box would mean to her. Touching the heart at her neck, she went to find her husband.

Daniel had been pacing at the bottom of the stairs for several minutes when he finally heard Eva call his name.

"Daniel."

She was a vision, a siren sent to enslave him. Wrapped in satin the color of the deepest ocean, he could see the curves of her breasts above a fitted bodice. The skirts fell in a waterfall of rippling silk and each step she took outlined the length of her legs. The hem lifted slightly at the front and was caught in place with tiny sparkling diamonds and Daniel was vastly relieved to see an underskirt of darker blue beneath. Had he glimpsed her skin, he would have carried her straight back to whence she came and slaked the lust gripping his body. Her maid had piled her luxurious locks high, leaving one long ringlet to rest on her shoulder. Light glinted above, picking out the small diamonds tucked into the sable curls. He noted the heart necklace resting on her creamy skin.

"You look beautiful, my love."

She took the hand he held out to her. "And you are so handsome, my love."

Eva had never spoken to him so openly and it warmed him to his toes.

"Thank you for my gifts" She brushed a kiss over his lips, then ran a hand over his chest, which made him suck in a deep breath. "The music box, Daniel, it is the most beautiful thing I have ever owned."

"I saw it and thought of you." His eyes roamed her face.

They stood toe to toe, both her hands in his, pressed against his chest, their eyes focused solely upon each other.

"Are you scared, Duchess? Are your knees quaking beneath that lovely gown?"

"Not now, standing in your arms. All my fears flee when you are near."

"Then I will make sure to stay close." His kiss was soft and achingly sweet and left them both breathless.

"The first guests have arrived, your Grace."

With reluctance, Daniel placed one last kiss on his wife's lips before turning to face his grandmother's butler.

"Come, love, let us greet our guests."

Daniel felt Eva stiffen as he led her forward. "All will go well, sweetheart. I am here at your side, as is your staunchest ally."

"Our grandmother really is sweet, you know, Daniel."

"If you say so, my love."

Minutes later, they stood beside the Dowager Duchess, who was dressed in a stunning shade of emerald with a turban to match. Around her wrists and neck, she wore rubies.

"Grandmother, you look beautiful," Eva said, slipping into a curtsy, then kissing her cheek.

"As do you, child," the Dowager Duchess said, examining her granddaughter.

"The Countess of Braithwaite!"

Daniel tucked Eva in between himself and his grandmother so she was flanked on both sides. Then, squeezing her hand, he turned to greet their first guests.

"My cheeks hurt," Eva whispered some time later.

"Scowl for a while, then," Daniel said out the side of his mouth.

"Oh, look, Daniel, it is Simon. Surely he will not mind if I do not offer him a brilliant smile."

"I heard that," Simon said, hugging Eva, which was totally inappropriate but made her laugh. "How are your cheeks?"

"Sore."

"Dear God, must I shake your grandmother's hand? I fear she'll bite me," Simon whispered.

"I do not bite, Kelkirk!"

"Be nice to him, Grandmother, he is very dear to Daniel and I," Eva admonished as the Dowager Duchess lowered her brows.

"If you insist," the elderly lady said with ill grace. Offering Simon a smile through her clenched teeth, she then sank into a curtsy.

Daniel coughed a couple of times to stop himself from laughing at his friend's surprised look. "Come, Duchess, I believe we may now join our guests."

"Really, Daniel?" Eva looked relieved.

"Really," he added, taking her hand and placing it on his arm.

They circled the ballroom, talking along the way, and then as the music started, Daniel led Eva onto the dance floor.

Everything around her stopped as she moved into Daniel's arms. Eva knew other couples were taking the floor for the first waltz, but all she could see or feel was her husband.

"If you keep looking at me like that, love, I will disgrace us both," Daniel growled.

Eva just smiled and blew him a kiss. When the waltz finished, he reluctantly handed her into Simon's care.

Daniel had looked everywhere for Huxley but the man had vanished. He and Simon had chased every lead and run down everyone associated with him but still they had not found him. Simon believed he had left London but Daniel didn't. Huxley had tried to kill him to get at Eva. Those were not the actions of a man who would simply walk away from what he wanted. Eva was not safe until Lord Gilbert Huxley resurfaced.

He had advised her to stay near people she knew when possible this evening, and his grandmother's staff had been given strict instructions to watch over her. Huxley was not to be allowed into the house under any circumstances; however even with these precautions in place, Daniel was still going to be vigilant.

Walking through the crush of bodies, Daniel took the time to study the room. Eva and his grandmother had done a wonderful job - the room was exquisitely decorated. Huge wreaths of fabric decorated the walls and fresh flowers stood in large vases, sending a sweet scent to mingle in the air with the perfumed guests. Servants in emerald green and black uniforms were scurrying around with trays of champagne. From the size of the crowd, Daniel gathered everyone had accepted the invitation. It would be a success and Eva would be launched officially in the eyes of society, and he was pleased for her. He knew she would always retain her innocence and enthusiasm for everything new, yet she would soon be one of the powerful ladies of the ton, someone many would try to emulate. Looking over several heads, he located his grandmother seated with her friends and headed that way.

"Will you do me the honor of dancing with me,

Grandmother?" By the stunned look on her face, Daniel guessed he had never asked his grandmother to dance before and was instantly ashamed of himself.

"Please," he added.

"Of course she will," Lady Dunbar snapped, giving the Dowager Duchess a shove in the back.

"Get up, Beatrice! We were just saying last night that we never get to dance anymore, and here you have an invitation from one of the most handsome men in the room." Lady Fairlie winked at Daniel.

"You flatter me, Lady Fairlie." Daniel bowed deeply. Dear God, he couldn't remember the last time he had blushed in company, yet his grandmother's cronies could always make him feel like he was wet behind the ears.

"I want to thank you, Grandmother," Daniel said as he gently steered her around the room seconds later. He wondered if she was nervous, because in truth he had not seen her dance in many years. "For this night, for helping Eva, but most of all for being the one constant in my life, the only person I could truly rely on," Daniel added, realizing that it was, indeed, the truth. Shaking his head, he wondered if loving Eva was making him soft.

"I am proud of you, Grandson, proud of what you have become."

Was that a tremor in her voice?

"But I will not be happy until you produce a great grandchild!"

Smiling over her head, he met his wife's gaze and held it for several seconds before her partner turned her away. He would keep their secret for a while longer.

The night for Eva was both pleasure and pain. Pleasure at her acceptance and success with the hundreds of guests, pleasure at her husband's and grandmother's obvious pride in her, but dear Lord, her feet hurt and she was exhausted. Her slippers were far too tight and if she was going to get through the entire evening she would need to change them and soon. Realizing supper was only a few dances away, Eva knew she had to make her move now.

"If you will excuse me, Claire, I must see to something."

"Shall I come with you?"

"No. I can manage and will return shortly."

Eva skirted the room and slipped out of the ballroom.

"May I be of assistance, your Grace?"

Waving her hand vaguely at the footman who had appeared before her, Eva shook her head and walked toward the stairs. "I will return shortly," she added over her shoulder as she started to climb.

Eva released a breath as the quiet enveloped her. She could still hear the music and soft rumble of voices but it was nice to be on her own. Daniel would not like that she had left the ballroom unescorted, but it was only briefly and she would have returned before he noticed her absence. Walking down several long hallways, she finally found her room. A lamp had been lit and the curtains drawn. Eva looked longingly at the bed but knew it would be some time before she could lie upon it. Kicking off her slippers, she sighed as her cramped toes stopped aching. Molly had packed several pairs of slippers in case the first pair was ruined in some way. At least Furban wasn't here so she didn't have to worry about his little teeth gnawing on the satin. Unfortunately, it was Daniel's clothing and footwear that he chose to drag around the house, not hers. Yesterday, she had watched as he ran past, followed by a scowling valet, with one of Daniel's neckties in his mouth.

"I am most pleased to have finally found you alone, your Grace."

Eva watched in horror as Gilbert Huxley emerged from behind the curtains and walked toward her.

"I would ask you to leave this room at once, Lord Huxley!"

"I think not, your Grace. When I leave, you will be accompanying me."

"Don't be ridiculous. I would never leave my own ball." Eva was pleased at how calm her voice sounded when inside her chest, her heart was thumping painfully.

"I didn't say it would be voluntary, Berengaria. And much as I want to throw you upon that bed and rut you until you scream, we must leave now before your husband appears."

Eva felt the color drain from her face. "He will kill you for this."

"He will have to catch me first and with all the noise going on below, I fear we shall be well away from here before he even notices you're missing."

"No!" I will never leave with you," Eva began edging toward the door.

"Unfortunately you will have little choice in the matter, my dear."

Eva watched him walk toward her as one would a venomous snake. "Why are you doing this?"

"Because you have always belonged to me and I should never have listened to your father when I wanted to take your innocence. The duke may have been your first lover, Berengaria, but I will be your last."

"No!" She screamed as he lunged for her – she heard her bodice rip as his hands caught the edge. Raking her nails down his cheek, Eva fought with everything she had. Lifting her leg, she tried to knee him in the groin; however, he was too quick and twisted his hips.

"You won't escape me, Berengaria!"

She saw the cloth in his hands and knew his intent was to drug her - in seconds she would be unconscious. Stomping down with her foot she then jabbed her fist into his stomach. His grip slackened as the air whooshed from his body, and that gave her enough time to run. He blocked her way to the door, so instead, she ran around the bed.

"If you touch me again, I will kill you!"

"You are stronger than you were, Berengaria. But that only makes me more determined."

"Eva!

She watched as the door opened and Daniel charged into the room. Horrified, she then saw Gilbert Huxley pull a wicked looking sword from his belt.

In one glance her husband took in her ripped bodice and the nail marks down Huxley's cheek.

"You'll die for this."

"No, Daniel, do not fight him, I beg of you!"

"What the hell is going on?" Simon bellowed, running into the room seconds later, followed by a footman.

"This room is getting crowded," Huxley said, swishing

his blade from side to side, his eyes never leaving Daniel. "Your wife is delectable, Stratton. I wish I had time to really taste her," he added.

"Did he attempt to abduct you?" Daniel bent to pick up the piece of cloth Huxley had tried to smother Eva with.

"Daniel, please -"

"Eva, tell me the truth!"

"Yes," she whispered.

"You." He pointed to the footman. "Two doors to the left from here, you will find my late grandfather's blade. Bring it to me."

"You cannot fight in this room, Daniel. It is not big enough," Simon said.

"Open those doors. They lead to a larger, private balcony. We will fight there."

"Daniel, no!" Eva cried.

"Simon, take care of Eva."

She could feel his anger. It filled every corner of the room, yet he would not look at her. Gilbert Huxley was his sole focus. His words were clipped; his body, tense - ready to strike. Gone was her amiable husband, in his place a cold, hard man whom she barely recognized. Never had she been so scared in her entire life. "Daniel," she whispered, taking a step toward him.

"Simon, take Eva from the room at once!"

"No. I will not go!"

"Madam, you will do as I say," he said in cold, clipped tones.

"I will not!" Eva dragged a blanket off the bed to cover herself.

Simon walked to the glass doors, which led to the balcony and threw them open.

"I have the sword, your Grace."

Daniel wrenched off his coat and gloves then took the blade from the servant. "Outside," he said with a nod of his head to Huxley.

Eva watched an evil smile tilt the corners of Gilbert Huxley's mouth as he backed toward the doors and then slipped outside. Silence filled the room, the only sound the swishing of Daniel's blade.

"If something should happen to me this night, make sure Eva is cared for and kept away from her family," Daniel said to Simon. "She is with child. I will ask you to visit my solicitor and make the necessary changes."

Dear God, he was discussing her in such a calculated manner - as if she were not standing right there, only a few feet from him.

"He has the rest of the details in my will."

"No!" Eva cried, running around the bed toward him. He caught her and briefly held her close. "You will not leave me, Daniel."

"Never doubt my love for you, Eva."

"Stop him!" Eva tried to hold him as he pushed her toward Simon.

"Eva, he must do this, and in order for him to win, he must focus solely on Huxley. Do you understand?"

Eva stilled, as if all the air had been sucked from her lungs. Looking up into Simon's eyes, she realized no one could stop the fight and that either Huxley or Daniel would die this night. "I cannot lose him."

"He's good, Eva." Simon placed his hands on her shoulders. "So is Huxley. However, I believe Daniel can take him if he fights with his head."

"Can he?" she whispered. "I-I mean will he fight with his head?"

Simon nodded. "As long as he has no distractions."

Eva gulped a deep breath and then nodded. It was obvious she could be a distraction.

"I will not distract him, b-but I will not leave. If my husband is injured, I wish to be here to tend him."

"All right." Simon took her hand and followed Daniel outside.

Light from the room lit the small balcony and the moon sat high in the night sky illuminating both men as Simon and Eva joined them. She bit her lip to keep herself from calling out as she saw them facing each other. Simon clenched his fingers around her slender ones and she was glad of their strength at that moment, as her knees were struggling to hold her upright.

"Ready to die, Stratton?"

"Even if you win tonight, Huxley, you will never get your hands on my wife. She is protected now from scum like you. And tonight I will extract long overdue revenge for the part you have played in tormenting her. No one frightens my wife and lives to see another day."

"En garde!"

Eva shivered at the first clash of steel, the sound so loud in the night air. The music from the ballroom below drifted toward them, the happy sound so at odds with what they were watching. She felt a wave of hysteria swell up in her throat.

"Focus, Daniel," Simon said softly.

They seemed to be locked in some sort of deadly dance for several seconds, each circling the other, gauging weakness, looking for opportunity. She didn't want to watch but could not draw her eyes from the scene. Huxley lunged and blood appeared on Daniel's arm. Daniel lunged and Huxley retreated and each time Eva felt as if a fist was clenching tighter around her heart.

"Have faith in him, Eva." Simon tightened the grip on her fingers, his eyes never leaving the two men.

They were both fit. Huxley was the shorter, yet he was fast, his movements quick and concise. Daniel's moves were elegant and seemed to flow more easily from one to the other.

"Keep moving, Daniel." Simon's voice sounded calm when, in fact, he was far from it. Next to him, Eva could feel the tension in his body.

She didn't know how long the fight had been going on; time seemed to stand still. The night air was now filled with the harsh breaths of both men as they continued in their deadly combat. Occasionally, a burst of laughter drifted upwards from below.

"Your wife has beautiful breasts," Huxley rasped.

Eva held her breath as Daniel lunged, his feet leaping forward. His blade sliced through Huxley's shirt and into his side. Huxley gasped and dropped his sword as the front of his shirt was swiftly drenched in blood.

Simon stepped forward, pushing Eva to one side. She gripped the stone balcony, watching as both men reached for the fallen man.

"Kill me, you bastard. For God's sake put me out of my misery!" Huxley cried.

"Simon, is that footman still here?"

"I am, your Grace." The man materialized out of the shadows.

"Have my coach brought around to the back entrance and say not one word of this to anyone," Daniel ordered.

"At once, your Grace."

Daniel tried to ease his breathing as he spoke. "Eva, get another blanket from the bed," he said without looking at her. If he did, he would have to touch her, pull her into his arms and hold her and never let her go. He couldn't allow himself to do that until he had the matter of Huxley cleared away. Only then would he take her back to their house and lock the bedroom door.

"I have the blanket," Eva said a short while later. He noted she had pulled on a cloak over her torn dress.

"Good girl. Now lay it over him and then go to the steps along the end and see if the carriage has arrived.

"Where are you taking him, Daniel?" Simon said, still holding his hand on Huxley's injury.

"Is the Imperial still in port?"

"Aye, I believe so," Simon nodded.

"I think Lord Huxley needs to make a new life for himself in America," Daniel said.

"I will not!"

Daniel knelt beside Huxley so he could see into his pain filled eyes.

"Heed me, Huxley, because if you do not take this

opportunity I give you and you choose to remain in England, then I will hunt you down and this time I will not aim to wound you."

"B-but America," the man groaned as Simon pressed harder.

"America will offer you more than you leave behind in England."

"Wh-why?" Huxley said.

"Because killing you would mean I'd have to leave for France and you have caused my duchess and I enough trouble already."

"The carriage awaits, Daniel."

"Simon, take his legs. I'll get his arms," Daniel said, slipping his hands under Huxley's shoulders.

"Go to your room now, Eva, and change your dress and go back down to the ballroom. Simon will escort you when he returns."

"But, Daniel…"

"I need you to do this for me, love. No questions or arguments. There is too much at stake."

Nodding, Eva hurried inside just as Molly appeared.

"Your Grace, I was just about to tidy up."

"Pl-please, Molly, don't ask any questions just help me change quickly."

"Tis lucky we have a spare," the maid said, noting the ripped bodice. She instantly whisked the dress over Eva's head and then went to collect the other one. This one was emerald green although the style was not dissimilar to the last. It was scalloped around the hem with silver thread and had a silver underskirt. Slipping on a clean pair of white gloves, Eva noted her hands still trembled. Tears filled her eyes as she looked at the white slippers Molly was slipping onto her feet. Had she not come up here to change earlier, none of the events she had just witnessed would have happened.

"You are ready now, your Grace." Molly helped her to stand.

"Thank you."

Simon was waiting outside and took her arm as she walked through the door and silently they returned to the ball.

"I will stay with you until he returns, Eva."

They slipped into the ballroom and then followed the flow of people into the supper room. Forcing a smile onto her face, she unclenched her fingers on Simon's sleeve and let him lead her to the buffet table.

"Eva! I have looked everywhere for you."

"Hello, Claire. I-I had an accident in my dress and was forced to change."

Claire looked from Eva's fearful gaze to Simon's anxious one but said nothing. Instead she said, "I shall get you both something to eat if you will find seats for us, Simon."

Simon found Eva's grandmother and her friends and lowered her into a chair beside them. He then stood behind her chair, resting one hand on her shoulder.

"Is all well, Granddaughter?"

"If you would be so kind as to not ask any questions, your Grace," Simon said in a voice only she could hear. "We have had an incident that the duke would rather keep between ourselves. Therefore, I would ask that you keep the duchess at your side until he returns."

The Dowager Duchess looked at Simon and her granddaughter, then she nodded and started to talk, including both Simon and Eva in the conversation. If both chose not to add much, it went unnoticed.

Before long, Claire returned, moving to Simon's side. Eva heard her begin to question him. Her tone was gentle, unlike the other times they had conversed. No one commented on the duchess's pale face or shadowed eyes. They all just stayed close to her side, listening as the Dowager Duchess and her elderly friends talked endlessly of amusing stories from their past.

When Daniel walked into the ballroom, he was once again the immaculately attired Duke of Stratton. His arm had been cleaned, stitched and bandaged and stung like the devil beneath his jacket. His eyes swept the room but could not find his wife. Prowling around, he finally felt his body relax as he saw Eva's head beside Claire's. Simon stood at her back and his grandmother to her right. His heart eased at the scene; they had formed a circle around his duchess, protecting her. Nudging Simon aside, he moved into position behind her. Placing one hand on her shoulder, he caressed the soft skin.

"I hope you are not telling stories of my youthful indiscretions, Grandmother." He felt the shudder that ran through Eva at his words and tightened his fingers on her. He stood there for a while, talking and stroking her skin until she slowly relaxed.

"Come, Duchess, it is time for our second waltz." He took her hand in his. "Thank you," he then said to each of the people who had cared for her while he could not.

"It's all right now, love," he whispered as she gripped his fingers tight. "I am here, Eva, with you," he added soothingly, dancing her slowly down the room. "Look at me, love," he coaxed.

"I was scared I would lose you."

Daniel felt her despair like a fist to his stomach as she looked up at him. The blue depths were wide with remembered terror. He had vowed to keep her safe from those who would hurt her, and again he had failed. "You will never lose me, Eva."

Lowering her eyes, she kept them trained on his necktie for the rest of the dance.

For the remainder of the evening, Daniel watched Eva closely. Her smile was brittle as she danced and chatted and he knew her well enough now to see the turmoil hidden deep inside.

"We will leave soon, love," Daniel whispered in her ear as he stood at her side. Her only response was a quick nod. Finally, an hour later, the guests started to depart.

"Come, sweetheart, let's go home."

"I don't understand."

"We need to be in our own home tonight," Daniel said, leading her down his grandmother's front steps and into the waiting carriage. They were silent on the journey. He held her close to his side. She stared out the window into the darkness and Daniel wanted to tell her how proud he was of the way she had gotten through the evening, yet knew now wasn't the time. First, they would have to discuss the duel.

"I will say goodnight, Daniel," she said as soon as they entered the house. "I am in need of sleep. Therefore, I shall see you in the morning," she added in a tight voice.

Daniel admired his wife's slender ankles as she picked up her skirts and ran from him up the stairs. If she thought she would be spending the night alone, she could think again.

"Will you require anything further, your Grace?"

"That will be all, Wernham," Daniel said, following his wife. His valet helped him remove his clothing and then Daniel dismissed him. After washing, he slipped on his dressing gown and moved to the connecting door between their rooms.

Pushing the door open, he saw Eva lying on the bed, still dressed in her gown and slippers, with the puppy nestled under her arm. Closing the door behind him, he watched her eyes widen as he stepped up to the bed.

"I want to be alone," she whispered.

"I think not, now get up and I will help you undress."

This time it was her turn to say no.

Daniel lifted the sleepy puppy and walked back into his bedroom, where he placed him on his bed and then closed the door. Eva had moved as far to the opposite side of the bed as she could. Leaning on the mattress, he grabbed her ankles and tugged her gently toward him.

"Daniel, your shoulder!" She tried to wriggle free from his grasp.

"My shoulder is fine," he said taking her hands and pulling her to her feet before him.

"I want to be alone. I-I need time…"

"Time for what?" Daniel said, undoing the buttons at her back and pulling the dress from her shoulders.

"To…" She struggled to put her thoughts into words. "To come to terms with what happened tonight."

"I don't remember needing isolation when you were nearly killed in that carriage accident." Daniel unlaced her corset and tried to ignore the generous swell of her breasts. "In fact, I needed only you that night."

"You should not have fought that duel!"

Now that was better, Daniel thought. The look of terror had left her face to be replaced by the flush of anger. Sinking to his knees, he untied her stockings and rolled them down her thighs.

"Would you have had me thank Huxley instead for mauling you and trying to kidnap you, or perhaps I could have taken off one of my gloves and slapped his face?" Daniel now stood before her. She was gloriously naked, and his body fired to life.

"I would have you live, damn you!"

"As I do." Daniel removed his robe.

"But I will not allow you to fight a duel every time someone challenges me."

"It was more than a challenge, Eva, as you very well know. Huxley hurt and terrified you and let us not forget that he also shot at our carriage."

The bandage around his arm drew her eyes and he saw the terror as she remembered the moment he got it.

"I-I could have lost you," her fingers shook as they traced over the cotton.

"Never." Daniel hauled her into his arms, then tumbled them onto the bedcovers. Covering her lips with his, he kissed her hard. She struggled against him but Daniel held her closer and deepened the kiss until he felt her resistance flee. Only then did he ease back.

"You gave yourself to me, Eva," he whispered against her neck. "Body and soul," he added, running his hand over her breasts in soft strokes. "And I will protect you with my life if and when I believe it is necessary."

She shuddered as his fingers moved over her stomach. Daniel watched as she arched toward him as they delved into her silken core.

"You are mine as I am yours, Eva." Daniel moved down her body, kissing and licking until he reached his goal. "Do you understand what that means?"

He ran his tongue down the dew-drenched folds between her legs, tasting her essence.

"I-I understand."

He sucked on the hard little bud between her legs until he felt the pressure build inside her. Only then did he climb back up her body and drive himself deep inside her slick heat.

"We belong, Eva," Daniel rasped as he withdrew and pushed slowly back into her.

"I love you, Daniel, so very much, now and forever."

Her whispered pledge drove Daniel over the edge. Thrusting into her until she clenched around him, they scaled the heights of passion together.

"And I love you, Duchess, forever and always," Daniel said, gathering her close in his arms as he felt sleep pulling him under. Resting a hand on her stomach, he imagined their child and dreamed of the future that now dawned bright and beautiful before them.

## THE END

CPSIA information can be obtained
at www.ICGtesting.com
Printed in the USA
LVHW112209080921
697407LV00015B/158

9 780473 254230